Surviving Elvis Week

Vanessa Grace & Amy Bea

INFINITY
PUBLISHING.COM

Copyright © 2009 by Vanessa Grace & Amy Bea

All rights reserved. No part of this book shall be reproduced or transmitted in any form or by any means, electronic, mechanical, magnetic, photographic including photocopying, recording or by any information storage and retrieval system, without prior written permission of the publisher. No patent liability is assumed with respect to the use of the information contained herein. Although every precaution has been taken in the preparation of this book, the publisher and author assume no responsibility for errors or omissions. Neither is any liability assumed for damages resulting from the use of the information contained herein.

This is a work of fiction. Names, characters, places, and incidents either are the product of the author's imagination or are used fictitiously. Any resemblance to actual events or locales or persons, living or dead, is entirely coincidental.

ISBN 0-7414-5501-3

Published by:

INFINITY
PUBLISHING.COM

1094 New DeHaven Street, Suite 100
West Conshohocken, PA 19428-2713
Info@buybooksontheweb.com
www.buybooksontheweb.com
Toll-free (877) BUY BOOK
Local Phone (610) 941-9999
Fax (610) 941-9959

Printed in the United States of America

Published October 2010

For Elvis Fans Everywhere –
you make the journey worthwhile.

&

For our Families, who love us in spite of our craziness.

Acknowledgments

Thank you, first and foremost, to our parents for believing in us from the very beginning. Thanks also to the rest of our family and friends for your unconditional support.

Thank you to our first and most supportive readers: Ivan Fuller, Amanda Pellicotte, April Olson, Mark Woodley, Marshall Mikesell, Sue Carrizales, Cori Neufeld, Ann Rapkoch, Shiela Reynolds, Valora Freeman and Linda Wadman. We appreciate your friendship, advice, insightful reading and humor.

Thank you to our wonderful Editor, Sarah Cypher (www.threepennyeditor.com) for transforming our caterpillar of a tale into a butterfly. And to cover designer, Kristen Summers (www.redbatdesign.com). You are amazing.

Thank you, above all, to the men who put up with nights of neglect as we pound away at our computers, Geof Rapkoch and Wesley Trautman. Thank you, Geof, for always being there. Thank you, Wes, for providing the means to turn our dream into reality.

Finally, we'd be remiss if we didn't thank Dr. Timothy S. Jones, formally of Augustana College, for providing the spark of inspiration that became *Surviving Elvis Week*.

Chapter 1: Stella

We found Elvis between the rusted '67 Ford and the fender-less Citation. He wore his gold jumpsuit. Pink and turquoise stars exploded from his cape. His knees were bent in dance, and one hand held a microphone to his unnaturally wide mouth. His eyebrows were definitely not the same size—hell, they weren't even located in the right places. Even in his worst years, when the end was near, Elvis never looked as bad as he did spray-painted on the back of the Sun Tours Express.

He seemed to be saying, "Run as fast as you can and don't look back. Never look back!" I interpreted the monstrosity as a sign and urged Jessica to heed the warning, but she put a camera in my hand. "He's perfect," she whispered. "Take a couple of pictures."

I obediently centered Elvis on the camera screen, and took a few quick snaps. The whole scene made me ill. Pink and turquoise paint had been slathered over the rusted chrome. Behind cracked windows, the interior décor was just as bad: age-stained seats and a layer of grime coating the ceiling. Shuddering, I turned from the bus.

Pete's Pump 'N Pack might not be the rendezvous point for every Memphis-bound tour, but for the Sun Tours Annual Fourteen-Day Elvis Extravaganza there could be no other. Located on the corner of Fifth and old Main, Pete's P-N-P was the proud star attraction of an otherwise demolished block.

However, on this early August morn, Jessica and I had little time to admire the view. The Annual Elvis Extravaganza was due to launch from Pete's at 12:09 p.m., the 9 being no accident, but a minute painstakingly selected by Marion Common, the tour coordinator, to represent Elvis's Life Path Number. That left little more than four hours for my partner and I to complete our initial documentation.

Jessica murmured into her recorder, "First impressions. After trudging through the slums of Minneapolis, we found Elvis. Refer to pictures. All this gas station needs is a stick of dynamite. That mud better come off my suitcase."

"It's not mud."

"What?"

"It's not mud."

"Great, just great."

A woman driving a maroon Volvo pulled into Pete's. Her black hair was cut bluntly to her shoulders, and she wore a navy blue, Fifties style polyester suit complete with heels and red lipstick.

She waved in greeting. "Hi, I'm Marion Common, your tour guide. You must be Stella and Jessica from *Olympus*. I'm sorry I'm late."

"Actually, I think we're early by, like, four hours," Jess said as she glared at me.

"I was worried we'd hit traffic and miss the bus," I explained and returned Jess's stare. She'd made me late plenty of times. I wasn't going to ruin our one chance at professional redemption.

"Oh, I understand. I'm the same way," Marion said. "I'm so excited to have you both on the tour. Imagine, two big-time travel journalists covering our little adventure. Give me a couple of minutes to organize my things, and I'll give you a tour of Cybill."

"Cybill?" I asked.

"The bus." Marion turned to go, but stopped and asked, "Would you like to meet Pete?"

"You mean there really is a Pete of Pete's Pump 'N Pack?" I asked. I gestured for Jessica to flick on her recorder again, but it was already running.

"You really should meet him," said Marion. "It all started with Pete. He was part of the Flying ELVI in Las Vegas. He moved to Minneapolis after he retired to be closer to his daughter and her family. He missed being Elvis, so he bought an old bus from Grey Hound, renovated it, and that's how the Fourteen-Day Elvis Extravaganza came to be. This year marks our twenty-third trip. Five years ago, Pete sold his company to Sun Tours. I've been with the company for three years."

We followed Marion into Pete's, which was a typical gas station and convenience store save for the pictures of Elvis on one wall and Pete's awards on the other.

"Pete?" Marion shouted. Her voice was so loud I wondered if Pete was in the store or in the next state. "Pete, are you here?" We heard a toilet flush and assumed it was Pete, so we waited. And we waited. And we waited.

Jessica turned off her recorder. "Should someone go check on him?" she asked.

"Oh, no. He's coming. He's an older gentleman and moves a little slower these days," explained Marion. Apparently 'an older gentleman' meant someone born during the time of Christ. The man who appeared from the men's room and made his way inch by agonizing inch down the chip aisle couldn't have been more than three feet tall or weigh more than one hundred pounds soaking wet.

"Pete," yelled Marion, "I'd like you to meet Stella Smith and Jessica Bernard from *Olympus*. They are the reporters I told you about."

"Who?" asked Pete.

Marion screamed louder, "Stella and Jessica. The reporters." Pete stared blankly. With veins popping out of her neck, Marion bellowed, "Stella! Jessica! Reporters!"

"Oh, that's nice," said Pete. Marion smiled as if she finally got him to understand who we are, but everyone knew he didn't have a clue. We shook his hand gently; it was as delicate as a bird's skeleton.

"I told Jessica and Stella about your career as a Flying Elvis. They wanted to see your awards."

"Oh, that's nice," said Pete. Marion smiled. We smiled. Pete smiled.

"Well, we'd better get going. Lots to do. Just wanted to meet you."

"What?" asked Pete.

"We have to go now. The Annual Elvis Extravaganza starts today. Remember?"

"What?"

Marion pointed at the three of us and screamed, "We," then pointed at the door, "must go," then pointed at her watch, "now."

"Oh, that's nice," said Pete. His head bobbed a little, either in farewell or because he had palsy.

Marion held the door. "Usually his granddaughter is here helping him. She must be in the back." The sun turned her black hair red revealing a poor dye job. She led us across the cracked asphalt and into Cybill's shadow. "Well, here she is. Did you know the actress Cybill Shepherd actually dated Elvis briefly?" Marion didn't wait for an answer. "That's where the bus gets her name. You will probably want a picture of the back. A local artist painted a really nice mural of the King."

"Who was probably drunk when he painted that piece of crap," Jess muttered behind me. Louder, she said, "We already got a picture of the back. You're right, it is nice."

"Oh, well then maybe a picture of me at the door," Marion giggled. "At my post, if you will."

"Sure," I said and stepped back to photograph the enthusiastic creature called Marion. She had fastened a large pin of Elvis's head to her collar and "I'm Elvis's #1 Fan!" was opposite her "Hi! I'm Marion, Your Favorite Tour Guide!" nametag. She posed in front of the camera looking like she just kissed Elvis in front of Pricilla and didn't care.

She pushed open the door with the flat of her hand, waved us up the steps and started jabbing one gold fingernail all around. "The driver sits there. I sit here. There are eight rows totaling thirty-two seats. Getting all this? We have blankets and pillows in the overhead compartments. See here, aren't they cute? They're Elvis, see. I made them myself. I found the fabric at an outlet store. Can you believe it? How about a picture?"

I did as commanded. The combination of air freshener and industrial cleaner was dulling my senses, making me obedient. Maybe that's how this whole thing worked, because how else could you put up with pink and turquoise seats pocked with cigarette burns and various stains?

"And there are TV/DVD players every four rows for watching Elvis movies!" Marion cheered. "What's your favorite Elvis movie?"

I thought about coming clean and saying, "Lady, I've never seen an Elvis movie and, God willing, I never will," but instead I improvised, "*Harum Scarum*."

"Oh, that is a good one. And what's yours?"

"*Charro!*" Jess lied.

"Oh, that's a good one, too. Mine is *Clambake*. As you probably know, Elvis made over thirty movies and we can usually get through our favorites two or three times." Marion said, expecting us to be excited, but the prospect of sixty plus hours of Elvis movies didn't make me excited; it made my ass twitch.

Somehow Marion read my mind, or my ass, because she said, "You'll be happy to hear we renovated Cybill's facilities. We put in all new stainless-steel, automatic, sensor-operated, state-of-the-art sink and stool." Marion led us to the back of the bus and gave us the reveal: It was impressive, a picture of Elvis hung by the sink. I wasn't sure how I felt about Elvis watching me pee.

"Maybe another picture?" Marion asked and I obeyed.

Stepping into the adjacent kitchenette, Marion pulled down a covered tray from one of the compartments. "Are you hungry? I've stocked our fridge with all of Elvis's favorites. I got the recipes from *Are You Hungry Tonight?* And for a special treat, I made Elvis-shaped cookies." She lifted the plastic wrap. Indeed, a hundred little Elvises. "Would you like one?"

We'd eaten a bagel that morning, and nothing since. I took one and bit off Elvis's head. Jess had a sweet tooth; she took two. Marion's cell phone saved us from the rest of the tour. She stepped outside to get better reception; we followed her off.

"What do you think?" I asked Jess.

"Don't ask," she replied. "Marion's affection for this pile of crap is an indication of her loose hold on reality." The sun reflected in white streaks across the top of her imitation Prada sunglasses, but even without seeing her eyes, I knew she was getting herself worked up. "Yes, she's one of those anal people who are too perky to live long. Sooner or later someone will have to put her under to spare the rest of society from her unrelenting enthusiasm."

"But for an Elvis fan this bus is Heaven. And that's what we are at the moment: Elvis's biggest fans."

"In that case, I love it," she conceded.

"That's the spirit."

Marion returned. "That was Mr. Nelson, the owner, just calling to make sure everything was a go. He wanted me to tell you he's happy to have you on board. I told him he has nothing to worry about. I've done this tour three times now, and I've got it down to clockwork. The others should be arriving shortly."

After another long, awkward stretch of small talk next to the Coke machine, our fellow tour members began arriving. Marion put on her biggest plastic smile and walked out to make her greetings.

"Thank God," I said, "Her attempt to become our best friend is making me twitch."

"Calm down," Jessica said, "One more Incident and we're fired. Here comes Elvis."

An Asian man with a pompadour and sideburns hugged Marion. "Hello, beautiful, how've you been? I can't believe it's been another year. Are you ready to hit Memphis again? What's this you were saying about a couple of journalists?"

"They're here," Marion explained and was going to introduce us when he interrupted.

"Oh, excuse me. How rude! I'm Lester Chen, but you can call me Elvis." Lester laughed. He continued in a voice of a pubescent choir boy, "Actually many people confuse me with the King."

"As did I," said Jess. "You look just like the image on the back of the bus."

"Oh, I know!" Lester laughed again. "I'm so excited. This is my eighth Elvis Extravaganza. When I moved from Vegas, I thought I'd miss the Elvis culture, but then I found this tour on the web. Don't you just love Marion?" He hugged her again. "She's the best guide we've had so far. Actually, she's the only guide who has returned after their first year. Have you seen Cybill?"

"Yes," Jess answered.

"You know she's named Cybill after Cybill Shepherd because—"

"Yes, we know."

"Well, I don't mean to brag, but I'm an Elvis expert, practically Elvis himself, so if you have any questions. No one knows more about the King than me, except maybe Marion. In fact, I brought some books from my Elvis library that might be helpful in your research. Right now I'm reading *The Tao of Elvis*, which is so good. But I also brought *Elvis: Collected Poems on an American Icon* and *Elvis and You: Your Guide to the Pleasures of Being an Elvis Fan*. I'm sure you'll want to read that one. Here, let me get them."

"Lenny, don't you want to load your luggage first?" Marion asked.

"Oh, you're right. Okay, I'll be right back."

When he was out of earshot, Jess said, "Those sideburns are fake."

"Yeah, I want to yank 'em off," I added.

And the Asian Elvis was just the beginning.

"Oh, it must be this year's winner!" Marion squealed as a long white limousine bounced its way over potholes, stopping beside the decrepit bus. She ran to greet the yellow sweatpants-wearing woman, and didn't waste any time dragging her over to meet us.

"Stella and Jessica, this is Char. She won the trip from the Rockin' Fifties Diner in New Jersey. They do this every year."

Char jerked free. "Let go of me, woman. I'm tired. I'm hungry. And I've been traveling too long to be making chit-chat. Who's gonna get my stuff?"

Before the dust settled on the limo's hood, a BMW van bumped over the curb and three twenty-somethings hopped out.

"They're Elvis fans?" I asked. "They're too young."

"We're too young," said Jess.

They had matching Elvis T-shirts and duffel bags, proving their devotion and rightful places on this tour. Marion pointed them in our direction.

"Yo, Marion says you're writers or something."

"Or something," I mumbled.

"Yeah, that's cool. I'm Matt. This here is Luc. He's from France. And this is my main man, Marcus. It'll be cool having you chicks on board."

"Thanks," I said. The kid was likable with his curly sandy-brown hair, a confident swagger and an easy grin. Luc had chalk white skin, rich blue eyes and coal black hair. He was a delicacy of a guy, and the delicious French accent made him irresistibly interesting. Marcus was the quiet one, and had the ruddy paleness of a fourth-generation Minnesotan. All three were roommates at the University of Minnesota.

"So are you guys really Elvis fans?" I asked.

"Are we Elvis fans?" Matt mimicked in an exaggerated tone.

"I take that as a yes," Jess said.

"King of Rock and Roll, man," Matt confirmed. "Say, are you chicks going to be asking questions and stuff for your article?"

"And stuff," I said.

"Cool. What do you want to know about Elvis? We know everything there is to know. Go ahead, ask."

"Okay," I took the bait. "Who knocked Elvis's 'Don't Be Cruel' off the top of the charts after eleven straight weeks?"

Matt's eyes rolled back into his head as he thought. "Let's see that would be, uh, that was, uh. Help me out guys."

"Elvis," answered Marcus. "He knocked himself off with another hit. 'Love me Tender' became number one and 'Don't Be Cruel' fell to number two."

"Say, that's right," said Matt. "You were trying to trick us."

"Oh, darn," I said. "You got me."

"Yes, we did," declared Matt. "See, between the three of us, there isn't anything we don't know about the King. Take the bus. Bet you didn't know Cybill is for—"

"Cybill Shepherd," Jess interrupted.

"Oh."

As they headed inside Pete's, Jess eyed their butts and said, "Good thing I don't have any rules about younger men."

I smirked. "They're not too much younger. So they're fair game."

By now Pete had hobbled outside and settled on a bench with another station attendant. Jess said she wanted Pringles and a Coke, so we went inside—and found the next three tour members.

Three Asian women were arguing next to a rack of motor oil. Although we couldn't understand their language, there was no mistaking the tone. I asked them if anything was wrong.

"We lost," one said.

"We supposed to meet someone," explained another.

"You mean Marion?" I asked.

"Maybe yes," said the first.

"No, that not it," said the third.

"Okay, maybe no," mused the first.

"But you are supposed to meet someone here?" I asked.

"Yes," said all three.

Silence.

I sighed. Jess shrugged her shoulders. A lot of help she is. "Why are you meeting this person?" I asked.

"For tour."

Ah ha. Now we're getting somewhere. "Then you do mean Marion."

"No that not it."

"But you are meeting a woman to take you on a tour."

"Yes."

"What kind of tour? A tour of what?"

"Of Sunset . . ."

"Sunrise . . ."

"Sun Tours?" Jess offered.

"Maybe yes."

"No, that not it."

"Okay maybe no."

"I think maybe yes," I said then turned to Jess. We walked behind the motor oil. "Why don't you grab us something to eat while I take them to Marion. Maybe once they see her, they'll remember. I don't know what else to do."

"Sounds good," Jess agreed. "Let Marion deal with them."

I returned to the ladies. "Why don't you come with me?"

"Where you take us?"

"To the lady you're supposed to meet."

"Who?"

"Marion."

"That not her name."

"Well, why don't you come meet her anyway, just in case."

"No."

Listen you old bag, I thought, *you can sit here and rot for all I care.* "I'm only trying to help. Now come on."

As I herded them away Jess murmured, "Maybe I want a Coke? No, that not it. Maybe Pepsi? No. Maybe Mello Yello? Maybe yes."

I led the ladies over to Marion, who was trying to placate Char with a thick layer of optimism regarding the bus's air conditioning. "Marion," I said, "I believe these three ladies are part of our tour."

"Yes?" Marion looked at the women and confusion crossed her face. "I was expecting a trio of older women, but . ."

"But what?"

"Oh, nothing." She turned to the first. "Are you Elizabeth?"

"No that not it."

"Oh," sighed Marion. "That's odd. I guess they wrote down the wrong name when you made reservations."

"It probably is her name," I explained. "She just doesn't know how to say much else."

"No, that not my name," she insisted. "My name Sachi Uchiyama."

"Saucy?" Marion asked.

"Sachi."

"Saky?"

"Sachi!"

"Sucky?"

"Sachi!" the woman screamed, then rambled furiously with her companions in her native tongue.

"Okay, okay," Marion said. "Could you spell that for me?"

"What?"

"Could you spell your name for me, please?"

"What you want I to do?"

"Spell your name."

"Sachi!" the woman screamed again, not understanding what Marion wanted, or deciding that the spelling of her name should be self-evident to any polyester-wearing tour guide in Nowhere Ville, Minnesota.

"Okay, well then that's you," Marion muttered as she crossed Elizabeth off her list and wrote something that probably wasn't even close to the woman's name. To the second she said, "And yours?"

"Midori Iwamoto," the second woman said quietly.

"I'm sorry, what?"

The third lady helpfully screamed, "Midori Iwamoto!"

Marion flushed. People were beginning to stare. Marion sighed and scribbled nonsense. "And you are?"

"Harulu Okudara," said the first loudly and proudly.

Over her shoulder, I saw Marion write *Helen*. "Okay then, you're all checked in, so if you want to get your things. I'm sure one of these boys can help you."

"We not going with you."

"We supposed to meet lady for sunset tour."

"Sun Tours," I corrected. "This is your lady."

"Yes, I'm a lady. The guide of Sun Tours," Marion assured.

"That not it."

I turned and all but ran away. Jess had confiscated one of the rickety lawn chairs outside Pete's and moved it into the dwindling strip of shade. "What did you get for snacks?"

"A bag of Doritos and a couple of Little Debbie Nutty Bars."

"Well where's mine?" I asked.

Jess licked Doritos powder off her fingers and shrugged. "You were busy jabbering with those old ladies and those Elvis cookies didn't tide me over."

"I was trying to help unlike you who said she's going to get some food for us to share and then eats it all!"

"You're welcome."

"I'm going to get some food."

But Marion had pawned the Japanese ladies off on Marcus, and was at my sleeve again. "Jessica and Stella, I'd like you to meet Mary. She'll be joining our tour, and I hope you'll make her feel welcome."

I'm five years old with my mom asking me not to throw sand at the fat kid. She was a petite Latino woman with caramel skin and dark lashes framing deep, troubled eyes.

"Nice to meet you, Mary."

"Nice to meet you."

Silence as we stared at each other. I looked longingly at Pete's. If only I could get away. I needed a Snickers and Munchies Trail Mix. Perhaps a Slurpee. I could almost taste the blue raspberry syrup.

"Mary's a nun," blurted Marion interrupting my thoughts. "Oh, gosh, then, gee, do we call you Sister Mary?"

"No, please call me Mary."

Marion laughed. "I think it's just perfect having you here," she said. "Don't you think it's just perfect?" she said to us, and it was obvious we had no idea what made it just perfect having a nun on the tour. "Her name's Mary?" And we still didn't get it, so Marion explained, "Like Mary Tyler Moore." Not getting any warmer. "I'm sure you know Mary Tyler Moore played a nun in the Elvis movie *Change of Habit*. Well, actually she wasn't really a nun, she was—"

"Oh of course," gushed Jess, "*That* Mary Tyler Moore. I thought, well, never mind. But you're absolutely right. She is just perfect. I love *Change of Habit*. When she wore that thing on her head. What's that called?"

"A habit," I didn't feel like playing the game.

"Yes, habit. Let's watch it three times."

"At least," Marion declared. "Oh, it's just perfect." She giggled. "Oh, I'm sorry Mary. You'll have to excuse us. Others are arriving. I hope I didn't embarrass you, but it's just perfect."

"Perfectly annoying," said Jess through her teeth.

"Come on," I said. "I think we're supposed to follow Marion."

"Perfect." Jess's smile took on the crazed look of a serial killer. "That will be perfect. Isn't everything just perfect? I'm perfect. Are you perfect?"

"No, actually, I hungry."

"Oh," Jess's smile vanished. "Yeah, sorry about that. Want me to go get you something?"

"We have any money?"

"Ursula the Sea Bitch gave us a stipend."

"I'll be fine. We better follow Marion before she breaks her arm waving us over."

Marion introduced us to an African American father–son duo from Milwaukee, Eric and Elliot Preston. Eric's manicured nails indicated success, but his piercing eyes, stern chin and economy of words implied it was hard fought for. Elliot's torn jeans and offensive T-shirt were enough to know he has hit the rebellious years. They didn't look like Elvis fans, but neither did we. They looked like they wanted us to leave them alone, so we did.

From there we had the pleasure of meeting Passengers #11 and #12, Elvis and Priscilla Presley. They had the outfits and the look down pat. Marion introduced them as Vince and Ella Morelli.

"And wouldn't you know they're honeymooners," Marion gushed.

"Really? Whose idea was it to take this tour for your honeymoon?" Jess asked.

"Mine," said Vince, "but Ella agreed it would be perfect considering Elvis is the whole reason we're together. You should put us in your article."

"Oh, that would be perfect," I said.

"Here, take a picture so your readers will know how much we look like Elvis and Priscilla."

I snapped the photo and we left on the premise of meeting other tourists. "Did you see Ella's face?" I murmured to Jess. "Doesn't seem like an Elvis Extravaganza is her idea of *perfect*, as Vince put it."

"If Elvis is the only thing going for them, I fear for their marriage," Jess added, but she was the pessimist when it came to love.

A Mexican showed up in a turquoise ruffled shirt unbuttoned to his navel and black leather pants. He strutted right to Mary and started an earnest conversation, centered on a pamphlet he produced from his briefcase. It must have been a solicitation for sex because her reaction was instantaneous. The nun poked her finger repeated into the ruffles of his shirt. From this distance, I could only make out "First Commandment" and "sinners."

Marion veered toward the scene wearing her big plastic smile and tried to mediate, but only succeeded in raising the volume on the nun's chilly, stiff-backed, righteous anger. Finally Mary turned up her nose at the piece of paper and removed herself from their company.

Marion started to follow, then hung back to console the dejected Mexican.

"We need one of those papers," Jess whispered. "A bag of Doritos says he's got more in that briefcase of his."

The Mexican was a handsome man with dark chocolate eyes. I noticed his eyes immediately because they were magnified to about twenty times their normal size behind a pair of thick, black glasses. To make matters worse, the frames kept sliding down his nose.

"Excuse me," Jess said. "Are you okay?"

He nodded, shrugging his indifference, and pushed up his glasses. "It's okay. I'm used to it." He had an Antonio Banderas accent, and I could see Jess start to melt into the asphalt and the wheels turning between her ears, getting stuck on the phrase she'd proclaimed over dozens of pink martinis in the years I'd known her: Latin men are so yummy.

Before she forgot herself, I said, "Can I get one of your pamphlets?"

He looked at me like I'd just brought his dead grandma back to life. With an extra flourish, he pulled out a crisp paper from his briefcase. "Here you are." He presented the sheet with pride. "Take it, read it. If you have any questions, don't be afraid to ask. My name is Thomas Gold."

"Nice to meet you. I'm Stella and this is Jessica."

"Oh the reporters," Thomas said. "I have a great angle for your story."

"That's nice," I said and walked away. The pamphlet was an advertisement for a church, a church dedicated to the worship of Elvis Presley. I'm surprised Sister Mary didn't have Thomas burned at the stake.

Marion waved us over to the tailgate of an enormous Chevy, where a couple in Western gear were unloading matching luggage. "Billy and Tansy, I would like you to meet Jessica and Stella, the journalists I was telling you about."

"Well how do," boomed Billy, holding out a beefy hand. He had salt and pepper hair, a shiny belt buckle the size of his fist and a rope necktie. "This blushing lil' lady is my wife, Tansy." Tansy shook our hands, but remained aloof.

"Where are you two from?" Jess asked.

"Texas," Billy said with Lone Star State gusto. "And you?"

"Denver," Jess answered for us. I couldn't focus on anything except Tansy. She was unlike any woman I had ever seen. She applied her makeup with a palate knife and only God knows how she got her hair into the shape of a helmet, but the most fascinating part about her were her boobs. Enormous doesn't even come close. They had to be fake. I imagined her saying to her plastic surgeon, *"I'd like boobs the size of my head please."*

Suddenly, I realized I'd spent an abnormal amount of time staring at another woman's cleavage. I tried to join the conversation, but shouldn't have.

"Nice boobs—blouse. Nice blouse. The color really accents your, um, eye shadow."

Awkward pause. "Thanks," Tansy said.

I tried to save myself, but again, shouldn't have. "Where did you get them, I mean, it?"

"Target."

"Oh. That's . . .nice."

Jess came to my aid, "Well, we should meet the other passengers."

"Yes, yes, of course," Marion was quick to break the tension.

"I can't believe you said that," Jess hissed as we walked away. "What's wrong with you?"

"I didn't mean to. I've never seen boobs like that; they're unreal!"

"Stel, there's a thing called an inner voice," Jess admonished. "Use it."

Tansy found a friend in Passenger #16, a woman of similar physique except this woman had dark auburn helmet hair and her boobs were a smidge smaller. Other than her name, Maggie, we didn't get much out of her.

"Isn't it funny," I said to Jess, trying to act normal again as we walked towards yet another new arrival. "Some people hog our attention, vying for that fifteen minutes of fame, while others treat us like we have some sort of communicable disease."

Jess shrugged. "Everyone has a great story idea. They just don't want to do the work."

I continued to stew in my usual obsessive compulsive manner until I saw him and nothing else mattered.

"Is this Sun Tours?"

While we'd been talking to the boob sisters, a white Datsun rattled to a stop and parked behind all the other cars. The driver saw the knot of us talking, assumed that someone here was in charge, shouldered his duffel bag and waited politely for Jess and I to finish our little catfight.

I didn't answer his question, but stared stupidly as Jess transformed into master seductress without missing a beat. "Yes, it is. And you are?"

"Don."

"Don, that's a nice name. Are you going to join our tour?"

"Yes."

"You don't look like your typical Elvis fan."

"I'm more a fan of a fan, I guess."

"Really, how mysterious," Jess continued exchanging mindless banter with a man I thought only existed in magazines, airbrushed to perfection. He reminded me of Mr. October with wavy blonde hair, blue eyes and sun-kissed skin. He wore his clothes in the haphazard, stylish fashion that said, "I paid two hundred bucks for these worn-out jeans because I'm just that cool."

"Are you a big fan?" he asked.

"Oh me? I'm a writer," said Jess in a tone meant to impress. "I'm on assignment. Perhaps I'll interview you."

"I'm not sure I'd have much to say," Don argued. That's when he noticed me - drooling at Jessica's elbow. "What's your name?"

"Yeah." And that's all I said. Just yeah.

"Yeah?" Don asked. "Your name's yeah?"

"Oh," I said and laughed like a deranged idiot. "Yeah, my name's Yeah. My parents couldn't decide if they wanted kids, so my name's Yeah and I have a twin sister named No Way in Hell." I was hysterical, and nobody else was laughing. "I'm kidding. I have a name, of course I have a name. I'm just—"

"This is my writing partner, Stella," Jess interrupted my psychobabble. At that, he stared at me for the longest time, then turned and walked away without another word.

Jess took my shoulders and turned me slowly to face her. "Stel, I realize you have few social skills, but if we're going to save our careers, you've got to get it together. You can't gawk at everyone then blurt out something bizarre. What's gotten into you?"

"I don't know. I guess I'm all shook up."

"Not funny. On second thought, maybe you shouldn't speak. Why can't you just be normal?"

"Normal? Look around you, Jess." I said, pointing to Lester. "We have a grown man wearing a jumpsuit."

"He's an Elvis impersonator."

"Exactly. We left normal hours ago. We have to spend the next two weeks with Elvis fans. Don't you get it? Elvis fans aren't like other fans, Jess. They're a breed apart. And we're going to learn more than God ever intended strangers to know about each other." As I said this I looked around and thought, *so these are the types of people who love Elvis.* And then there's Jess and I.

Chapter 2: Jessica

And then there's Stella and I. I was glad at least one person on this tour would listen to my smart-ass comments and not think less of me, which is pretty much the basis of our friendship.

#

We met as freshmen at Northwestern in Chicago. Both in pursuit of a Bachelors in Journalism. The class was Early American Lit. The assignment, Crevecoeur's *Letters from an American Farmer*. A blond-haired, blue-eyed cheerleader stood at the front of the class offering her thoughts. I'll admit her nonsensical review of Crevecoeur's *Letters* was painfully simple and off-the-mark. I preferred to daydream rather than listen to her prattle which made any listener dumber. Then she said, "And when Crevecoeur calls America an asylum, I just don't get it. I mean, isn't an asylum where they put crazy people? Like on Looney Tunes?"

Our professor tried to tactfully explain, "Well, there are a couple of different meanings for the word 'asylum'."

"Like what?" asked the dumbfounded cheerleader, which was too much for Stella who shouted, "A place of refuge! He's calling America a place of refuge" in a tone that said 'just sit down and shut up you stupid, silly girl.'

The class fell into a stunned silence. Except for me. I was in the back, laughing.

After class, I found Stella at lunch, sitting alone as usual. I pulled up a chair. "So, you didn't like Alexandra's presentation?" I asked.

"I know I embarrassed her, and I feel bad about it," Stella said into her Caesar salad. Then looking up she explained, "But it was Crevecoeur after all, and she was killing him! I mean, Crevecoeur, the man who first defined what it meant to be an American. Who wrote, 'Here individuals of all races are melted into a new race of man, whose labors and posterity will one day cause great changes in the world.' And she has the gall to stand up there and say, 'I don't get it. Isn't an asylum a place for crazy people?'" Stella mocked, flinging hearts of romaine in her impassioned tirade. "It was Crevecoeur after all," she concluded as if that explained everything.

"Exactly," I agreed. We both laughed and a lasting friendship was born.

As we walked to our dorm rooms after lunch, I asked, "So, how do you get along with your roommate?"

"I don't have one. I think the Dean could sense I'm not good with people. Do you have a roommate?"

"Yes. She scares me a little. So I spend most of my time in the library. My own personal asylum."

Stella laughed. "Well, you're welcome to move in with me, but you might regret it," she offered.

I did move in, and I never regretted it. Not even after The Incident. Not even now.

#

"Do you know what they'd do to us if they discovered our secret?" Stella asked.

"Which secret?" I asked. "That we don't like Elvis?"

"Don't even say it out loud."

"Or that we're not travel journalists?"

"We are now."

I suddenly came to the realization I wasted four years in higher education. I was covering an Elvis tour, for God's sake. Four months ago, Stella and I wrote for one of the top newspapers in Chicago. Then The Incident happened. Then we were fired. Three months with no work. We were shunned by all decent journalism societies. We used dishwashing liquid to wash our hair. We couldn't call our parents; there's such a thing as self-respect. But we were not above begging our former editor, Bruce, who in turn begged Ursula at *Olympus*.

Ursula is Ursula St. Claire, a woman with coal black hair, green eyes, and a chip on her shoulder. She built *Olympus* from nothing into a magazine with a quarter million subscribers, a fact she never tires of sharing. We nicknamed her Ursula the Sea Bitch, after our first meeting.

#

"I know about The Incident," Ursula said, "and that kind of shoddy journalism will not be tolerated here."

"I'm sorry. What 'shoddy journalism' are you talking about?" challenged Stella. "I know you're not talking about the story we ran on Mayor Jenson because that story is true. No matter what you've heard."

"Then why did the editor of *The Tribune* recant it?"

"Jenson's henchmen made him."

Ursula threw her head back in a disbelieving laugh. "Okay, Stella. It's good to learn this lesson early in your career. It's not always what you say, but what you don't say, and good journalists know when to leave a story alone."

"Oh really," Stella was not backing down. "When is that? When the story will embarrass a mayor who is running for governor?"

"When you don't have a credible source."

Touché. I kicked Stella and whispered, "Enough for now. We need a job, remember?"

After a thirty second stare down between Ursula and Stella, Ursula continued, "I've decided to give you a chance out of respect for Bruce. Don't make me regret my decision. I'm putting you both on our travel and leisure section. That should be safe enough. Your first assignment will be Elvis Week in Memphis."

"Great, when do we fly out?" I asked.

"Oh, you're not flying. You're going by bus. You'll start in Minneapolis. You will be immersed in Elvis lore, surrounded by Elvis fans and steeped in Elvis travel sites. My readers want details. Do you think you can handle it or maybe I'm asking too much."

We bore this snide remark with indignant silence. I could hear Stella grinding her teeth. Fearing another confrontation, I moved to bring the meeting to a close. "Thank you, Ursula," I said. "We won't let you down."

"See that you don't. You can get the details from Lucy on your way out."

We rose to leave, but Ursula called me back, "Jessica, wait. There's something I want to ask you."

We both turned around, but Ursula clarified, "Stella, you may go." I knew Stel was hurt by the dismissal, but she left without comment while I returned to my seat.

"I'm curious about your involvement in The Incident," Ursula said leaning back in her chair.

"Excuse me?"

"From what Bruce tells me, the story was all Stella. He even said he heard you trying to persuade Stella to leave it alone." Ursula paused, waiting for my confirmation. Knots started forming in my stomach.

Begrudgingly I answered, "That's true, but I believed Stella. I still do. The story is true."

"Of course." Ursula rolled her eyes and leaned forward. "I can understand defending your friend on the press room floor, but getting publicly involved at City Hall..." Ursula trailed off. She didn't have to finish; we both knew what happened at City Hall. Hell, it seemed the whole world knew what happened at City Hall. The Incident made the front page of every major newspaper in the US and earned over two million hits on YouTube.

"Your point, Ursula?" I was growing impatient wanting this interrogation to be over.

"Just be careful who your friends are. That's all I'm saying." Ursula turned her attention to her computer monitor. "I have a lot of close friends, but none of them are worth my career. You understand?"

I felt my face flush and anger pulse through my veins. I considered my words carefully so she would understand. "It's funny who moves through your layers of familiarity. It's not always who you'd expect or even choose sometimes."

Ursula leaned on her elbows and waited for an explanation.

"Someone comes into your life by a seemingly unrelated series of events," I continued. "They start as an acquaintance. Similar interests, hobbies, points of view move these two acquaintances toward a friendship. The term 'close friend' is bestowed on those select few who come to know you better than you know yourself. These friendships have been forged by good times, a few laughs and a listening ear."

I paused and took a few deep breaths. I wanted to say this just right. "Then there are rare occasions when someone comes into your life unexpectedly, and they become something more, something beyond 'close friend,' something we don't have a word for – like sisters without the bloodline." I looked Ursula square in the eyes. "Do you know what moves two people to this level of friendship?"

"More good times?" Ursula answered noncommittally.

"Pain," I whispered. "Shared pain. When something happens to you, the person who gets you through the pain, who shoulders that pain with you, becomes something more."

I stared Ursula down through a sheen of unshed tears. "I would defend Stella with my life. And she would do the same for me. It's not something most people can understand."

After a long pause, Ursula conceded, "Okay." I don't think she understood, but it didn't matter. I'd said what I needed to say. Ursula continued, "I'll be counting on you to keep Stella in check on this assignment." She dug through a drawer. "Here. Take this cell phone. I'll be checking in from time to time. You may go."

In the hall, Stella waited for an explanation. "What was that about?"

"Nothing."

Unconvinced and seeing the look on my face, Stella asked, "Are you okay? Did she say something to upset you because I'll-"

"Stella, it's okay," I assured. "It's nothing. We have a job. Let's get some lunch and celebrate."

Stella debated a couple of seconds, then hooked her arm in mine and marched out the door. As we left, Stella called out our motto, "Don't let the bastards get you down!"

#

Two weeks later, here we are. Although this assignment is just one step above obituaries, I'm grateful to still be writing.

"Did anyone think to check if Pete sells pink martinis?" I asked. "It's going to take more than pop and chips to survive this group."

"Too late. Look, the others are boarding Cybill."

Marion stood next to the door holding a clipboard. She greeted each person by name and then handed them a large manila envelope from the boxes at her feet.

"Now don't open it until we're all seated. Then we can open them together!" she trilled. "Welcome to Sun Tours!"

I got our envelopes and seat assignments and pointed Stel toward the back. Don sat across the aisle, but we had other problems. The passengers who'd boarded before us had tried the windows. Only five would open. As I made my way to my seat, I felt an icy tickle of fear grow in my throat. This is it. No going back now. Those bus doors are the gates of Hell and I'm trapped on the wrong side.

Chapter 3: Stella

I'm trapped on the wrong side of hell with Marion posing as Satan's Gatekeeper.

She barked out orders as everyone attempted to find their assigned seat. Don's seat was opposite Jess's and mine. I grew impatient waiting for Jess to stow her bag in the overhead, so I ever so casually bumped her with my hip. She shouted as she flopped into the seat, but I didn't care. My attention was focused on two huge biceps and one chiseled chest. I took inventory of his physique as I said hello in what I hoped was a sultry voice. In my mind, I was saying all sorts of clever and cute things. Apparently none were coming out of my mouth because Char barked, "Girl, you gonna stare at him all day or can I sit down?"

Don was about to say something brilliant, I was sure—to the tune of *you're the most beautiful woman in the world and I love you.* I was about to ask him to marry me when Char ruined my moment. I took my seat and smiled sheepishly at Don, and at least he returned the smile. I added good teeth to my inventory. Teeth are important. Our children will be beautiful.

Marion picked up a microphone. It squealed to life then swallowed the first three rows in static for several seconds of her spiel.

"Excuse me. If everyone can take their seats, please. No, Char that isn't your seat. I have you sitting in seat 15, not 17." Char exclaimed, "Oh, hell," and began moving her gear. Marion continued, "Thank you. Some of you might think the seating chart is silly, but it is necessary for what I have planned. We'll get to that as soon as everyone is settled. The time is 11:57 and I would like to start at 12:09. Thanks!"

We could only guess at and dread whatever Marion had planned. The tour members griped; the seats were already uncomfortable. The nun seemed to be deep in prayer, but in reality her seat was bent at a 45-degree angle. Two of the college guys and one of the older ladies shared the same predicament. On the other hand, Thomas and Lester's seats kept falling back, which I found hilarious until my head flopped into the lap of another member of the Japanese Trio. I attempted to right my seat by pulling on the lever. The seat flew forward and slammed into my back. I leaned back to lock it in place, and flopped into Midori's lap. Or was it Sachi?

"What you doing?" she asked.

"I don't know," I replied. I gently squeezed the lever. Slam. Squeeze. Flop. I sighed and stood up, not knowing what to do about my seat.

Char's caterpillar eyebrow arced up to her hairline. "Girl, what do you think you're doing? Don't you know how to work a seat? Never travel by bus? Is that beneath you?"

"My name's Stella. Not girl," I snapped.

"Well, excuse me, Miss Hoity Toity. It's like, oh my God, it's just a seat."

Okay, Char, you want a go-around, let's go. I can exchange insults with the best of them. I was preparing my attack when a large hand fell on my shoulder. I turned to find out who was keeping me from ridding the planet of this woman's insolence.

"What the hell do you want?" It shot out of my mouth before I could contain myself.

The man answered, "I'm the bus driver, honey-cakes, so just cool it. Let me help you with your seat." He gave my seat a kick and the thing popped into place. I mumbled a thank you. I suppose he was waiting for me to say something, but all I could think about was how I was going to kill Char and make it look like an accident.

The driver introduced himself. "I'm Gus."

"I'm Stella."

"First tour?"

"Yes."

"Love Elvis?"

Aware of everyone's stares and a warning glare from Jess, I answered, "Oh, yes. His biggest fan."

"Well, you're on the right tour." Indicating the bus, he stated, "Yes sir, this ol' girl's name is Cybill. In case you don't know, she's named after—"

"Yes, I know!" I practically shouted.

"Okay then. Cybill has carried us safely to and from Memphis twenty-three times now. She may look a little worse for wear, but she's a true lady. She ages gracefully." With that, he winked at one of the old ladies.

She giggled and asked her friend, "That man wink at me?" Her voice was so loud her hearing aid battery must be dead.

Gus continued, "Yep, just sit back and relax. Don't let these seats worry you none." He banged on my seat again and concluded, "There ain't nothing broke on this girl that I can't fix. And you'll be happy to know this year we installed some real fancy shitters."

"Bathrooms," Marion squealed into the microphone, "He means bathrooms. We installed the latest technology in our bathroom complete with a sensor toilet and sink. Now Gus, thank you for your help, but could you take your seat?"

Gus moved to the front of the bus. When he reached Marion, he asked, "Miss me, sweetie?" He grabbed our guide and gave her a big kiss.

"Gus, please!" Marion smacked his arm. "Now everyone, take your seats so we can start."

I peered at my seat and told myself to show no fear. As I sat back down, I muttered to Jess, "At least the shitters on this bus will work" using Gus's quaint terminology.

Jessica didn't acknowledge my comment because she was busy recording the events in her journal. "Are you listening?"

"No."

"I need you to casually look over and read Don's expression. Is he's looking at me?"

"No."

"You didn't even look."

Marion continued, "We'll begin with a video."

Jess nudged me and whispered, "Shush, Beelzebub speaks." What appeared on the screens of the mini-TVs was repellent. An Elvis impersonator, looking worse than the spray painted cartoon on the back of the bus, jiggled, sang, and carried on about Elvis and the great things to see and do in Memphis. After the video, Marion asked us to pull out our folders and turn to page three. Page one was a welcome with smiling Elvis faces, and page two was an index. What I found on page three caused my heart to sink with horror. It was titled, "The Sun Tours Annual Fourteen-Day Elvis Extravaganza Itinerary," and a quick flip of the folder revealed twenty-seven color-coded pages.

Jess whispered, "She has everything in here, planned down to the minute."

The thought of Marion controlling every moment of the next fourteen days, which totaled three hundred and thirty-six hours of our lives, made my heart pound harder in my stomach. "This can't be happening. We have to escape. We don't belong among these people."

Jess agreed, "We've just landed in the seventh level of hell with Nimrod handing out our condemnation."

"She's not going to read this thing, is she?"

"Yes, I believe so."

"It's practically a novel."

"I hope you're comfortable."

The August heat set in. The bus became a rank sauna. Tansy tried to keep her face on, but her foundation streaked down her cheeks, and when she wiped the sweat from her upper lip, she smeared lipstick up to her nostrils. My flesh began to bubble and slide off my body. The sound of snoring harmonized with the buzz of the microphone, lulling me into a trance. Out of glazed eyes, I stared at Marion, this nonsense-speaking blob at the front of the bus. The emergency exit began to call to me, but suddenly, two hours later, she neared conclusion.

"Okay. The time is 2:31. Only a couple more points. You will notice in your Fun Folders, I have included attractions that we won't be able to visit. I've noted the nearest mile marker on your maps just in case you ever get the urge to take in more Elvis sites on your own. Finally, a word about the seating charts. In order for everyone to get to know each other, I've scheduled seat rotations. There is a new seating chart every day. Okay?" Upon receiving no response, she said, "Well, I guess we can get going. Everyone settled? Gus, are you ready?"

"Ready for lift-off. Boys and girls, hang on to your hats 'cause here we go!" It took several turns of the ignition key before Cybill kicked to life with the roar of a 747 and the tremors of a 6.0 earthquake. Gus popped in an Elvis sing-along tape and began to sing along. Smoke billowed out of Cybill's backside and engulfed the entire block. One minute Pete was waving goodbye and the next he was swallowed by exhaust.

Something exploded and Cybill lifted off the ground and crash-landed ten feet down the road. Once her wheels re-established contact with the earth, Cybill tore through downtown Minneapolis traffic. Gus seemed to be the only one unaffected by the chaos.

The rest of the bus was a whirlwind of airborne tourists and duffle bags. Bodies were flopping like fish on the shore. I landed at the bottom of the pile, somewhere in the center aisle, but thanks to Fate, so did Don. We lay with our face inches from each other. I stared into those arctic eyes until I noticed a spare set of teeth on his shoulder. I think I said something brilliant like, "You have teeth on your shoulder!" Over the din, we heard one of the old ladies gurgle for them. Don and I separated, and like a true gentleman, he picked up the not-so-pearly whites and returned them to their owner. Maggie was the only casualty. A hurtling bag had knocked her unconscious.

After we settled back into our seats, I pulled out my journal, taking my cue from Jess. For this assignment, we agreed to keep separate journals where we'd record our impressions, sort of stream of conscious, then share with each other at the end of each day. We hoped this would provide enough of a story to meet Ursula's approval and earn a second assignment.

Day 1: First Impressions, I wrote. What do I say about this cast of characters seemingly taken from a Neil Simon play? *Damn, I'm good*, I thought. But doubt quickly crept in as my mind returned to City Hall and The Incident.

"What is it?" asked Jess as if reading my mind.

"Nothing," I replied. "Just thinking about the time I called Mayor Jenson a lying sack of shit, and how that got us into this mess. Why did I do that?"

"Because Mayor Jenson is a lying sack of shit," Jess explained simply. "And he had just told the entire city of Chicago that your article shouldn't be printed in *The Tribune* but rather in Grimm's *Fairy Tales*."

"Oh yeah. How could I forget."

"And that's not what got us into this mess. I'm sure we could have salvaged our positions at *The Tribune* had you not proceeded to punch the mayor's assistant and start a riot in City Hall."

"True." Jess was such a pragmatist. I lay my head on her shoulder. "I'm sorry I got you involved."

"I'm not. The mayor's assistant deserved it."

"Yes he did. He called me a 'delusional dike suffering from PMS and penis envy.' I don't even know what he meant by that, but he did deserve a punch in the face for saying it." *I would do it again in a heartbeat*, I thought. "However, I'm glad you backed me up because he would have killed me."

"What are friends for?" Jess said and put her head on top of mine. "Besides why are we talking about this again? I thought we agreed to leave The Incident in the past, and take this assignment as a fresh start."

"I'm trying, but The Incident keeps rearing its ugly head, making me believe everything I write will result in another public crucifixion."

"Stella." Jess took my chin in her hand. "It's Elvis Week. That's the assignment, not Watergate. Lighten up. It's going to be okay."

I laughed. "Okay. Well, then I'm not writing because I just don't feel like it and not because The Incident has made me lose all confidence."

"Fine," Jess said scribbling away. "Then re-read the itinerary instead. Or listen to Marion."

Along the route to our first destination, Marion peppered the view with commentary about the sites. The constant ringing of the microphone began to drill a hole in my brain, and somewhere between Owatonna and Saco, Minnesota, I prayed for salvation.

Chapter 4: Jessica

Salvation came in the form of Albert Lea, Minnesota. It grew up like a weed in the cross section of Interstate 90 and Interstate 35. It was one extended rest stop—a long chain of gas stations, hotels and fast food joints. After Marion's incessant jabbering coupled with no lunch, I was almost desperate enough to eat the piece of jerky I found on the floor.

"Okay, folks," Marion announced. "This is the end of the road for today. I didn't want to do too much on the first day. We'll be eating at Shake, Rattle & Roll before ending the day at the Albert Lea Guest Lodge." As Cybill cruised the main drag, Marion pointed out several shops that were just down from the diner. We had a two-hour break in which to eat and shop before the bus transported us to our first hotel. "The company pays for the meals purchased at the diner. If you would like to eat elsewhere, I'm afraid you'll be on your own." The microphone crackled as she turned it off.

"Dear God, I thought she'd never put that damn thing down!" I said as I grabbed my carry on.

Thomas, the Mexican with the Elvis church, gave me an understanding smile. "I'm going to run across the street to Wal-Mart. I need aspirin, lots of aspirin."

Stella was pretending to write in her journal, but was really watching Don. He was making no apparent effort to get off the bus, so I told her to meet me later.

At Wal-Mart, I bought earplugs, aspirin and more memory cards for the camera. Outside, I looked for one of my fellow tourists, hoping to pair up with them and ask discreet questions. The beginning of our article was starting to form in my mind. I was halfway excited when I caught up to Maggie, the red-headed boob sister. Stella joined us and we began walking towards the diner.

"So, how's Don?" I asked.

"I'm hopeless. You can have him."

"What?" asked Maggie.

"Stel has a crush on Don," I teased.

"Who doesn't," Maggie said. "Although he's a little young for me. So, you talked to him?"

"Not really," said Stella dragging her feet along the cracked sidewalk. "I can't say anything halfway intelligent in his presence. When I got off the bus, he was standing there. He opened his mouth to speak and, what do I do, I blurt out that I need to go to the drugstore right away for supplies. He probably thinks I'm on my period."

Maggie and I laughed at my hapless friend. "That's real smooth," I said. "Haven't I taught you anything?" Stella remained silent. "Oh well, at least you have your e-mail lover."

"Who?" asked Maggie.

"She met a man on eHarmony," I said. I was having too much fun filling Maggie in on the details. However, karma paid me a lesson as I stumbled into a pothole and nearly twisted my ankle. Maggie and Stella stepped around the hole where the sidewalk should be, but wasn't.

"For the last time, we didn't meet on eHarmony," Stella said, glaring at me, her face red. "We both belong to the same Shakespearean forum online. We chat now and then, but we are far from lovers."

"Thought you said he wanted to meet?" I asked. I wasn't letting it go. Screw karma. I don't often get a chance to put Stella on the spot.

"Yes, but that doesn't mean we will. How do I know he isn't some serial killer?"

"A serial killer who belongs to a Shakespearean chat group?" Maggie asked.

"Yes, have you read *Hamlet*? Murder, bloodshed, conspiracy." Stella said this as if it were a logical explanation.

"So the only man in your life besides the one who raised you is a Shakespearean serial killer?" I asked. "You are hopeless." I held the door to the Diner open for Maggie and Stella.

The Diner was a typical mom and pop place, where the shakes were made with real ice cream, grease was considered a legitimate ingredient, and no one had heard of the veggie-burger. The booths were a reddish brown vinyl with pictures of famous people from the Fifties: James Dean, Marilyn Monroe, the young Beatles. Lester and Vince fought over the Elvis booth while Thomas started a tribute to the King on a jukebox. I gritted my teeth. Thirteen days, I thought: thirteen days, five hours and forty-five minutes.

Stella and I joined the father-son duo.

"Eric Preston," said the father, reintroducing himself. "And this is Elliot, in case you forgot."

I appreciated his thoughtfulness; I'm terrible with names. "Thanks, I'm Jessica and this is Stella."

"I know. You're the reporters."

The way he said "reporters" made it sound like an accusation, so we kept the conversation light. We chatted about inconsequential things while we ate our burgers and fries. Stella peppered the otherwise adult conversation with obscure Elvis trivia. Twenty minutes later we'd finished and sipped on bland coffee. Elliot drew on a napkin while Eric related a story only he found amusing.

"You folks through with that?" The voice was whisky warm with just a touch of Southern Comfort. "I can clear that out of your way, ma'am."

"Sure," I replied. Time stopped. Before me stood a very young, very handsome Elvis.

He gave me a crooked grin and bent to grab my plate. Eric was still talking. Elliot was still drawing. The jukebox was still wailing and the waitress was still making the rounds. I gave Stella a slight elbow.

She turned, saw the young Elvis and started laughing. "That's great. Do you do this for every tour?"

"Yes, ma'am," Elvis replied. "We bus every table for all our customers."

"No, I mean dress up like Elvis. Or did you do it just for us?"

"I'm sorry, ma'am. I don't know what you mean. I didn't dress up like Elvis." He took Stel's glass and turned to walk away.

"Wait," Stella said grabbing his elbow and causing a cascade of silverware and glasses. He bent to clean the spill as Stel jumped out of the booth to help. "No, I'll get it. I'm sorry."

With her face within inches of Elvis's, Stel asked, "So you look like that normally?" I couldn't help her. I could only watch in stunned disbelief.

"Yes, ma'am," said Elvis. "I'm afraid I do. My mama gave me this face."

"That's not what I meant. I'm sorry, uh, what's your name?"

"D.J., ma'am."

"D.J., I'm telling you, you look like Elvis," Stella persisted. Upon standing, she appealed to Eric and Elliot for confirmation. "Don't you guys think he looks like Elvis?"

They looked at Stella, looked at the busboy, looked back at Stella and answered in unison, "No."

"I wish I looked like Elvis. Then I'd get more girls." The busboy laughed, and even his laugh sounded like the King's.

Stella was about to argue when I interrupted, "We need to use the ladies room, excuse us." I hooked my arm through Stella's and dragged her away.

Inside the closet of a restroom, I said, "Who did you see?"

"Elvis, of course," Stella returned.

"Okay. I saw the same thing, I think."

"Well, thanks for backing me up out there." Stella turned her back on me and pretended to straighten her hair in the mirror. "Eric and Elliot looked at me like I'd lost my mind."

"I'm sorry," I knew she was embarrassed. "But didn't you notice we were the only ones on a bus full of Elvis fans who thought so?" I asked.

"Yes, they're obviously blind or crazy."

"They are crazy. That's a given, but that still doesn't explain things." I leaned against the bathroom door. "I've been thinking of an angle for our story, and this just added another layer."

"Other than me making an ass of myself I don't see how this plays into our story," said Stella, still pouting because I didn't defend her.

I fanned my hand in front of my face as I visualized the opening paragraph, "A characteristic of Elvis fans so blinded by their enthusiasm they can't see the real thing when it's in front of them." I turned to see Stella's reaction expecting excitement, but she just crossed her arms and gave me one of her looks.

"We should get a picture of him for proof," I said. "Let's go."

As we exited the restroom, we heard Marion instructed everyone to hand the cashier their tickets on the way out. I snapped a picture of Elvis as he restocked the napkin dispensers.

The bus didn't shake as much as before. Still, Marion waited a couple of minutes before reaching for the mike. She beamed. "Okay, ladies and gentlemen. When we arrive at the hotel, I'll give you your room assignments and keys!" I was curious to see what kind of accommodations Marion arranged. My vision of the life of a travel writer included wild adventures at exotic ports, fancy restaurants and plush hotels. So my disappointment when we arrived at the Guest Lodge was beyond even my power to describe.

"I know it's not what some of you are used to," Marion said, "but I thought it would be unique and fun."

"Unique is one word for it," I whispered. "Shithole is another."

The bus shuddered toward a cluster of cabins surrounding a two-story building. Each cabin was painted a different, hideous color. "The Albert Lea Guest Lodge has recently come under new ownership," Marion read from a brochure. "Bette and Daryl Sharp are delighted to offer their guests a unique experience complete with indoor swimming pool and sauna. The theme-colored cabins come with queen-sized beds and color TVs. Enjoy your stay!"

"Maybe they're still in the process of remodeling," Sister Mary offered.

"Maybe nothing. This place is a dive," Char said loud enough for the entire bus to hear. Most nodded in agreement, except Lester who yee-hawed in delight.

Stella collected our key and I grabbed our two suitcases. She came back with a sour look on her face and said, "We're in the magenta cabin."

I handed her a suitcase. "What, not the olive green cabin?"

"I know. I wanted orange, but magenta it is. Also, we're sharing with Mary."

Our cabin included magenta walls, magenta curtains, magenta furniture, everything magenta. Except the carpet, which was magenta and some colorful stains.

"I think," Stella said as I laid my suitcase on the pink atrocity of a bedspread, "that magenta just became my least favorite color."

"It's like someone drank a bottle of Pepto-Bismol then puked all over," I added. "I should write that down." As an afterthought I wondered if Mary might be offended by my comments, but she just giggled. At least, I think she giggled. A half laugh, half snort came from her smiling lips. I flashed a timid smile at her, then shifted my attention to a strap on my suitcase. Having been raised Catholic, I was unsure how to act in such an intimate setting. The thought of seeing her in pajamas just seemed wrong.

"It's a little warm in here, isn't it?" Stella broke the silence, having no qualms over rooming with a nun. She pushed a few buttons on the air conditioner and a fan hummed to life. "Lukewarm at best. And wasn't there supposed to be a TV?" We scanned the room. No TV.

"I could call up to... Where's the telephone?" Mary asked. No telephone.

"Do we have a toilet at least?" I asked.

Mary opened a pink door. "We have a full bathroom, complete with a pink toilet," she announced. From the tiles on the floor to the shower curtain rings, everything was a God-awful hot pink. "Well," she mused, "It could be worse." Stella and I turned our incredulous gazes towards her. She shrugged. "We could be sleeping in the burnt yellow cabin down the way."

Char, the Extravaganza Winner, shared that particular cabin with Maggie. We heard all about their cabin when they wandered over to escape their furnace, which was set at ninety-five with a broken temp controller. Our air conditioning kicked in after Mary adjusted a couple of levers, and the five of us started playing cards.

"One look at this dump," Char said, "and you go color blind."

Mary frowned. "You can't go color blind by sleeping in a room that's all one color."

"The hell you can't! It affects your vision all right. After five minutes in that room, I walked outside and everything had a tinge of yellow to it. The sky looked green, for heaven's sake. I'm wearing my mask tonight so I don't suffer permanent damage. I suggest you do the same. I don't know how you girls are going to describe this place in your article. 'Course I could tell you a story or two about dumpy hotels." Char laid down her hand. "Gin."

We threw in our cards. Maggie, who I pegged a quiet observer in the game of life, began to shuffle for another round.

"The fact Marion chose this hotel tells you a lot about her, doesn't it?" Char continued her assessment.

"What do you mean?" asked Mary. I stood on the pretense of getting a glass of water, but I was really looking for a way to get away from the conversation. I was pretty sure I knew what Char meant, and I was equally sure Mary wasn't going to like it.

"Who in their right mind would choose to stay here?" Char spread her flabby arms to indicate the pink room. "Clearly that woman has issues. Does she have a man? No. Does she have kids? No. I bet she's a pervert."

I spat the water out of my mouth trying to stifle a laugh. I guess I didn't know what Char meant. I'd thought she'd say something offensive, but didn't imagine her calling Marion a pervert.

"Char," Mary reprimanded. "How can you say that? You don't even know her."

"I'm just calling it like I see it."

Mary and Maggie frowned in disagreement, but neither seemed inclined to leap to Marion's defense. Stella made subtle nods towards the door, indicating we needed to vacate the premises.

"Well," I said, "I think I'll wander around for a bit. See if I can find a TV and catch the news or something. Stella, would you like to join me?"

"Sure."

"I think I'll go for a walk myself," said Maggie, her shadowed eyes careful not to meet Char's. Mary began picking up the scattered playing cards.

Char sniffed. "Well, I guess I'm left to my own devices. I think I'll retire for the evening." She mustered a surprising amount of grace and swept from the room, almost quickly enough to hide the wounded expression on her face.

The evening air felt refreshing after the stuffy room and antagonistic conversation. I took a couple of cleansing breaths and listened to the city preparing for sleep.

"Can you believe Char," Stella muttered after a few moments. "She has the nerve to criticize Marion when she's wearing yellow sweatpants."

"I know," I agreed. Stel and I began walking along the road to no place in particular.

Our ringing cell phone stopped us cold. Only one person had the number: Ursula. The woman who held our future in her ball-crushing fist. I fumbled with the phone trying to dig it out of my pocket.

"Tell me what you've got." No pleasantries from the Sea Bitch.

"Ah… It's been an eventful day," I said. "We've gone from Minneapolis to Albert Lea."

"Albert Lea? That's only about an hour from Minneapolis. What the hell took you so long?"

Stella had crowded in to hear Ursula. "Good question."

"What?" Ursula asked.

I glared at Stella. "Nothing. I mean, we asked good questions of the other passengers. A couple of them are Elvis impersonators, and I think they would make an interesting sidebar to the article."

"I'll be the judge of that. What about the Guest Lodge?"

"It's… colorful." I shifted from foot to foot and looked to Stella for help. She only shrugged.

"Get pictures," Ursula ordered. "And Jessica?"

"Yeah?"

"Mess this up and I'll have no problem yanking the article and ending your pathetic careers." Click.

"Thanks, Ursula. You have a nice night, too. Glad you called, you wench." Stella laughed and started walking again. "Take pictures," I muttered in disgust. "Like we wouldn't take pictures."

"Exactly. We covered the Kurntz–Meyer investigation. We can handle a two bit trip to Memphis."

I sighed. "Don't let her get to you; it's just what she wants. She wants us to fail and you know what I say?"

"What?"

"Screw it. Let's make the most of this gig. We don't have much choice. Eventually people will forget The

Incident and we can go back to writing Pulitzer Prize winning exposes."

"You're right. We may be on a tour full of freaks, staying at a crap hotel in the middle of nowhere, but what the hell, let's live it up."

In spite of the words, Stella seemed sincere, and it made me feel a little more at home with the gig we'd taken to save our souls. We had reached the edge of town and paused to watch the setting sun.

My thoughts turned from Ursula to my mother. When my mother found out about The Incident, she seemed almost happy. Not that she wanted me to fail, but now she figured I'd come home, meet a nice man and start a family. She never understood why I left for Chicago and majored in journalism in the first place. She can't imagine a woman wanting any life but her own. And I do want her life – the husband, the kids. But not right now. Right now I just want to get my career back on track. And if takes becoming an Elvis fan, so be it.

The sky turned from orange to blood red as the last sliver of sun hung on the edge of the horizon. I took a deep breath and let it out slowly. Then without speaking, Stel and I turned around and began walking back to the Lodge.

"So, speaking of our article...what did you get?" I asked.

"Not much. Just jotted a few lines on each person." Stella admitted, "I doodled mostly."

"Oh, good." I laughed. "That's a start. Well, while I was writing my first impressions-"

"While I was writing my first impressions," Stella imitated.

I chose to ignore her mocking tone and continued, "One main question keeps coming to mind."

"Yeah, and what's that?" Stella asked and casually stepped over the sleeping homeless man.

"How does Elvis continue to appeal to such widely different people?" I stopped walking and stared at Stel. Let her think on that for a moment. "I mean, everyone on this tour loves Elvis," I continued.

"Except us."

"Except us." I started walking again. "And they come from all walks of life, all backgrounds, both genders, multiple nationalities, and span in ages from teenager to geriatric."

"True." We paused in the Guest Lodge driveway.

"That's the angle of our story," I said. "We focus on these people and their stories to answer the eternal question of the Elvis mystique."

Stel thought about it. After awhile she shrugged, "I like it."

"Good."

"Want to go for a run?" she asked.

I considered her offer. I should, but I don't feel like it. I didn't answer Stella as my attention was drawn to the multicolored cabins. *Take pictures*, I thought. All of a sudden Ursula's condescending tone, my mother's disappointment in my chosen career and everyone's pity and poorly veiled glee at my fall from grace after The Incident started to burn a fire in my soul like I have never felt before.

Damn it, I was born to be a writer. At a young age I was watching the nightly news with rapt attention, devouring every word of *Time* magazine and provoking my uncles into political debates. I memorized Martin Luther King Jr.'s speeches and the *Declaration of Independence*. I would repeat them aloud as if I were the one igniting the people to revolt, to take a stand. Words have the ability to open a person's mind to a different reality and the power to bring change. And mine will. Mine will.

"Jessica, you want to go for a run?" Stella repeated her question bringing me out of my reverie.

"No, I'm tired. I just want some sleep."

Chapter 5: Stella

"I just want some sleep!" I moaned in frustration, kicking off the comforter.

"What's wrong with you?" Jessica murmured.

"Sorry, I didn't mean to wake you. I'm so tired, yet I can't sleep."

Jess groaned and shifted, gaining an extra inch of room. She's sneaky that way. "What's keeping you up?"

"Oh, nothing really. Just a spring poking through the mattress that's tearing a gash in my leg."

"Yeah? Well, I'm sleeping on some sort of lump in the middle of my back. And all my blood is running into my eyeballs." She rolled to her side, trying to relieve the pressure. "Perhaps we should flip and put our heads at the foot of the bed."

"No. Then the spring will be at my shoulders. I'd hate to slit my throat by accident."

"No, I don't love you! I can't! I've given my word!"

"Jess, what the hell?" I sat up to look at her.

"That wasn't me!"

"So, who said that?"

"Mary, she keeps saying she doesn't love someone."

"Hmmm. Interesting. The time is 2:37."

"Stel, go to sleep."

#

He was half-naked in swimming trunks that left little to the imagination. He beckoned to me, the sun glinting off his teeth. He dove into a natural pool beneath a waterfall. Surfacing, tiny water droplets clung to his bronzed body. He signaled for me to come to him. I stepped seductively into the water. I began to slink my way over to him when at step five I vanished beneath the water. Surfacing with seaweed in my hair, I gagged. I pushed my hair back and looked at my dream man in embarrassment. He only smiled his gorgeous smile, making me feel adorable rather than clumsy. He pulled me close and was about to speak. I held my breath waiting for what he would say, waiting for him to kiss me.

But he didn't speak and he didn't kiss me. He pulled his hands away to reveal that algae had slimed my back. I tried to wipe it off. He helped by holding me under the water and scrubbing my back with his feet. He kicked me and kicked me and I was at the bottom of the pool and I couldn't breath, but I couldn't move because his foot was in my back.

"Don, stop! No, Jess. Jess! Get your damn knee out of my back!"

"W-w-what?"

"You're hogging the bed. Move over."

She mumbled a sleepy "fine" and moved over a whole inch. I gave her a shove and gained another foot. I attempted to return to my dream minus the algae, but with no success.

Why was I dreaming of Don anyway? I let my thoughts wander as I stared at the popcorn ceiling. I don't normally go guy crazy. In fact, I hate girls who fall apart just because they're in the presence of an attractive male.

In the last five years, I've had a handful of dates and one serious boyfriend. Which if I was honest, I'd admit I only tolerated him because he took me to the ballet, and I liked the attention. But I was never that interested.

I've always been independent. Jess says it's because my parents abandoned me when I was an infant. They left me in a barn on an Amana colony farm in Iowa. The couple who raised me did so lovingly, but always at arms length. So Jess thinks I never get attached because I live in fear of rejection. But I think it's because I like being on my own.

And Jess can't talk. She's really hard on men. They either play by her rules or she's moving on. No waiting around to see if it'll work out, if he'll change into the man she's always dreamed of. Nope, with Jess, it's 'this is how it's going to be or that's it.' And for that, I admire her. At least she knows what she wants.

And what do I want? Until the debacle in Chicago, I would have said nothing. But lately I've been wanting someone…I had to think for a moment, and as I did, I noticed the water stains on the ceiling looked like Nixon. After awhile, it became clear.

I don't need someone to take walks with along the beach at sunset. I don't need a guy with a good sense of humor. I need a man who'll stand between me and everyone trying to rip me apart. I want someone who will keep the world at bay.

Who'll pick me up after I've lost the fight and say, 'Get up. You've taken a hit, and you feel pretty shitty. Get back out there. You know who you are. You know what you're worth. And if you've forgotten, I'm here to remind you. Stop being afraid to try. Even if your worst fears materialize, I'll love you anyway. I always will.'

If only that kind of man existed. I sighed and rolled toward Jess. *I really need to find him*, I thought as I looked at my friend – drooling, snoring, hair matted to the side of her face. She's adorable, but for some reason, she doesn't do it for me. I laughed out loud at my thoughts as the alarm blared to life.

The stupid thing had an alternative sounds feature, but instead of waking to a gentle violin sonata or the ocean surf, dogs barked, roosters crowed, neighbors bellowed good morning, and I swear I heard the grunting of pigs, but I can't be certain of that. It featured every animal on the farm, but no off button. I yanked the plug out of the wall after checking the time – 6:35. I concluded no more luscious dreams were going to happen. However, I didn't get out of bed until 7:00.

Jess and I moaned and groaned our way out of bed. We went through our usual morning grunting, neither of us able to make sociable English until noon. Mary was her ever-pleasant self as she prepared for the day. The tug of a comb and a washcloth was all she needed to be radiant. I hated her for that.

I moved toward the shower with a Texas-sized headache building I was sure not even a gallon of coffee could cure. I climbed into the shower and stayed there for forty-five minutes mentally preparing myself for the day.

I like the temperature of my shower to be just below scalding. As the hot water rained down my body, easing every stiff muscle, I remembered Mary's nighttime confession. She's always smiling, but her eyes betray her.

I pushed aside thoughts of Mary for thoughts of Don. I jumped out of the shower to find something nice to wear; however, in an attempt to 'blend' Jess and I packed touristy clothes. Then I spied Jessica's blue sundress. I slipped it on and dried my hair. Spent a little extra time on my makeup and was done.

When I emerged from the steam-filled bathroom, Jess and Mary were ready to go.

"Nice dress," said Jess. She wore jean shorts and an Elvis t-shirt.

"Thanks."

"Took you long enough."

I addressed the look Jess was giving me. "Don't even start. You know I have to ease into the day. Ease. No rapid movements. I have to get used to the idea of functioning."

Marion arrived at our door, calling "The time is 8:20. You should be making your way to the main Lodge for some breakfast. I want to leave promptly at 9:09. That gives you exactly forty-nine minutes."

At the Lodge, Jess shuffled to the coffee machine and muttered, "I feel run over." A glance around the room convinced me the rest of the tour felt the same.

The three college students looked the worse for wear. They probably haven't seen this side of noon in years. Eric Preston was perfectly starched as expected. Only his eyes revealed his restless night. Elliot was wearing the same clothes as the day before. As was our driver, Gus. If smell was any indication, he's worn the same outfit for weeks. Billy Butler, our resident Texan, was in a red John Wayne outfit with white stitching. Tansy wore black shiny pants, which were creeping up her butt and a pink V-neck blouse. One of the Japanese ladies wore a slip and argued with the other two about the location of her skirt. Vince and Ella, the honeymooners, were their regular soppy selves as they fed each other breakfast. I didn't catch what they were wearing because I was too grossed out to notice. I stifled a laugh at Brother Thomas and Lester. They dressed as if competing in an Elvis look-alike contest. I wasn't sure who was winning.

And there was Don. He was dressed in a muscle flattering polo shirt, carpenter jeans and loafers. He walked by our table and I could smell his seductive cologne. I sighed, "Delicious."

"What's delicious?" Mary asked. "This?" She stared at our dry toast and bitter coffee. Jess knew what my comment was about so she tactfully changed the subject. I phased out of their conversation and began plotting how I was going to get Don to talk to me. I watched as he walked across the room without speaking to anyone and sat at a table in the corner. He's not a morning person either. Perfect.

Marion hurried into the room. She had on a soft green version of yesterday's Fifties outfit. "Good Morning Elvis Fans! It is good to see your cheery faces!"

"Honey," Char announced, as loud as her orange blouse, "I bet the homeless of New York slept better than I did last night."

Marion had no clue how to respond, so rolled right into regaling us for a half an hour with the day's activities, which was a word-for-word repeat of page seven in the itinerary. The only thing remotely interesting was the mention of the mud sculpture of Elvis.

"Okay gang, let's load up," Marion cheered. "The time is 9:17, so we are already eight minutes past schedule."

As we handed Gus our luggage, Marion cornered Jess and I. She walked us around the front of the bus. "I was thinking it would be nice if one of you or both would speak on our way to the first stop of the day." She stared at us expectantly and waited for her answer.

"Speak?" Jess asked.

"Yes, to pass the time on the bus."

"Speak?" I asked.

"Yes."

"About what?" Jess asked.

"Well, about what you are doing on the tour." Marion clearly didn't think this needed explaining, but she tried. "You know, how you became interested in Sun Tours. Why you love Elvis."

Jess took a quick intake of air which she tried to cover with a cough.

"Maybe a little about yourselves," Marion continued. "Other accomplishments from your careers in journalism."

Immediately I saw the tour's reactions as Jess and I explained how we actually don't like Elvis, followed up with our crowning achievement in journalism – the infamous Chicago City Hall Riot, better known as The Incident.

Apparently all of this played across my horror stricken face because Marion asked, "That wouldn't be a problem, would it?"

I made a vague guttural noise, still unable to process what was happening and how this was all going to play out.

"I just thought it would be interested for everyone."

"But we're here to gather your stories about why all of you love Elvis." Jess weakly tried to get us off the hook.

But Marion was not easily put off course. "Exactly. And I think everyone might open up more if they hear your story first." She probably has us down in her damn itinerary already, which means we were doomed before she even asked. She turned to me, the easy kill. "Don't you agree, Stella?"

"Uh," I shook my head and shrugged my shoulders like a human Bobblehead.

Marion took that for a yes. "Great, so after we drive down the road awhile, I'll just call you up to the front of the bus to speak. Okay?"

"Okay," Jess answered.

"Okay." Marion looked pleased with herself as she returned to the other passengers.

Once she was out of earshot, I turned to Jess, "I think I'm going to be sick."

Chapter 6: Jessica

"I think I'm going to be sick," I said, turning to Stel.

"That's what I said." Stel was doubled over with her hands on her knees.

"What?"

"I think I'm going to be sick."

"You too?" I asked. Stel threw her arms in the air for a reason I didn't understand. "Look, don't be mad at me. I didn't do this."

"I'm not mad at you. It's just..." Stel trailed off. We walked several paces away from the bus to move out of range.

"What are we going to talk about?" I asked.

"We'll tell them why we love Elvis just like Marion said."

"Except we don't."

"I know!" Stella shouted. She was becoming hysterical.

All of a sudden I found the situation funny. I started laughing, which irritated Stel. She really did look like she was about to puke, which made me laugh harder.

"Stop it. We're about to stand up in front of a group of strangers and make asses out of ourselves." She stood in front of me with her hands on her hips like my mother used to do when I was a naughty child.

"We can't talk about our careers," Stella lectured. "If we mention anything from our previous lives as political reporters for *The Tribune*, we risk them finding out about

The Incident. We can't talk about Elvis because we don't know anything about him they don't know already. And they'll see through us in a heartbeat." She punctuated every point by throwing her hands in the air.

"Once they know we don't like Elvis, they'll bludgeon us to death or kick us off the tour, which would be worse because then we'd have no story for Ursula, which means no second assignment, and before you know it, we'll turn to prostitution for money." Stel hit her fist on her leg. "Why do you keep laughing?" she shouted.

I realized I needed to intervene before Stel hurt herself. "It's okay," I reassured her. "I'll do it. You don't have to."

Stella threw her arms around me in a bear hug. "Really? You don't mind?" I should have remembered Stella would rather have her fingernails pulled off one by one rather than speak in front of a group. "But what will you say?"

"I'll think of something." As I said that, my nerves went away, and I felt better. I don't mean to brag, but I'm queen of thinking on my feet – comes from my acting days. Marion's request is really no big deal when I thought about it. I'll be fine. But I didn't tell Stella because I wanted her to be eternally grateful for me letting her off the hook.

"Oh, thank you, Jess." Stella gushed. "I mean it. You're the best. You know how I hate talking in front of people."

"I know."

#

As we boarded the bus, Lester called, "Hey, Jessica. Stella. I saved a spot for you."

It's not like we could say no, but we considered it. But then again, you have to admire a man who wears tight polyester shorts.

"As you know, this is my eighth time taking this trip," Lester said. He leaned across the aisle and planted his elbows on his knees.

"Yes," I said, concentrating on his face. His tight shorts were bunched around his junk which was distracting.

"Elvis and I have so much in common," he continued.

"Really?"

"Yes, I can't think of a time in my life without Elvis. It all started with my dad."

Great, here we go, I thought. Peril of the job. Everyone wants to tell you their life story. I looked at Stel and rolled my eyes. She pulled out her journal.

"My dad came to America from Vietnam in 1956 on a student visa," continued Lester. "He got a job running the projector in a theater. The first motion picture he saw was *Love Me Tender*, which was my—er—Elvis's first film.

"That's how my dad learned English, from watching Elvis movies over and over again. A year later he married my mom, a second generation Vietnamese–American. Because she was a citizen, Dad became a citizen. They moved to Las Vegas to work for Mom's uncle who owned a small bar. My father took my mother out to watch every movie Elvis ever made.

"When *Viva Las Vegas* came out in '64, Vegas became Elvis crazy. Even more than usual. My parents weren't affected by it too much. By then they'd had my older brother and sister and were busy raising a family. I was a big surprise when I was born in '71. At least that's what my great-uncle always said. Basically, I wasn't supposed to come along. But that's okay. Mom always said there was something special about me."

I gave Lester the response he was looking for, "Your mom was right." Stella stifled a laugh.

"She was right!" Lester agreed. "I picked up my parents' love for Elvis movies and it grew into loving all things Elvis."

"Of course."

"Shortly after my eighteenth birthday, my great-uncle hosted an Elvis Impersonator Contest at his bar. Eighty-three impersonators entered. Most were locals, but a few came from Reno, San Francisco, Los Angeles, even two from

Phoenix. The competition was fierce, because the grand prize was five thousand dollars. The night of the contest, the bar was filled. There was barely room to fit my siblings and their families and our cousins and neighbors. Great-uncle had rented a sound system and these spotlights that shined all different colors, which looked really cool whenever an Elvis took the stage. The whole room sparkled with color and light." Lenny's eyes glazed at the memory.

"I was dressed in my white jumpsuit, modeled after the one Elvis wore onstage at the International Hotel in Las Vegas in '69. They say Elvis's greatest performance was done in that suit. I always considered it my lucky suit, and that night, I was feeling lucky."

This time Stella couldn't help herself and laughed aloud.

"Impersonator after impersonator took the stage," Lester continued unabashed. "That night we heard every one of my, uh, Elvis's hits."

I didn't know if he confused himself with Elvis on purpose as a joke or if he was just that delusional.

"The impersonators were in rare form. Some weren't bad, a few just terrible, and some were so like me I was shocked. Anyway, I was the twenty-seventh contestant, and that night, I was the King. As they called my number, a wild cheer broke out, louder than any other contestant. I sauntered onto the stage. I looked over the crowd, in that moment, I could do no wrong. I nodded at the DJ. Slowly, the lights faded out, leaving a pale spotlight illuminating me in my white pantsuit." Lester made a grand sweeping gesture with his hands.

"I sang 'Good Enough for You' with such soul several people had tears in their eyes."

I haven't heard Lenny sing, but the pitch of his voice is enough for me to suspect there was another reason for the tears in their eyes.

"As the last note faded, the crowd fell silent. I could barely make out the faces of my family sitting at a front table. They looked stunned."

"I'm sure." But Lester was waiting for me to say more. "So, what happened next?"

"Someone in the front began clapping. I bowed again. Another person started clapping, but for the most part, everyone was in complete shock. I didn't blame them, because I had just ended the competition. No one could top my performance."

I just shook my head. What could I say that wouldn't sound completely sarcastic?

"I wasn't surprised when my number was called as the grand prize winner."

"Of course not."

"When I accepted my prize, the judge told me I sang one of his favorite Elvis songs. 'Son,' he said, 'the way you sang that song was a real tribute. It always reminds me of my marriage.'"

I couldn't remember the song, but I didn't think it was romantic.

"The judge told me not to let anyone stand in the way of my happiness. 'You have a real talent.' His words were a light bulb in my head. At that moment, I knew my destiny." He paused for dramatic effect.

Again, I decided to play along and give him his cue, "And what's your destiny?"

"Follow in footprints of the great Elvis impersonators and take my act on the road!"

"Sweet Jesus, it is not."

"It is! Say, do you want to hear me sing?"

"No," I answered, but Lester was already making his way to the front of the bus, and Stella was digging out the camcorder. Lester handed a tape to Gus who obligingly popped it in. The music played for two bars before Lester began to sing.

OH HO, my darling
What more can I do
Doin' the best
The best I can
But it's not good enough for you

But it's not good enough for you

A root canal without Novocain couldn't have been worse. Lester squealed, hitting notes only small dogs could hear as he serenaded us with "Good Enough For You." When he finished, Lester took a deep bow. The Japanese Trio clapped enthusiastically. They probably had defective hearing aids, which prevented them from hearing Lester's tortured rendition. Politeness forced the rest of the bus to clap.

"Well, thank you. Thank you very much." He waited for laughter that never came.

"Did you get it?" he asked Stel as he flopped into his seat.

"Sure did."

"Good. You'll want to use it in your article I suppose." It's official. He is delusional. "That's why I told you my story."

"And I'm glad you did," said Stel. "Good stuff." This satisfied Lester, who pulled out *The Tao of Elvis* and started reading.

My relief at being released by Lester didn't last long. "Marion is looking at us," I whispered to Stel.

"Have you thought of what you're going to say?"

"Shit no."

Stella screamed, "Bring on the Elvis movies!"

"What are you doing?" I hissed at her.

"Stalling."

It didn't look like Stella's tactic was going to work. Marion got to her feet and was definitely looking at us. But then Vince made his way to the front of the bus and handed Gus a tape.

"Looks like Vince is going to sing, so I'm safe for now." I took the camcorder from Stella.

"I wouldn't be so sure."

"It can't be any worse than Lester's wailing."

Chapter 7: Stella

It could be worse. It was.

It wasn't his voice, but his style. Vince rapped Elvis's "Are You Lonesome Tonight." The whole thing was just confusing and sad. Thomas looked as if Vince just committed a sacrilege.

"Ha, take that, Lenny," shouted Vince.

"Oh, please," mutter Lester.

Again we clapped out of politeness; however, Vince, being so proud of himself, didn't seem to notice or mind our lackluster response.

"Elvis is the reason my buddies and I started our band, *Vince and the Jordanaires*," he said. "Inspired by the talent and life of Elvis, we model our music after his. We sing techno and rap versions of Elvis classics, following the King's innovative style. We play at local bars and fairs. We're popular because we're really good, as you can tell."

Vince handed the mike back to Marion and strutted down the aisle. However, he didn't rejoin Ella. Instead he slid beside Maggie and started to openly flirt with her. Shocked by his behavior, I turned to catch Ella's reaction. As expected, her face relayed hurt and confused feelings, but when she caught me looking, she flashed a smile and turned to stare out the window.

"What a sleaze," I mumbled to Jess.

"Yeah, a real dirt bag," she agreed. "Feel sorry for Ella."

"She's pissed, but trying to hide it. Say, let me up. I'm going to go talk with her." I nudged Jess out of the way.

"Mind if I sit here?" I asked, but didn't wait for an answer. After acknowledging my presence with a nod, Ella turned back to the window. "So, are you enjoying your honeymoon?" I asked, trying to break the ice.

"What's that supposed to mean?" Ella snapped.

"Nothing. Wow, relax." Not the reaction I expected. "I was just wondering if you're having a good time on the tour."

"Oh, yeah, it's nice. You?"

"Well, we haven't done much, but yeah."

Again, Ella nodded then showed me the back of her head as she returned to staring out the window. After a few moments of awkward silence as I searched for something to talk about, Ella asked, "Is there something you wanted to say to me?"

"I'm just trying to have a conversation to get to know you." I didn't know why she was being so hostile.

"No, I don't think that's it at all."

"No?" I asked and waited for her to tell me what I meant.

"No. You saw Vince sit down beside Maggie and felt sorry for me–this new bride who's already lost her husband's attention."

Damn, she did know what I meant, I thought. My face flushed in embarrassment.

"But you know what?" Ella continued. "You can just save your pity; I don't need it. I'm not one of those insecure, jealous wives who expects her husband to never talk to another attractive woman again. I'm confident in my relationship. I know Vince loves me. Me, you got it?"

I shook my head yes. Wow, I really hit a nerve.

"And all those other women don't mean a damn thing because he loves me."

"Of course he does." *All those other women*, I thought. And since we were already into it, I just asked, "Are you happy?"

"Happy with what exactly?" This time I could see Ella's nostrils flaring since they were only inches from mine.

But I pressed on anyway, "Happy being married."

"Why wouldn't I be? What the hell kind of question is that to ask a newlywed? You've got a lot of nerve."

"I'm sorry. I'm not trying to upset you. I just thought it might be hard being so young and newly married to a man who is used to receiving a lot of attention because of his band and all." There, I said it. I might regret it, but I said it, leaving the door open to see if Ella wanted to walk through.

She didn't. She pretty much slammed the door in my face. "I'm very happy. You got it?" She said loud enough for everyone on the bus to get it. "Now, if you're looking for some controversy to make your article more interesting, you can go-"

"You want to feature us in your article?" Vince interrupted, which was good because my sympathy for Ella had wore off, and I was about to adjust her hostile attitude.

"I thought you would," said Vince, sitting down across the aisle. He leaned his arm on the back of my chair putting his breath and face too close to mine. "Why don't you tell her how we met, sweetie."

"Yes, tell me how you met," I said in a challenge to Ella.

Ella returned my smirk and began reciting their story on cue. "I heard his music on the radio and liked it. When his band came to town, my girlfriends and I bought tickets. He was the only thing my girlfriends could talk about. Our seats were right up front."

"Her friends thought I was the hottest thing, so they wanted to be real close," interrupted Vince. "Isn't that right, honey? Didn't your friends think I was hot?"

"Yes."

"A real sex machine or something. You get a lot of that when you're famous. It comes with the territory. Doesn't it, love?"

Ella's 'yes' was a little less enthusiastic than before, and she wouldn't look at me.

"Continue, babe. Stella is waiting," urged Vince.

Ella began again, "So after the show we stood in line to get his autograph-"

"I put my cell number next to my signature," Vince interrupted again wanting to tell the story himself. "I asked her when she planned on calling me. Very audacious of me, don't you think?"

I doubt Vince really knows what 'audacious' means.

Vince continued, "She was speechless, so I suggested she stop by my hotel room later where a bunch of the gang and our followers were going to have a party. I doubted she would have come if her friends hadn't brought her. They concocted some lie to her parents and stayed all night. Ella and I talked 'til dawn. She was just so kind and sweet, like an untouched angel. She was so easy to talk to." Vince reached across my lap to stroke her cheek.

"She completely understood the pressures of being famous and talented even though she didn't have any experiences like that. So what if she was younger than me– it's only by three years. It didn't matter. We were fated for each other. After that first night, we were inseparable. Except of course when I need to have my space, when the band and I record albums, and when I travel."

"Of course," I said, looking at Ella.

"We were married the weekend before this trip. We felt there could be no better honeymoon than celebrating our love for each other by demonstrating our love for the King. After all, he introduced us in a way." Vince laughed, but Ella didn't.

"Well, that's very nice. Thanks for sharing," I said. I stood abruptly and returned to my seat without another word.

"So, how'd it go?" Jess asked, having heard the whole confrontation.

"Wonderful," I said sarcastically. "Remind me never to feel bad for someone and offer my friendship."

"She was probably hurt and embarrassed and took it out on you," Jess said. "Here, try these."

"What are they?"

"Some chips Mary gave me."

I tried a few. "Wow, these are spicy." I coughed, then continued, "Ella accused me of wanting to use her troubles to make the article more interesting. Can you believe it? I'd never do that."

"I would." Jess was rubbing her neck. I noticed her face was red and eyes were watering.

"You would not."

"I'm putting it all down right now." Jess scribbled in her journal.

We smelled Marion's signature Chanel N°5 perfume before we saw her. "Hi Marion. How are you?" I asked pretending I had no idea why she was standing beside us. I hope Jess had some time to prepare.

"Good," said Marion. "And you?"

"Good." Silence as I couldn't think of any way to get Jess out of having to speak. However, when I looked at her, I could tell she was not doing well at all. "Jess, are you okay?"

"No," she choked. She seemed to be working very hard to breath.

"Jess, what is it?" But she couldn't answer.

"What's wrong?" Marion asked.

"I don't know," I answered. "Mary, can I see your bag of chips, please?"

"Sure. Why?" Mary handed me the bag, and I instantly saw the problem.

Processed in peanut oil, I read and then jumped out of my seat, practically knocking Marion over in my panic. I grabbed Jessica's bag from the overhead storage. What were we thinking? "She's allergic to peanuts!"

"I'm so sorry," wailed Mary. "I didn't know."

"Of course you didn't. It's going to be okay." I said this more to Jess and myself than to Mary. I was scared, very scared, but trying not to show it. Jess was really struggling. Hives had already formed down her neck. I quickly grabbed Jessica's EpiPen and administered the shot with trembling hands.

After I returned the syringe to its case, Jess grabbed my hand and looked into my face for reassurance. "It's going to be okay," I repeated.

"Is she going to be all right?" Marion asked still standing in the aisle. "Does she need medical assistance?"

"No, she'll be fine. But she won't be speaking today. I'm sorry." I thought this would be the end of it, but I was wrong.

"Of course not. You'll have to speak for the both of you."

"What? No, I, uh, Jess was, you see I can't." But Marion didn't hear my protests because she was already walking to the front of the bus.

"Well, folks, we still have about forty miles to the first Elvis site," Marion announced. "So, to pass the time, I've asked Stella to speak."

"I can't," I whispered to Jess while staring at an impatient Marion.

"You have to." Her breathing still came in labored gasps.

"You did this on purpose."

"Yes, Stel. I ate something that would make my throat swell shut just so you'd have to speak because I'd rather die than talk about Elvis."

"I would."

"Well, Stella?" Marion persisted.

I made my way to the front and wondered if everyone could see how hard my heart was pounding. I took the microphone from Marion and turned to face the crowd. It was a few minutes before I managed to say, "I'm sorry, Marion, what did you want me to talk about?"

Marion looked completely exasperated. I wasn't trying to be difficult. It was just hard to think with this ringing in my ears. "I thought you could give us more of an idea of what it is the two of you do," she explained.

"Well, we're reporters. So we report on things, you know, like people, events and stuff." Oh dear God, help me,

I prayed. Every word came out like I was reading off a teleprompter. What's wrong with me?

"And do you always write about travel or do you report on other things?"

"Other things." I was looking at everyone, but at the same time not looking at anyone.

"Like…" Marion coaxed.

Here goes. "Politics and stuff."

"Oh, that's interesting." Marion looked at the rest of the tour as if to say, see, isn't that interesting? "And do the two of you always work together?"

"Most of the time."

"Why?" I could tell by the way it came out Marion didn't mean to ask that question, but I answered anyway.

"Because we're friends."

"Yes, but friends usually don't work together, or at least they don't stay friends for long." Marion laughed and asked the rest of the tour, "Am I right?" A few people laughed and mumbled in agreement.

"And usually a magazine only sends one writer after a story," Marion continued, but sensing she insulted me, she quickly clarified. "I mean, so there must be a reason, a certain style of reporting that requires two writers."

"Well, after we graduated from Northwestern with our bachelors in journalism, we were fortunate to both be hired by the same publication in Chicago."

"Oh, how nice. What magazine would that be?"

"It was a small newspaper. You wouldn't know it," I lied. I could see Jessica laughing in the back. "Anyway, we have complimentary styles, and we collaborated on some of our early pieces, so I guess it just grew from there."

"That makes sense. I understand," said Marion.

But as I looked at my friend who might have suffocated had I not been here, I thought, *no you don't understand.* And for some reason, I wanted her to.

"I don't have parents," I blurted, which caught everyone off guard and seemed random, but to understand what Jess means to me, they need to know where I come from.

"What do you mean, you don't have parents?" It was Elliot who asked.

"I don't have parents."

"Everyone has parents," said Marion pragmatically.

"I don't." I'm not sure why I was doing this, and I could tell by the look on Jessica's face neither did she, but since I've started. "The people who brought me into this world, you could call them my birth parents, but I don't. They left me in a barn when I was just a few weeks old." I waited for this news to work its way around the bus.

"That's awful," said Tansy. She shook her head and Billy put his arm around her.

"I suppose it would have been if Glen hadn't found me while he was doing chores," I continued. "So the people who raised me, you could call them my adopted parents, but I don't. They did the best job they could being older and never having children of their own. They are Amanas, so I grew up on a farm in Iowa. And I grew up knowing I was different. From the very beginning, Glen and Louise told me what happened."

"I'm sorry," whispered Marion.

"It's okay. I had a good life. Glen and Louise are practical and kind and loving from a distance." Again, I looked at my friend. Tears sprung to my eyes, but I didn't care. "When I left for college and met Jessica, I didn't expect her to become the only family I've ever known. She's so much more than a friend to me. Something else, but I'm not sure what you call it."

"You soul sisters," said Harulu, one of the oriental trio.

I laughed, "Yes, I suppose that's it. You hear that, Jess, we're soul sisters."

"Yes we are," she answered, and the rest of the tour laughed.

"So, Marion, you're right," I continued. "It is a bit unusual for two writers to cover one story, but I've always been a bit unusual. And I suppose it won't always be this way. Our careers will eventually take us down separate paths. But I'm grateful for everything we've experienced so far, good and bad." *Yes, even The Incident*, I thought. "And no matter what the future brings, she'll always be my soul sister."

With that, I gave the mike back to Marion and returned to my seat.

"Thank you," she said and addressed the rest of the group, "Isn't this a great way to pass the time?" No one answered.

"Thank you, soul sister," Jess said as I sat down.

"Whatever. Don't talk to me. I'm still mad at you."

"But you did great." She shoved me with her shoulders. "I mean it, Stel."

I shoved back. "Thanks. Are you okay?"

"Yes, just a little shook up, and my throat itches."

"We have to be more careful about that, Jess."

"I know, I know."

Marion interrupted my lecture. "And we are right on schedule. If you look ahead you will see the quaint town of Defiance, Iowa, home of the Giant Elvis Mud Sculpture! Yeah!" She cheered at her own announcement.

"Finally, our first tourist trap," said Jess. "I wonder what it'll look like."

"I don't know. She said Giant Elvis Mud Sculpture, so, and I'm just guessing here, but it'll probably be a big pile of mud in the shape of Elvis."

Chapter 8: Jessica

"A pile of mud in the shape of Elvis," I echoed Stella's comment. "I can't wait. Get the camera ready. This will be the thrust of our article."

Glistening silver light marked the water tower, standing proud at the edge of the town. At this angle, only the massive letters of D, E and F were visible. However, Defiance never came into clear view as we turned onto a gravel road.

Marion read about the attraction from a brochure. "Ernie and Harriet Osborne are credited with the discovery of the Giant Elvis Mud Sculpture. Although called a sculpture, it is, in fact, a natural wonder. No tools or human hands created or modified the likeness of Elvis. The Osbornes, upon discovering this natural miracle, erected a building to protect the mud from the elements. This was a slow process, as no one wanted to vibrate the ground too much for fear of disturbing Elvis's face. The Osbornes and hundreds of volunteers dug the foundation for the building by hand. They also carried every brick 100 yards to build the Center that encases this Gift from Graceland."

It was like God lost a piece of Memphis on its way to Tennessee. Billboards with Elvis in various costumes doing various gyrations popped out of the cornfields. "Nine Miles to the Eighth Wonder of the World!" read one sign. "Elvis Lives On! In Nature!" said another.

Ernest and Harriet Osborne were not the American Gothic couple I expected. They were more like *Green Acres* minus the pig. Ernest looked his part in bib overalls and faded t-shirt, but the pair of black satin slippers on his feet ruined the hard-working-farmer getup. Harriet had on hot pink beachcombers, matching sunglasses, a floppy straw hat, flip-flops, and a colorful plastic beach bag. Both were standing next to a large brick building located on a circular drive. In the center of the driveway, a life-sized statue of the King emerged from a clinging tangle of wild roses planted at his feet.

The group chattered with excitement as they disembarked. I snagged Stella's arm. "Come on. I didn't get a good shot of the Elvis Statue on the way up."

"Why? It's not the mud sculpture."

"I know. But someone decorated the statue with roses and I want a closer look."

"Are you taking pictures?" Char asked as she got off the bus behind me. "Can you take mine too? I'm going to get my money's worth on this trip, somehow."

"But I thought you won this trip."

"Yes. So?"

"Never mind."

"Could you take my picture, too?" Don asked.

Assaulted with Stella's pleading face and feeling somehow threatened by Char, I agreed to be the photographer as we walked to the statue.

"Just push the round button," instructed Char. "But first you need to focus it. No, wait! Move over so you capture more of my good side. And don't get me from the waist down. Can you hurry up? I'm getting stuck by these damn thorns."

Somehow I managed to snap a picture without hurling the camera at her head. As Char climbed down, she ripped the lei of fake roses from Elvis's neck and stuffed them in her purse.

Don smiled as he handed over his camera. "Just do your best," he said, then pulled a stunned Stella into the pose with him.

After taking a picture of Stiff Stella and Dynamite Don, he collected his camera and studied the statue. "You know, it almost looks as though the roses are trying to pull him into the ground." I had to bite my lip to keep from commenting on the irony; nature trying to restore the balance.

"Well, thanks again," said Don as he walked away.

"Wait," called Stella, but he kept walking. "No, please," she said in a tiny voice to herself. "Thanks for the picture" She sighed, "I love you."

I laughed at my melodramatic friend.

Char shouted back to us, "Hey! The group is going inside the building!"

We squished into a small room that doubled as the entry to the main exhibit and a gift shop. My cheek was pressed against a rack of postcards. Everyone swarmed over one another like mice on a sinking ship.

From a safety point behind the front desk, Harriet addressed the group. "In a moment I'll be opening the door to our exhibit hall. We ask that you stay on the marked path at all times. Please do not cross the railing. We also ask that you do not handle the dirt. Do not pocket any dirt. Do not drop any garbage or personal items over the railing. Photographs are allowed, but please do not use flash as it may cause the exhibit to deteriorate. Please keep your voices low. We are trying to preserve a natural monument, and disturbances of any kind will cause irreparable damage."

Harriet, despite her tacky pink outfit, had a flair for the dramatic, and her speech made the hair on the back of my neck tingle. I wished I'd had room to breathe so that I could have enjoyed it more. And thank God the door to the exhibit hall swung out instead of in, or someone would have perished. I peeled myself off the postcard rack and joined the group pushing through the door into a padded cell. Thick foam rubber covered the walkway. I assumed this cushioned the vibrations. The railing was also encased in foam rubber. The walkway and railing hugged the padded wall in the circular room. A large stump in the center showed valiant attempts at re-growth.

Harriet continued her dialogue in *dolce voce* as she moved around the walkway. "As you can see, nature tried to reclaim its gift to us several times. Had we permitted the continued growth of the tree, the limbs, leaves, and roots would have completely destroyed Elvis's body."

Due to the squishy walkway and Harriet's caution, the group seemed content to move extra slow, which increased my anticipation. I watched the faces of those in front of me for a hint of the treasure that lay before them. One by one, curiosity gave way to disbelief, shaky hands raised cameras to document the moment. People spoke in excited whispers to each other and pointed.

With some quick maneuvering and liberal use of my elbows, Stel and I reached an opening at the railing to view the Eighth Wonder of the World. My eyes saw, but my brain could not comprehend. I gasped. I stared.

Stella whispered at my elbow, "Dear God, what is that thing?"

If this was Elvis ala nature, then nature was cruel. His legs were twisted and gnarled—old tentacles that came from their host, the dead stump. The roots came up and joined together, thrusting out in a crude portrayal of Elvis's famous pelvis. His torso was comprised of a moldering pile of leaves and compost. A branch had fallen across the compost heap and created the illusion of arms. One arm extended into a long, sharp point, the other branched out into seven smaller twigs, resulting in a deformed hand. The head was three times the size of the body.

At one time, someone must have dumped dirt behind an old tree and the elements had done the rest. Then time, or more likely Ernest, stamped down the earth into a remarkable Elvis-looking pile of dirt. Especially if you tilted your head to the side and squinted.

"Isn't this the most incredible thing you have ever seen?" Marion was next to us and bounced on the foam rubber like a terrier puppy. Gus was to her right and didn't reply. He stared at Nature Elvis with a dreamy, far-off look in his eyes. I wondered what he was thinking, then wondered if he'd tell us his Elvis story sometime during the tour. I bet he had a doozy.

Harriet managed to untangle a few from the group and moved them towards the door, encouraging them to browse in the gift shop. I moved along with the first few, but stopped to zoom in on the crowd that lingered. Eric whispered to a bored Elliot. Tansy, Billy, Maggie and Don made an interesting foursome in the center. Stella remained behind, shooting dejected looks toward Don. Char and Marion were in the midst of another pow-wow, and it looked like Marion's cheerfulness was winning. The Japanese Trio took turns taking each other's picture and trying to get the Elvis figure in the background. None of the three ladies was tall enough to make this possible.

I decided to conserve the rest of my memory card and moved into the gift shop for mementos. I had chosen three postcards when a morose Stella joined me.

"He spent the whole time talking to Maggie. Probably likes her boobs."

"What man alive wouldn't?"

"If only I had bought a pair of boobs instead of wasting that money on a college education, how much better my life would be," Stella lamented as she absentmindedly picked a postcard off the rack, realized it showed a picture of Ernest in Christmas boxers with "Santa's Helper" across the top, and quickly put it back. "If you were a real friend, you'd give me some of what you've got."

"Sure. The minute they start to sag, they're all yours. Now, on to more important matters. Which shot glass should I get?" I held out two choices.

"The one with the mud Elvis head on it. I'll get the tree stump one and later we can drown our sorrows."

"Girls, the bus will be leaving in exactly twenty-two minutes!" Marion announced, approximately two inches from our ears. "What did you think of the sculpture? Did you get a picture? This would be a get addition to the article, don't you think? Have you seen Gus?"

"The driver? No, I haven't." Stella looked at me.

"The last time I saw him, he was inside the exhibit hall."

Marion brightened. "Then that's where I'll find him. Bus leaves in twenty-one minutes."

"Come on. I need to find a bathroom," said Stella, moving toward the facilities that were a good hike across the parking lot. Not wanting to risk the Sun Tour's idea of a portable john, I joined her. Maggie followed, which nixed any private conversation time.

Coming out of the restroom, we saw the others standing around the bus. Someone yelled, "Go get Marion!" We rushed to join the crowd.

Marion walked up to the door of the bus and the crowd pushed in closer. She began reading a note aloud: "After three years, Elvis has shown me the way. I must find my destiny. Take care of my baby." Her reaction was immediate. "Take care of his BABY! He can't do this! We leave in nine minutes! HE CAN'T DO THIS!" Marion moved away from the group and began to pace and rant in circles. I maintained the presence of mind to videotape the unfolding drama.

"What was that all about?" asked Brother Thomas from the back of the crowd. "Whose baby is she talking about?"

"It's not a baby. It's a bus."

Chapter 9: Stella

Gus has left the building.

When I realized the magnitude of the situation, my first thought was, *Sweet freedom!* Now it's not our fault if we quit this crazy tour and go home. Ursula might understand. Our work here is done, even if we never made it to Memphis.

Every vein in Marion's neck had doubled in size. Jess's mouth had formed a tiny smile, and we held our breath, fascinated.

Marion sputtered, "He's a . . .well, he's just a . . .well, he's a . . .well, a *bad bus driver* to be blunt about it!" She started pacing in the driveway. "I just . . . he can't . . . this can't happen . . . to ME! I had this trip planned. He knew the plan. I gave him three copies even though it's the same doggone plan we've used the last three trips." She abruptly stopped, turned to the crowd and asked, "How can . . . I just don't . . . what do we do now?"

No one answered.

"I mean where did he even go?" Marion held her arms out and spun in a circle indicating the vast expanse of farmland. I thought for a minute she was about to start searching for him. I could see her running in ever widening circles across the countryside determined to drag Gus back by his ear while the rest of us just stood in Harriet's driveway. But she didn't.

Marion took a deep breath. "This will not get me down." She began pacing again. "I am on top of this.

Everything is fine. I'm fine. We'll be just fine." It must have been something she had heard on a self-help tape. "So he wants to take off. So what? Am I going to let that upset me? No." Marion's voice jumped three decibels. "I am not upset! This is me being anything but UPSET! Not over something as trivial as being dumped by our ass-slapping, sloppy, sorry excuse of a piss-poor bus driver!"

Marion kicked the stand where smokers put their cigarette butts, hurting her foot in the process. The members of Sun Tours looked at each other like, isn't someone going to do something? But no one did.

After limping a few steps, Marion continued her tirade, "I couldn't think of anything better than to be stranded in this Godforsaken place with no hope of food, water, or a copier. Good riddance to that . . . that . . . freak of science, crash course, pedestrian killing, dumb, dumb, dumb, dumb-ass driver!"

Shocked back to reality by the meanest thing she had probably ever said, Marion turned to the group. Her face arranged itself into a beatific smile. "Don't worry," she soothed. "I'll figure something out. Give me a minute. Mingle amongst yourselves."

No one mingled.

Squatting with pump-clad feet spread apart and swaying her arms around like a dancer, Marion progressed through a series of tai chi moves to re-establish inner harmony and absolute control. Finally, she turned to the statue of Elvis and fell to her knees. With uplifted hands, she intoned, "Tell me, what would you have us do? Talk to me, Elvis."

After a moment, Marion rose to her feet and faced us. Her hands were clasped delicately at her waist, and the beatific smile had settled deep into the Revlon-clogged creases of her face.

"Elvis has spoken," she announced, which was funny because I didn't hear a thing. Lester and Thomas looked roused, and a murmur fluttered across the group. "When faced with difficulty," Marion said, "the King always pressed on. In *Viva Las Vegas*, did he give up when he lost his money and didn't have an engine for the race?"

"Why, no!" cried Lenny. His sequined shirt glittered as he looked at the faces around him for agreement. The murmur elevated to nodding heads.

Marion cheered. "That's right! And when everyone was betting against him in *Clambake*, did he back out of the race?"

"No!" The word erupted in unison. Jess even looked flushed, and an electric tingle shot down to the soles of my feet.

Marion was in her element now. "Did Elvis ever give up, back down and turn away in defeat?"

"Hell no!" We were on fire. We were ready to do anything. If she had asked, we would have picked the bus up and carried it into town.

Marion shouted, "Then tell me, what did he do?"

Lester answered, "He won the race and got the girl every damn time!"

"Yes, that's right! Now we have our own race, members of the Sun Tours Elvis Extravaganza. A race against time. We are now thirteen minutes past schedule." She held her clipboard up like a victory torch. "This is what we're going to do. We are going to drive back into town, check into a hotel and call for an emergency replacement driver. Who's with me?"

"We are!" We war-whooped our way onto the bus. We slapped high-fives and gave hugs all around like we just recovered the holy land from the disbelievers.

Marion bellowed over the din, "Can anyone drive this thing?" This brought an abrupt silence. Then Billy swaggered up the aisle, back straight, arms held a little out from his sides as if he was ready to wrestle a steer. "Well, ma'am, I have some experience with tours. I could sure give this lil' missy a try."

"Good. Get your butt in the seat." Empowered by her conversation with Elvis, Marion was back to her gleaming self.

Billy seized the wheel. He grabbed the mike and yee-hawed. "All right, ladies and gents. Hold on to your hats 'cause here we go!"

Cybill took off with her usual lunge and lightning. Billy seemed to have a bit of trouble with the girl. He shouted, "She has more kick than I reckoned for, but don't panic none, folks. Everything is fine."

But we could tell everything was not fine. We careened down the road, into a half dozen potholes. My jaws clacked and somebody's day bag went airborne.

Marion added her assistance, screaming orders and warnings. "Look out!"

"I see it," Billy answered.

"No, over there."

"I see it."

"Well, that doesn't mean you have to aim for it."

"Can't miss 'em all," said Billy as we hit a particularly large pot hole.

Sitting in the second row, I watched the Osbornes become a tiny speck in the rear view mirror. I glanced out the side window and read billboards such as "Thanks for Visiting the Eighth Wonder of the World" and "Elvis Loves You." Screams coming from Marion and Tansy brought my attention back to the road.

They were both yelling, "Swerve. Hard right. Right, man, right! A raccoon! Turn now!"

Billy obeyed, and Cybill leapt the ditch and crashed through a fence into a cornfield. Like a wild boar, Cybill took down the vegetation. Jess's fingernails were talons in my arm. Leafage flew by the windows. We were lost in the jungles of Iowa.

Marion's voice rose above the screams. "Billy, where the blazes are you going?"

"Lady, I'll be damned if I know. I'm just trying to find the road again!"

"Just stop this thing already. Stop!"

Billy slammed on the brakes, and Cybill came to a sliding halt, but not before crashing into something solid.

"Oh, my Elvis!" screamed Marion. "You've hit Elvis. You've decapitated the King!"

Billy shot back in defense, "I hit a billboard! It's just one of those blasted billboards advertising the mud sculpture. There's the road right there."

"But look what you did. You killed Elvis."

"Elvis is dead, lady!"

Like the shot heard round the world, that sentence hung in the suddenly noiseless air. A shocked Marion stammered, "H-h-how dare you say that?"

Billy, also shocked by his behavior, quickly apologized. "I'm sorry. I didn't mean it. Look Marion, don't cry. I'm real sorry. Oh, don't cry, ma'am. It's just driving this bus is harder than it looks and your screaming got me all flustered. Hey, chin up now."

Marion cried, "B-b-but what do we do n-n-ow? What about Elvis? I mean he's just staring at us with those big blue eyes."

Upon hitting the windshield, Elvis's face had cracked in two along the jaw line. The two parts had begun to slide off the glass, the bottom sliding faster than the top. At Marion's question, Elvis suddenly got a dopey grin on his face—as if he were mocking Sun Tours. Char was the first to begin laughing.

Hysteria overtook the group. When the tension had vanished, Billy rounded up the men to help push the bus out of the ditch. Everyone except Marion disembarked Cybill, and in fifteen minutes we were ready to rock and roll. Billy took over wheel more carefully, and somehow, he managed to drive Cybill into Defiance.

We stopped at the first hotel that appeared large enough to handle the tour, which wasn't tough. The entire town seemed vacant. The hotel was simply named Hotel as far as anybody could tell. It had Tex-Mex faux-adobe architecture, painted egg-yolk yellow. The yard included a sole pathetic cactus among some brownish boulders, which was an attempt to hide the dying grass and patches of barren earth.

As usual, Char took one look and voiced her unsolicited opinion, "We can't stay here. This is a big yellow dump."

"Do we want to risk taking Cybill around town trying to find something else?" asked Marion.

She got an immediate "Hell no!" from the group. We were all in desperate need of a shower, a nap and room to breathe. So it was settled. Marion walked through the screen door minus the screen that led to the office. We contemplated our fate, which promised to be another sleepless night.

Looking over my fellow tourists, I unexpectedly caught Don's stare. He arched his eyebrows in a "this should be great" expression. I smiled and nodded in agreement, then looked away before my face could reveal my jittery emotions.

Matt, Marcus and Luc stirred to life. "So this is where we're staying?" asked Luc.

"Yes," groaned Char.

"Cool! This place is trippin'," argued Matt.

"Yeah, it's so uncool that it's cool," explained Marcus. "Ya know what I mean, bro?"

"No," said Char. "And I'm not your bro."

"Hey!" called Vince. He was leaning toward the office window, his nose an inch from the glass. "Look at this. There's a bar advertising Karaoke tonight. We should check it out later. Don't you think, honey bunny?"

By the time Marion returned with our room assignments and keys, Ella and Vince had gotten Karaoke on the agenda for the entire group. As I wondered what Don would wear to bed and if coed room assignments were possible, Jess jingled the key in front of my nose and said, "I said, we are bunking with Maggie tonight."

Our room was cheap, basic and moderately clean. Guarding the entrance of the bathroom was a stuffed carcass. The animal was some sort of cross between a jackrabbit and an antelope. Maggie said, "I don't know what that thing is, but its beady little eyes are creeping me out."

We dropped our luggage on the cowboy bedspread. Frontier paintings decorated the walls. "I bet Billy is enjoying this," I said. "The home of his people."

At Smiley's Diner, everyone ordered the usual greasy burger, fries and a shake. Tansy joined Maggie, Jess and myself. I asked if either of them had spoken to Don. They said yes. So far, he had conversed with everyone except me. I found this behavior perplexing.

Lester approached our table with a beaming smile, a missing sideburn and stack of papers. "I wrote down my Elvis story so you can use it in your article. Are you going to join in on the singing?"

I stared at him like he'd lost his mind. There's no way in hell we're letting Lester Chen and his fake sideburns write our article. However, I focused on the karaoke and said, "Yeah, count me in. We should do a duet."

"Really?"

I thought, *No, not really.* But I said, "Sure."

"Great!" He turned to Jess.

She chimed, "Count me in, Lenny. If Stella is going to sing, I've got to see it. Plus, I could use a stiff drink."

"Great. How about you, Tansy?"

"Well, did you ask Billy?"

"He's coming."

"Well, then, of course I am."

"You, Maggie?"

"Umm, no."

"No? Why not?" cried Tansy. "Come on, Mags, you have to come with me."

"Well, Eric and I are going to play Trivial Pursuit with Elliot tonight." Tansy, Jess, Lester and I gave a knowing 'Oh.' Everyone had noticed the undercurrents between Eric and Maggie.

After dinner, we returned to our rooms to prep for a night on the town. After getting moderately comfortable in the sparse room, I sorted through my luggage. I managed to pass the bathroom guardian without its horned, hairy self falling on me. I put on a white off-the-shoulder top to accent my tan and blonde hair and the jeans that made my butt look good, according to an ex-boyfriend. I touched up my eye makeup to make my baby blues pop. I checked my figure in the mirror. I wished my reflection showed a woman with more boob and less butt; however, overall I was happy with my appearance. I wanted to make Don drool over me at Karaoke.

The woman's lib part of my brain was chastising me for thinking a man's attention would help me regain the confidence I've lost since The Incident. It's just so damn frustrating because writing is something I know I can do well. It defines who I am. There are athletes, movie stars, doctors, lawyers. I am a writer.

Writing has always brought me praise, a few awards and the admiration of my peers. I never expected it to bring me pain, a pink slip and public humiliation. Especially when I didn't do anything wrong. The story was true.

So the wounded part of my heart was telling me the musky scent of man might make me feel better or at least forget my troubles for awhile. And this is good enough for me. Having silenced my internal critic, I started singing "Slow Hand" by the Pointer Sisters, "*'Darlin', don't say a word cause I already heard what your body's saying to mine.'*"

From the bedroom I heard Jess explain to Maggie, "This is something Stel does. Just ignore her."

"*'I'm tired of fast moves, I've got a slow groove on my mind,*'" I let it out.

Jess shouted at me, "Are you done in there?"

I ran out of the bathroom, jumped on the bed and continued singing, "*'I want a man with a slow hand. I want a lover with an easy touch.'*" I fell onto the bed and clutched my hands to my heart. "*'I want somebody who will spend some time. Not come and go in a heated rush.'*"

"I'll just leave you two alone," Maggie said. "I don't want to keep Eric and Elliot waiting." She picked up her purse from the desk and crossed the room to the door.

"Jess, why aren't we dating?" I asked still lying on the bed.

"Because same sex marriage is illegal."

I snorted. "Not in Vermont."

"Can we go now?" Jess asked.

I don't know why she's in a hurry, but I sat up and looked around the room for my shoes. Without Maggie's nervous, quiet energy flitting around, the room seemed at once bigger and more private. Jess was holding out my shoes, looking annoyed.

"Oh, thanks." I took my shoes, threw one on the floor and started fighting with the tiny strap of the other. "But really, Jess, why are two fairly attractive, fairly successful women like us doing still single with no prospect in sight?"

She sighed. "Well, you're certifiable."

"After everyone we've met, you think I'm certifiable."

"It was enough to chase Maggie from the room."

"Fine," I said, fastening the first buckle. "If I'm crazy, what's your excuse?"

"I'm trying to salvage what little career we have left. I have no time for a man."

"Speaking of our careers, so far for our article we have Lester's destiny of becoming a world famous Elvis impersonator regardless of the fact he's Vietnamese and can't sing, and an Elvis-like mud sculpture."

"I know." Jess applied some lip gloss.

"Somehow I don't think Ursula will be excited about either," I said, finally getting the last shoe on. I sat up and the blood rushed from my head. "Hey, you look nice."

Jess wore black capris and a rose v–neck shirt that drew out her porcelain skin and ample bosom. Her black hair framed her face. "Thanks," she said in a flat voice, "so do you. Now let's go."

#

The whole crew was at Harvey's Hangout by the time Jess and I arrived. Jess, being the career-oriented nerd she was, brought her notes. We scooted to the bar and surveyed the scene. Our little band of Elvis lovers tried to blend with the locals. It was difficult with Thomas dressed like Elvis from *Wild in the Country*.

Jess asked, "Are you really going to sing with Lester?"

"Why not? He can't sing. I can't sing. We'll be a hit." I was about to ask Jess if she had spotted Don yet, when three hicks walked my way. They couldn't be more than sixteen. I saw them coming from the corner of my eye, felt their attention and ignored them. They wandered over anyway.

The tallest one asked, "Care to dance?"

I looked out at the still empty dance floor and answered, "No thanks. I'm, uh, visiting with my friend." I elbowed Jess.

"I bet you'll dance with me. Won't you, sweetheart?" asked the redhead.

"No. I don't care to dance. Thank you anyway." Another desperate jab to Jess as the three smelly guys leaned closer. She ignored me and started scrawling an outline for our article.

Without warning or permission, Goliath grabbed my elbow and roughly shoved me onto the dance floor. I tried to escape politely, but he had a tight grip on my arm. My heart was hammering as I frantically thought of how to get away from this jerk. However, I didn't want to show I was scared, so made some halfhearted attempt to laugh while pushing him away. He didn't get the message, or didn't want to get it. So I got pissed. I was just as mad at Jess for not helping, and put the full load of my anger into another shove. He stumbled back a step, and I tried to leave the dance floor.

"Hey, chick, what's your problem?" Again, he grabbed my elbow and prevented my escape. He leaned in, and I prepared to drop kick his redneck nuts when out of the cigarette haze strode my knight.

Don stepped between the thugs and me. "Leave her alone. She doesn't want to dance."

"Buddy, this doesn't concern you," said Redhead.

"You are bothering this woman and that is my concern."

Redhead didn't wait to debate the finer points. His fist came out of the air and landed an uppercut on Don's jaw. I screamed, bringing the attention of the whole bar to the scene. As one, the members of Sun Tours saw one of their own on the ground and sprung into action.

The fight opened up like a hole in the ground, and fists and arms and bodies tumbled into it. The locals took one side and Sun Tours took the other. I stood transfixed, backing up one slow step after another, not knowing what to do or why this was necessary—when that unforgettable Southern Comfort voice cooed in my ear.

"Why don't you step back here, out of the fray?"

I turned around. Standing behind the bar was that same dashing Elvis we met at the diner in Albert Lea. The living, breathing, lip-quivering Elvis. I stuttered, "Aren't you . . . haven't we . . . you seem familiar."

"I wouldn't know why, ma'am. Other than the farm, I've never lived beyond the city limits." He lifted up the gate on the bar for me, and I stepped over the tile and onto the rubber mat, which was tacky with spilled beer and liquors. He plopped down a fresh beer. He'd been swaggering about his work all this time at the bar. And once again I was face-to-face with a spitting image of Elvis and not one of these fanatics had noticed.

I asked, "Has anyone ever told you that you look like Elvis?"

"No, ma'am."

"What's your name?"

"Scott, ma'am."

"Okay, maybe I am crazy," I concluded.

"That makes two of us, ma'am. Look at them go."

Jess had climbed on top of the piano out of harm's way. Billy jumped in and took a right hook to the eye. This had Tansy all fired up, she started to kickbox the shit out of our opponents, gaining my admiration. The older ladies threw bottles from their booth and enjoyed themselves very much. Marcus, Matt and Luc were in the midst of the chaos living it up. Char sat on a barstool drinking and laughing at the bunch. Brother Thomas grabbed the karaoke mike and encouraged all to fight for the honor of the King while Vince cuddled a whimpering Ella in a corner booth

"It was sure gallant of that young man to come to your rescue," Scott said. "I was going to, but saw he had it."

"You mean Don?" I asked, but of course he meant Don. At that moment, Don had Redhead on the ground. "He was just being polite," I told Elvis or Scott or whoever he is. "We're part of this tour, you see."

"No he was watching you and jumped out of his seat the moment he saw you were not happy with the situation."

"Really?"

"You sound surprised. You should have more confidence in yourself."

"Tell me about it," I said, but Elvis was walking toward the other end of the bar.

In spite of Don and Tansy's ferocious efforts, the locals had the upper hand over the Elvis fans. Then something flashed across the dance floor, pushed Thomas aside and turned on the karaoke machine. It was Lester.

"*Holy smokes and sake's alive!*" he screeched.

Everyone stopped. Lester continued his torturous rendition of Elvis's "I Got Stung." By the time Lester hit the chorus, the locals and tourists had united in laughter. Redhead put down the broken bottle, Don righted a chair, and Goliath helped Billy off the floor. The rest of the evening was spent dancing, singing, and beer-guzzling. At two am, the townies and tourists left Harvey's Hangout knowing true friendships were forged.

As the members of Sun Tours staggered towards the Hotel, Lester cheered, "I really saved the day, didn't I?"

"Yeah, you saved the day." We had to give him that.

#

"Did you see Elvis?" I asked Jess as we climbed into bed.

"Yes, but I didn't want to say anything." She yawned.

"Why?"

Jess turned her back to me. "Because again we were the only ones who noticed, and I knew we'd have to talk about it, but I just want to sleep."

"C'mon, Jess, why do you think this keeps happening? Should we put it in the article?"

"You can't be serious." Jess rolled over to face me. She propped herself up with an elbow. "After The Incident, you want to run a story about Elvis sightings?"

"Well not when you put it like that."

"Goodnight, Stel." She lay on her back.

I stared at the ceiling for a moment. "Don't you want to know what he said to me?"

"No, I just want to sleep."

"You can sleep tomorrow. We're not going anywhere. We don't have a driver."

Chapter 10: Jessica

"We have a driver?" I couldn't believe what Marion was saying. Two minutes earlier I was roused from a deep sleep by someone knocking at the door. Now I was staring at a fresh-faced Marion who was telling me the tour would leave in an hour.

"Uh, okay, we'll be ready," I said and shut the door.

"Who was that," asked a groggy Stella.

"Marion."

"What did she want?"

"We have to get up. We have a new driver."

Stel sat straight up in bed. "No way."

#

We had to give Marion credit. Few tour guides could find a replacement driver and have him in place in less than twenty-four hours. We gathered at the Harvest Café around eleven for brunch, and to wait for him to show up. Marion referred to him simply as the General. Most of us were hung over and haggard. I know I was, and it probably had something to do with the four atomic martinis I quaffed on top of the piano, where I'd sat the entire night. This morning, I ordered black coffee and dry toast. The elderly ladies, Elliot Preston and a couple others tortured the rest of us by ordering greasy meals that smelled of burnt onions and rancid butter.

Stella and I slumped in a booth with Billy and Tansy. We dubbed Billy "Bossman" after yesterday's heroics, which earned him a black eye. Unaware of his new nickname, Bossman was trying to be his jovial self, but it was apparent last night's festivities had taken their toll. Tansy looked good in her leopard miniskirt, but she wore enough makeup to earn herself a job at the circus.

"Great news, group," Marion trilled, looking like her Kinko's box held a million bucks. "I spent yesterday afternoon adjusting our schedule. We should be back on track by four o'clock this afternoon, stopping for the night in Kansas City. We won't miss any time in Memphis! Now, I've scheduled some time to review the new schedule, so let's pass these around and open to page 2."

The group groaned. Marion frowned. "Now, what's wrong with my tour members?" In classic Marion Common fashion, she didn't wait for an answer. "I know what we need. We need to sing a song! And since it's mealtime, I know the perfect song. Does everyone know 'Johnny Apple Seed'?"

Only about a third of the group did, but that didn't stop her. She was armed with copies of the lyrics. She sang loud enough to compensate for those who didn't know the tune, loud enough to drown out the banging and hissing coming from the kitchen and the bells on the diner door. I mumbled the first two lines of the song, eyes down, trying not to be sick. That was the state of affairs when the General arrived.

He strode toward the group and stood at attention behind Marion's right elbow. He glared at us until one by one, we stopped singing. Only Marion was left belting out the Amens.

Marion noticed we had our eyes fixed on something behind her, so she turned around. The man looked her up and down, scrutinizing the Elvis pins and finally focused on her nametag. "You are the leader of Sun Tours?" he asked, his disbelief obvious.

"Yes." Marion's voice was barely a squeak.

"General Helix Arms, ma'am. I'm your replacement bus driver."

Marion recovered. "Oh! Welcome, General. We've been expecting you. Would—"

"I was expecting to meet the tour outside by the bus five minutes ago. Instead I find the lot of you in here, singing songs. Now we are behind schedule."

"Oh, no, General." Marion pulled a sheet from her box and handed it to him. "See? I managed to rework the schedule for a later depart—"

Helix stuffed the paper in his mouth, chewed twice, and swallowed. "There are reasons the schedule was set the way it was. I suppose some people would change the schedule on a whim, not realizing how it may inconvenience others. I see I'm going to have to take charge here. On your feet, civilians!"

Bewildered, we stood up. "I want you by the bus in five minutes with luggage in hand. Is that clear?"

Bossman stepped forward. "Now, just hang on one gall darn minute, partner. We're fixin' to eat."

Billy stopped mid-sentence when Helix's nose came within a pimple's distance from his own. "Chow time ended five minutes ago, *partner*. From the looks of it, civilian, you could afford to skip a meal now and then. Now, I gave you an order. Do you want me to repeat it?" The question was too ominous for an answer, and we ran as a mob for the door.

Five minutes later, each and every one of us stood in a straight line, chests puffed out, luggage by our heels. Helix paced in front of the group.

"On my watch there are rules. First, there is no talking. It distracts the driver. Second, each civilian is limited to one bathroom break and the breaks are spaced five minutes apart. Any closer and the up–down movement will distract the driver. There will be no picture taking as the flash will distract the driver. I want no arguments and only quiet activities, as noise will distract the driver. My understanding is there are certain videos that you may watch. I have chosen an appropriate one. The volume will be set at a regulated level so it doesn't distract the driver. I was ordered to get you to a certain place at a certain time, and by God, I will. Civilians! You will approach the bus in an orderly fashion, place your luggage in the luggage compartments and board. Is that clear?"

"Yes, sir, General, sir!"

He asked for it. Even the little old ladies heaved their luggage onto the bus like veteran soldiers. Once boarded, we sat in breathless silence. The only sound was the wayward automatic toilet, whose sporadic flushes sounded like nervous gulps. No one dared move. No one dared speak. Helix eyed us, gave a nod of approval, then pressed play on the DVD player. He adjusted the mirrors before reaching for the key. Even Cybill knew not to mess with Helix. She roared to life with only a sputter of protest.

GI Blues was the General's choice. I sat through one viewing, and since the video was set on automatic replay, the start of a second before my vision blurred. As I watched the flickering, silent screen, I envisioned the coming days with Helix as our driver. Eleven more days of *GI Blues* repeats and I will be homicidal. What was Marion thinking, hiring someone like Helix? How are Stella and I going to write an exposé about Elvis fans if we can't talk to any Elvis fans? If we can't write our article, we won't be paid. Then we'd have to take the third shift at a meat packing plant. We may as well end it right here, right now in the middle of this cornfield. Why are we driving through a cornfield, anyway? Where in the hell are we?

At some point, Helix had left the main highway and taken secondary roads and some gravel roads, with occasional trips down what appeared to be dirt paths through private property. The corn grew high enough to block the view, giving us only intermittent peeks at the landscape as we roared past an open pasture. As we caught one another's eyes in silent communication, it was apparent no one knew where Helix was taking us.

Marion summoned the courage to speak. In a whisper she asked, "Um, General? I know that you're in charge, but I was wondering if you knew where we are supposed to be headed because page eighteen of the revised itinerary says we should have arrived at Council Bluffs by four p.m. and it's after five."

The bus ground to a halt in a cloud of dust. Helix whipped around and narrowed his gaze at Marion. "Who is driving this bus?"

Marion cowered. "You."

"And who is in charge here?"

"You."

"That's right, Miss Busybody. Me. I have gone to foreign countries and have never, not once, gotten lost. I am taking a shortcut to make up for the time carelessly wasted by you. Any more questions?" Marion shook her head. "Good." He whipped back around and the bus started moving again.

I realized I had an intense need to pee.

A half-hour later, the need became desperate. Forced to give in, I stood up slowly, as to not distract the driver, and made my way back to the bathroom taking small steps, as to not distract the driver.

The toilet wouldn't flush until I jumped up and down three times and even then it only gurgled. The sink wouldn't produce any water until I violently waved my hands under the faucet and received a five second misting. The automatic towel dispenser wouldn't dispense any towels until I pried it open only to discover it was empty. So I wiped my hands on my pants. State of the art, my ass.

I slowly made my way back to my seat, as to not distract the driver.

An hour later, stomach rumblings were more and more noticeable. The cornfields seemed ominous after the third viewing of *GI Blues*. The initial fear of Helix dwindled, though no one seemed willing to take him on. I shifted my head subtly to see how the others were passing their time. Elliot caught my attention. He seemed to be shrinking. Bit by bit, inch by inch, Elliot sunk from view. When Cybill hit a bump in the gravel road, Elliot slid to the floor. He crawled toward the back of the bus. I watched as much as I could out of the corner of my eye, wondering what he was up to and knowing his army crawl would have made Helix proud.

Fifteen minutes passed. I was in the process of scribbling notes in my journal when Don murmured, "Hold out your hand." Sitting in the aisle seat, I complied. "Pass this forward." He pressed something cold and wrapped in plastic into my palm.

Sweet Jesus, a sandwich! Elliot had squirmed to the refrigerator. Marion's emergency snacks would save us from starvation.

"Here," Don whispered again. This time he pressed an orange into my palm, followed by another sandwich.

Stella kicked the back of Char's seat to gain her attention. Using the same method, we handed the food forward. Across the aisle, I could see Eric shuffling food forward to Bossman and Tansy. When everyone had something to eat, Elliot crawled back to his seat, looking only slightly dirty.

Stella and I divided our sandwich and orange. The sandwich spread was a cherry color, which we assumed was ham, but we couldn't be certain.

I took stock of our situation. We were six hours into our trip with Helix at the helm. Marion opened map after map, which couldn't be a good thing. Sachi, Midori and Harulu knitted. Sister Mary worked her way through her rosary. Matt, Luc, Marcus and Brother Thomas slept. Vince and Ella fed each other crumbs from their sandwich. Tansy repainted her face. Bossman appeared to be committing the road to memory through his one good eye. Elliot flipped through a graphic novel while Eric stared out the window, glowering at the cornstalks. The rest of us read or slept. I took the opportunity to record my observations and vent on paper.

At some point, I dozed off. When I awoke, the others were talking in undertones. "What's going on?" I whispered to Stella.

"It's after eight and we're still in the middle of nowhere." The setting sun turned the passing fields into a waving sea of red. "No one has any idea where we are. It's like Helix is driving around in circles. We were supposed to stop for the night two hours ago in Kansas City."

The murmurs grew mutinous. "Something better happen or Helix is going to have a revolt on his hands," I said.

Something did happen. Our cantankerous ride suddenly gave a loud sputter, shuddered to a halt, then died. We stared at the back of Helix's head, wondering how he'd handle Cybill's disobedience.

"Goddamn son of a bitch!" He stood up and began kicking the driver's seat, the dashboard, everything within reach.

In response, Cybill backfired twice.

"Down!" Helix bellowed. "Everyone, get down!" Helix lunged for his duffle. Stella slouched in her seat. I craned my neck, trying to see what Helix was doing.

Marion tried to calm him. "That was just the bus—"

Helix pulled out a semiautomatic handgun. With cries of terror, everyone hit the floor. Helix muttered, "Not again! Not again! No Vietcong bastard is gonna take me alive!"

Char screamed and threw her body over a cowering Lester.

Helix sprinted to the back of the bus. He cocked the gun and peered out the windows.

Billy tried to reason with him, "Now, see here—"

Tansy slapped her hand over her husband's mouth and pulled him further in the seat. "Shut up, Percy. He's got a gun!"

Helix slipped into the bathroom and we heard the door lock. No sound came from the commode. A few daring souls raised their heads. Matt and Marcus bolted for the front of the bus, taking refuge in the Helper of the Day seat. Ella sobbed. The Japanese Trio worked on what was now a large afghan. Don, Billy, Eric, Stella and I were on our feet.

Don kept his voice low. "What should we do?"

"Let's barricade the bathroom door." Billy held up a carry-on.

"Luggage isn't going to stop that lunatic," said Eric. "Besides the bathroom door opens in. We need to get everyone off the bus."

"And go where?" pointed out Char. "We are in the middle of a cornfield in Iowa. Didn't you see the movie where the corn was possessed by the devil?"

"Haven't you heard of a crazed man randomly shooting his hostages?" countered Don. "I'm with Eric. We need to get off the bus and hide in the corn."

A noise from the bathroom, and we were all ducking under the seats again. Helix raced to the front of the bus, waving his gun. Everyone screamed and did their best to vanish.

The door squealed open. Helix shouted, "I'm here you bastards! I'm not hiding from you any more! If you want me, you're going to have to come and get me!" He pounded off the bus.

Maggie closed the door then returned to her seat. Everyone threw their bags to the front, and the college boys erected a barricade so Helix couldn't get back inside.

"Quick!" Eric said. "Cover the windows so he can't see us!" We used everything imaginable to cover the windows that didn't have curtains. The elderly ladies draped their afghan over two windows. Tansy found a blanket and covered the large front window, using duct tape from God knows where.

The bus fortified, we sat in the dark, stunned. No one said anything for a good ten minutes. Sister Mary rose to check on Marion, who was catatonic.

Finally, Marion broke down into tears.

Lester made the first attempt to speak. "What happened?"

"I have no idea," Char huffed, "but I'll bet this cheap-ass company's pile of bolts finally kicked the can. The first thing I'm going to do when we get to Memphis is find a good lawyer!"

"Now, hold on," said Billy. "Nothing is gonna be accomplished if we focus all our attention on blaming someone for this mess. Let's not talk about suing just yet. Now, we should find out what's wrong with the bus?"

"G-g-g-gas." Marion sniffled. "We were supposed to stop for the night and fill up two hours ago." She buried her head in Mary's shoulder.

"No gas. And an idiot with a gun on the loose outside, so no one's leaving the bus to get some." Eric shook his head.

"We could radio for help," Maggie suggested.

"No go." Marcus spoke up. "When the General went ballistic, he kicked the radio receiver. It's broken."

"Cell phone!" said Don. "Shit, my battery is dead. Does anyone have a cell phone?"

Eric dug in his briefcase. "I've got one." He punched a few buttons. "No signal."

"Well, the only thing we can do is sleep here tonight and hope someone will find us tomorrow," Vince concluded.

"Good luck." Eric looked positively dour. "This is a private road. The only people who would come this way would be the owners of the field checking on their crops."

"It's harvest time," said Billy, looking like a pro in his Western shirt. "Farmers are much more likely to check their crops daily."

This gave the group hope. We foraged for food and pooled our resources. While we snacked, we assembled beds and designated floor space. The older ladies had first dibs. Everyone else made do with the seats, and I admit, I was grateful for Marion's cheesy Elvis pillows. Numb from the day, I lay awake, listening to the occasional *swoosh* from the bathroom and praying the next sound would be an innocent one and not a gunshot.

A gleaming star appeared in the window. I watched it for a while then adjusted the jacket to block it out. I hoped for comfort but it wasn't there.

Chapter 11: Stella

I reached for him, but he wasn't there.

I rose from our four-poster bed and walked down the spiraling staircase. The wooden floor felt cool under my feet as I crossed the foyer and walked out the door.

He sat on the steps of the porch staring at the night's sky. The wind swirled around him, flowing down the hill and into the cornfield. I wrapped my arms around his neck and planted a kiss on his ear. The soothing summer's breeze washed over us. For a long while, I simply held him close, drinking in his smell.

I whispered, "Baby, what are you doing out here?" But I knew.

"Looking at our land. I still can't believe it's ours," he answered.

I smiled and snuggled closer, sliding my hand across his bare chest. I kissed his neck, shoulders, back. He patted my arm. I changed tactics and knelt before him. He brushed my hair away from my face. I thought, *now we're getting somewhere*. But he pulled back and began talking about buying cows. When I pushed him onto his back, he asked, "What are you doing?"

I thought, *obviously I'm not doing it right or he wouldn't be asking*. He'd be taking off my lingerie. "I'm trying to seduce you. Maybe I'd have better luck if I looked like a cow."

He laced his fingers behind his head. "Probably."

I punched him and walked across the lawn. He was close behind. He grabbed me around the waist and tackled me to the ground. I'm sure he meant to be frisky and I laughed until I hit the ground and kept rolling. We rolled down the hill until cornstalks broke our fall. Still laughing, I stood up and looked for my husband. But he was gone.

"Where are you? C'mon babe, this isn't funny. Where are you?" Only the crickets croaked. I tried again, "Love, don't play games. Just come out. You're stupid if you think I'm coming after you." Nothing. "Fine. I'm going inside."

I started back up the hill, but stopped when I thought he might have been knocked unconscious. In a panic, I ran into the cornfield and called his name. I widened my search, but found nothing. Terrified, I began to cry.

Blinding lights appeared from everywhere and an alarm began blaring in my ear. Someone pushed me to the ground and I screamed.

"Don, save me!"

#

Slowly, I became aware of laughing.

I opened my eyes to discover I was in the aisle of the bus. My face progressed through the entire red spectrum, and I concluded with certainty I had uttered the last words of my dream aloud.

Char's eyes glittered in the darkness as she lounged on the seat above me, languid in the shadows. "What's Don gonna save you from, honey?" she wheezed between laughs.

"Nothing," I mumbled.

"Must have been something to make you scream like that. 'Don, save me!'" Her voice went high and mocking.

I wondered what it was in Char that made her capitalize on everyone's humiliation. My temper burned. Normally I would find some way to get even with Char for making fun of me in front of everyone. I'd say some cutting, sarcastic reply which would have the whole bus laughing at her. But since being forced to take anger management lessons after punching the mayor's assistant, I've learned "when you lose your cool during these episodes, you only hurt yourself and not the intended receiver." Or so my therapist says. So I counted to ten and turned my back on Char.

I tried to shake Jess awake. She lay over both our seats and a skein of drool ran down her face. We made quite a pair. The ringing in my ears persisted. "Does anyone else hear that?"

"Your tryst with Don left your head buzzing?" Char taunted.

"Shut up," I hissed. Screw my therapist. It would feel good to take Char down a notch. But before I could say anything, Lester jumped to my defense.

"No, I hear it, too."

Everyone's head was cocked at the same angle straining to locate the incessant ringing.

All heads turned toward the Japanese Trio as Ella said, "I think it's coming from one of them." Marion snapped her fingers with an 'I've-got-it' look. She announced, "Hearing aid."

Mary stepped toward Sachi. "Um, excuse me, Sachi, but I think someone's hearing aid is ringing."

"What?"

Mary tried again. "Hearing aid. Someone's hearing aid is ringing."

"Somebody singing?" asked Harulu, who joined the confusion.

Around and around they went, before they grasped the truth. "Oh, it you, Lulu?"

She cupped her hands over her ears and listened for a while. Then answered, "No. You?"

"No."

"Must be Dori."

Midori was fast asleep in a sharp tangle of limbs. Sachi gave her a shove and she grunted to life. "What is problem?" she asked her friends. After a flurry of Japanese, Midori pulled the hearing aids out of her ears and fiddled with them. The ringing stopped. She mumbled, "Sorry."

Everyone dispersed and debated who was going to exit the bus and go for help, until Matt asked, "Does anyone hear that?"

"It hearing aid. We get it," growled Sachi.

"Hey no, I hear the noise, too. It's coming from the outside," said Vince, ear pressed against his window. "Maybe it's Helix." All movement stopped instantly. We didn't even breathe. The sound of boots crunching cornstalks reached our ears. My heart began to pound in my stomach.

"Someone should see who it is," suggested Char.

"Good idea," I countered. "Why don't you do it?"

"Will you two be quiet!" hissed Bossman.

Vince moved the coat covering his window for a peek. As he leaned forward, someone knocked on the door. It was a staccato beating that sounded like the butt of a gun on metal. Bodies flew through the air and squirmed for the choicest spots under the seats.

Matt moaned, "Good God, we're going to die!"

Silence.

Another sharp rap.

"Should we answer that?" asked Eric.

Elliot snorted. "Sure, Dad, if you want to be ten inches shorter. That crazy fuck will take your head off."

"Watch your mouth."

Char opened her doublewide mouth. "Don't worry. Don will save us. Isn't that right, Stella?"

Oh that's it, I thought and felt my restraint tear. Without concern over the lone gunman, I jumped up and hissed, "You mistake of humanity! Tell me, are you a bitch by nature, or did you take classes? Because of all the bitches I've known you are by far the worst."

No answer. I felt Jess tug at my pant leg and warn, "Stel, get down."

Silence except for the relentless rattling on the door. I could see Char clenching her jaw muscles, but she didn't say anything, and she wouldn't look at me. The weight of my behavior made my chest feel tight. Why did I say that? Why did I let her goad me into losing my temper? What must everyone think of me? I was torn from my self-battery by the squeak of the bus door being opened.

Paralyzed, we listened as our visitor removed the luggage and stepped inside.

"Somebody do something!" begged Mary.

Still shaky with adrenaline and eager to redeem myself in the eyes of my fellow tourists, I crawled to the front of the bus. A shaky hand from Marion touched my arm. I waited until I saw his short-cropped hair silhouetted against the windshield, the low gleam of light on his sweaty forehead. Then I grabbed one of Marion's crates and heaved it at his head. The weight of the folders and books knocked him down the stairs and out the door.

In a flash of Xena power, I lunged out the door and hit Helix square in the chest. A flurry of arms that were more powerful than mine, and I was falling. I hit the ground, then scrambled to my feet. I don't know what I planned on doing to this man who was twice my size and trained for combat by the US government. Thankfully, Tansy had my back. She sprung out of the bus and nailed the guy square in the jaw, yelling, "Take that, you bastard!"

He flew into the air until he was parallel with the earth, then flopped to the ground in a big crash.

The trumpets of victory sounded as Tansy and I embraced. We hopped in circles as everyone poured off the bus. Congratulations were given all round. Matt clapped my shoulder and said, "You're one cool chick."

"Thanks." I glowed.

Eric approached the body as everyone quieted. As he turned the man over I thought, *I don't remember Helix wearing overhauls.* Eric lifted a cornstalk off the man to reveal . . .

The dark, handsome face of Elvis.

"Oh, shit," I moaned.

Jess ran to his side, her face white. "Mister . . . Uh, sir . . . whoever you are . . . Are you all right? Can you stand?

Oh, God! You're bleeding!" The tiniest spot of blood marked his chin. Jess shot me a death glare and turned back to Farmer Elvis. "No, don't stand. Don't move. Just rest awhile and tell me your name." Jess cradled his head in her lap. As expected, not a single tour member noticed his unmistakable resemblance to the King.

Jess pushed his greasy hair from his forehead. "Can you tell us your name and what you are doing out here?"

"I live here. This is my field," he croaked. He attempted to sit up and Jess helped him lean forward. She stayed kneeling beside him. He continued, "I was checking on my crop when I noticed this bus. 'Well,' I thought, 'That's unusual.' So, I came over to see what the problem was and ask if I could be of any assistance. When no one answered my knocking, I thought I'd have a look see. Sorry I frightened you."

Everyone gushed at once, "Oh, no, sir. We're sorry. Awful sorry. Don't worry about it. Real sorry." Marion took over, saying, "We've had a rough night. You see, sir, we ran out of gas, so we were forced to spend the night. When you knocked we thought you were, um, an animal or something."

Maybe she thought the news of an armed lunatic driver on the loose might upset him. She probably figured we'd done enough damage. Eric helped the man to his feet, and Jess was still glued to his elbow.

She asked, "What did you say your name was?"

"Oh, people round here just call me Tom."

"Oh." Jess and I established eye contact and attempted telepathy. Before I could read a clear frequency, she remembered she was mad at me for dropping a crate on Elvis's head. She turned away.

Tom spoke again, "You folks say you needed some gas?"

"Yes, man, we do. We need to continue our pilgrimage to Graceland," said Brother T, his gold jumpsuit catching the rays of the morning sun.

"That so?" Tom seemed confused, but too polite to question. "Well, my truck is just down the road a ways. I could drive someone into town and return with some gas."

"I'll go." Brother T volunteered and Jess was left with her mouth hanging open.

"It may take awhile. Town is about twenty minutes that way. How did you end up clear out here?"

"Wrong turn," explained Marion. "Would you tell us exactly where here is; I mean, what town are you referring to?"

"Webster, Iowa, ma'am."

"And is that near Kansas City by chance?"

"Not even close," said Tom. "In fact, you are on the opposite side of Iowa if Kansas City is your destination."

"Oh," Marion's face fell, but only for a moment before she pinned on her plastic smile. "Oh, that's fine. We'll be fine. You go on ahead now. We appreciate your assistance."

With that, Tom and Brother T walked down the road. The preacher's mouth was flapping so fast he could shame an auctioneer. I watched Brother's gold jumpsuit flash and glitter in the distance until they topped a hill and cornstalks got in the way.

#

To pass time, Luc, Matt and Marcus were off on another adventure. This time they had invited Elliot, and their voices rang across the field. Eric and Maggie were deep in conversation. Char sulked by herself and I felt the nauseous pang of regret. Marion sat on the road surrounded by her boxes. She was scribbling on her itinerary and mumbling, "Why, oh, why?" Don and Lester were talking, and I didn't have the gumption to interrupt.

I returned to the bus and dug out my journal. I jotted down a few paragraphs for our article. After several minutes, I felt the irritating need to pee. I considered finding a cornstalk, but concluded that if anyone were to discover me peeing outside, it would be Don.

I hesitantly entered the bathroom. By its spotless appearance, Cybill's loo seemed the essence of a modern facility. But I was not fooled. I had heard the rumors, stories of a vindictive toilet, flushing at random and spewing water three feet into the air. I thought such exaggerations were hearsay until I stepped forward and witnessed the six-inch cobalt-blue geyser in the bowl. Full of fear and trepidation, I unzipped my pants. The geyser sputtered higher. I slowed my movements to a slug's pace. The geyser ebbed, and disappeared into the toilet's throat. I held my breath and hovered over the seat.

I shouldn't have bothered.

The toilet had it in for me from the start. I heard the rumble, but was unable to dart with my shorts around my ankles. Cold water bathed my privates. The geyser retreated just as quickly, gurgling a kind of laughter.

I waddled to the sink, trying to keep my shorts out of the puddles on the floor. I grabbed several hand towels and began drying the little blue rivulets off my thighs and crotch. The toilet hissed in satisfaction.

I chucked the wet towels in the trash. In the bathroom's full-length mirror, I checked out my rear. Horror clutched my throat. I burst out the door and zipped up my pants while running down the aisle. On my way past the seat I grabbed my jacket and tied it around my waist.

Once off the bus I grabbed Jess by the arm and growled, "Come with me now!" We crashed through several rows of corn before I was convinced we had privacy.

"Let me go!" Jess yelled as she yanked free.

"Wait! You have to help me!" I wailed.

She started slapping her way through the corn, toward the group.

"Wait. Please. I have a blue ass!"

Jess turned, "You clobbered the man I'm desperate to talk to! And you hogged his attention all last night. Are we partners, or not?"

"What? You said we weren't putting the Elvis sightings in the article." I stumbled over a clump of dirt as I made my way to Jess.

"And I still say not in our article, but maybe an article for a different publication."

"Yeah, *National Enquirer,*" I interrupted. "Jess, did you hear me? I said, I have a blue ass—a bright neon blue ass!"

"I don't care what you have. You seem to be writing your own story."

"Jess, you're becoming as crazy as the rest of them. Now listen. Try to understand. My ass is blue. This is a problem for me. I need your help."

"What are you talking about?" Finally, I was getting through.

"I've been screaming at you for the last five minutes. I had to go to the bathroom, so I used the one on the bus. I heard a rumble, but I couldn't move in time and so, well, then, it just happened so fast, you know, and now, oh, Jess! What am I going to do? What if it doesn't come off?"

"What if what doesn't come off?"

"The blue dye on my ass."

"Your ass is blue?"

She can be so dense. "Yes! Are you stupid? Is English not your first language? Yes!" I threw up my hands in exasperation.

"How?"

"I took a magic marker to it. Wake up. The Clorox Blue from the toilet, you moron."

"Oh. You mean everything is blue… down there?" Jess's face crinkled in disgust.

"How the hell should I know? It's not like I can crane my face down there and look."

"I'm not looking."

"I'm not asking. Geez, Jess, you're sick."

"You're sick. You're the one with the blue ass."

"Jess, you have to help me."

Jess suddenly found the whole situation hilarious. She fell to the ground like she was about to pee her pants laughing. "Okay, no problem. I'll buy you some bleach when we get to town." Between gales, she wheezed, "I bet you look like you just made love to a Smurf."

"Nice, Jess. You're so sympathetic."

"Hey, Stel? You cold? Because your ass looks a little blue."

"I'm leaving now." I headed for the bus.

Jess yelled after me. "I bet you pee Kool-aid for months. Try explaining that to your gyno."

I yelled "Jerk!" over my shoulder and kept walking.

When we returned, the tour was ready to go with Billy at the wheel. Bossman started toward Columbia, Missouri—four hours down the road where everyone agreed we would spend the night. This would mean missing the Elvis Fun Park in Kansas City, but we'd be back on track by the end of day four. Billy drove like a kid just learning to drive standard.

Brother Thomas walked to the front of the bus and grabbed the mike. *This should be good*, I thought. And I wasn't disappointed.

"Can I get a 'Praise Elvis'?"

Chapter 12: Jessica

"Praise, Elvis!" I shouted, causing Stella to look at me like I'd lost my mind. "Why not?" I asked her. "I want to see where this goes." She rolled her eyes and readied the camera.

"Praise Elvis!" Lester squeaked, backing me up. That's what I'm talking about.

Brother Thomas continued in classic southern evangelist style. "Folks, we are on a journey, you know, a journey to see the King." He paced up and down the aisle, occasionally bumping off a seat. "And it has been fraught with trials and tribulations."

"This is great," I whispered to Stel. "It's like Martin Luther King Jr. meets Cheech and Chong."

Stel laughed, "You're ridiculous."

Thomas hung his head low, shook it side-to-side. "Now, my brothers and sisters, I didn't always love Elvis."

A murmur of shock swept the group. "Not love Elvis?"

"I know, I know," Thomas said. "I was young and foolish. My parents were among the disbelievers, may Elvis help them."

I wondered how Sister Mary was reacting to Thomas's sermon. I could only see the back of her head, but I could tell Thomas had her full attention.

Brother T continued, "As a young and reckless man, my one passion wasn't Elvis, but flying. There's nothing like flying, you know. You're a thousand miles up, floating in ghost clouds, and suddenly there's an explosion of color—

orange, red, yellow, purple. Man, it's like seeing for the first time. It's so brilliant you have to blink, and in that fraction of a second, it's changed and you've missed something.

"I worked for a small charter company based out of Sioux Falls, South Dakota. I flew everything from people and furniture to important documents and even human organs. I led a pretty average life until one fateful day when it all fell apart." He looked at each of us in turn, letting the suspense build. "After that day, my life would never be the same."

This is so good, I thought. I scribbled furiously in my journal just trying to keep up.

"I got an order to fly a cow vaccine to a big spread in Wyoming," Thomas continued. "I was twenty minutes from the ranch when the storm hit. And in that storm, I realized my mistake. I had miscalculated my distance from the ranch and dropped to seven hundred feet right in front of Devil's Tower. I was headed right for it and I knew, I knew, I was going to crash. And that's when it happened." Again, he paused for dramatic effect and scanned the crowd.

I smiled and wrote in my journal, he worked the audience with the skill of a master orator. I almost missed Brother Thomas's next lines.

"I was staring at this looming gravestone when light more complex, more brilliant than anything I'd ever seen, with colors I didn't even know existed, formed into a being in my co-pilot seat."

What in the hell does he mean by that, I thought and looked up from my notes.

Brother T lowered his voice to a near whisper. "I tell you, Elvis was with me."

I couldn't help it, I laughed out loud, so did Stel. But we quickly covered our laughter with a 'Praise Elvis!' when we realized everyone else on the tour was taking this seriously.

Thomas allowed the gasps to subside before continuing. "I remember thinking, this can't be real, but Elvis just smiled and said, 'Hello, Thomas. Looks like you're in a world of trouble.' 'Si,' I said, 'I'm going to die. There's no way to avoid that.'"

Thomas began acting out both roles, jumping from side to side. He tried to add Elvis's famous sneer, but his Mexican accent didn't make this possible. "'Tell you what, Tom. Why don't you listen to me and I'll see what I can do for you. You're a good man,' Elvis says this to me, 'a real good man and they are hard to find, you know. You take your dreams and make them realities. You take your talents and you use them for good. And you don't forget those who believed in you and helped you along the way.' Then he says to me, 'I need you to do something for me.'

"Me? What?" Thomas pointed at himself, then asked the crowd, "I mean, what could I do for the King, eh man?" He slapped Vince on the shoulder.

"So then Elvis explains, 'There are a whole lot of people in this world who need a good man like you to help them. They need someone they can trust, someone who can deliver my message to them. They need someone like you, Tom.' Then I says, 'Okay, man, just tell me what to do.' Because I would do anything for the King, you know.

"Elvis says, 'You will know when the time comes.' That's it. That's all he says to me, just 'you will know.' But before I could ask Elvis any questions he says, 'Now, about your problem. When I tell you, I want you to pull up as hard as you can.' That's when I remembered I was about to crash my plane."

I hate to admit it, but I had stopped writing and was on the edge of my seat, waiting to see if Thomas crashed or not.

Brother T continued, "'I can't, I says. I don't have the strength.' Elvis says, 'Trust me, Thomas. Trust the light.' Then he vanished." Thomas held his arms heavenward. "From the clouds I hear Elvis shout, 'Now!' so I pulled up as hard as I could and the wings of my plane tilted. A gale of wind caught the body, twisting it perpendicular to Devil's Tower. The wheels brushed the side of the mountain. I tell you, man, that's how close I came to collision.

"However, I wasn't safe yet. The storm had done a number on my plane. After clearing Devil's Tower, I sank like a stone, barely righting the plane and hitting the emergency beacon before crash landing at the visitor's center. The plane went through a grove of trees that ripped off the wings and smashed the windshield."

Thomas pulled off his glasses. "Shards of glass entered my eyes, permanently damaging my eyesight. When I got out of the hospital, I had these glasses and a fear of flying so intense I've never been able to get on a plane since."

"Wow, that's sad," whispered Stel.

"The loss of what was so precious to me took its toll, you know," Thomas continued. "I lashed out at everyone, including my fiancé, my family and my friends, until I had no one. When I told people about what happened in the plane, they laughed at me. I felt stupid, lonely and crazy.

"Then I met Joseph. Joseph is a leader of a church called The Order of the Blue Suede Shoes. They preach about how Elvis was sent to carry on the work of Jesus. Everything Elvis did, all his music, all his movies, was a way to reach people who had different values and lifestyles than they did two thousand years ago. The more he talked, the more I saw the truth in what he said. Hadn't Elvis spoken to me in my time of need?"

Brother Thomas was staring right at Mary who was pointedly avoiding him and staring out the window. *Oh, she has to be pissed*, I thought.

"I told Joseph about my own experience," Thomas continued. "He immediately invited me to come to his church. I retold my story before one hundred and fifty devoted followers. After I finished, a woman asked to sponsor my induction into the fold. Now I travel the world to teach people Elvis's message and to get them to join the Order, but mostly to show them the light."

#

"I have seen the light," said Stella

I gave her a drop-it look, but she continued. "I had me a vision of Elvis, once. It was about three days ago. He appeared on the back of this bus telling me to run like hell away from this band of lunatics. I know I'm going to regret not following that vision."

"Stel, you're impossible."

"I need a drink."

"Me, too. You believe any of Thomas's story?" I asked.

"Are you stupid?"

"Becoming more so by the minute."

"I know what you mean." The words came from Eric who was sitting by the window across the aisle. I didn't realize he could hear us.

"So, you're not about to join Brother Thomas's Order of the Blue Suede Shoes?" I asked.

He laughed, "No. At least, not any time soon."

Realizing Stel and I still didn't have much substantial material for our article, and going back to my first impression of Eric being a man of distinction earned through hard work and sacrifice, I took a chance. "So, what's your Elvis story?" I moved across the aisle to sit beside him.

"My Elvis story?" Eric repeated. "Why are you going to put me in your article?"

"Maybe," I smiled, hoping to disarm him. "Would that be okay? Stel and I are exploring how Elvis appeals to different people and how this has kept his image alive. I'm definitely interested to learn how a businessman such as yourself becomes an Elvis fan."

Again he laughed, but didn't volunteer any information. I let the silence stretch, knowing if you give someone enough time, they'll usually begin to talk.

"Okay," Eric conceded. "I guess you could say my love for Elvis sprung from my hate for my father."

"Really?" Not the beginning I expected.

Eric explained, "You see, I hit my teen years right as Elvis was coming on the scene. My father loved jazz. He said Elvis was trying to be black, and it angered him in a way I didn't understand. In addition, my father believed the way Elvis danced was like the Pied Piper leading the country on a super-slide into damnation. He blamed the whole Sixties episode on Elvis."

"A lot of people did," I said. "Do you mind if I take notes?" Eric shook his head no, and I turned to Stella who promptly put my journal and pen into my outstretched hand.

Eric continued, "My father was a respectable man. He worked his way to a management position with a large insurance firm based in Milwaukee, which was something for a black man in his time. He was proud of his position, his split-level home, his Cadillac and his obedient wife. So I did anything and everything to piss him off." We shared a laugh. "Man, I put him through hell." Eric paused, lost in the memory.

I wrote, 'who knew this quiet professional with his reserve demeanor disguised a rebellious youth.' I expected to hear tales of his rebel years, but instead Eric's tone grew serious.

"My father had it all worked out, how I would follow in his footsteps. I said I didn't want his business. He said 'Fine, go to college.' I joined the army instead. After basic training, I was shipped to 'Nam."

"Oh," I said looking up.

"You served in Vietnam?" Stella interrupted. She has a peculiar fascination with Vietnam which I don't understand. I shot her a look that said, 'Shut up. Don't scare him into silence with your weird war fixation.'

But Eric continued unfazed, "Not for long. I took a shot in the hip within the first month, but you probably guessed that from my limp." Eric paused and saw our confusion. "Oh," he remembered. "I forgot about this." He took off his shoe to remove a one-inch lift. "This makes me appear normal."

After an awkward silence, Eric continued. "When the air cleared after the attack, I discovered my buddy Gary and I were the only ones from our platoon left alive. He was hurt real bad. We found the radio and called for help, but Gary didn't make it. I must have passed out before the chopper arrived because I don't remember much of the flight back to base. The government patched me up and sent me home. I arrived in San Diego in October of 1962.

"Eventually, I learned how to walk with the lift. You can imagine I was pretty low at this point. I tried to tell myself I was lucky, but sometimes fighting off the anti-war activists was worse than 'Nam. I hitchhiked my way to Vegas where I met a woman who became my angel. Her name was Rose. We were two lost kids in need of a friend. When I met her, she was a cocktail waitress at the casino where I bartended.

"Rose was vibrant and alive and beautiful. We spent every moment of every day together talking, laughing, pouring out our souls to each other, dancing to Elvis and planning adventures we would never take. When I was with her, I didn't even care about the looks people gave us."

"What looks?" I asked.

"Rose was white," Eric explained.

"Oh." I really didn't know what to say about that, but thankfully I didn't have to as Eric continued.

"After awhile she convinced me I needed to make peace with my father. So I bought a Greyhound ticket, promised to come back for her and headed home. I forgave my father, as promised. I tried to find Rose, but she had moved, and I had no way of tracking her down. In my heart, I knew my father would never approve of Rose. A poor white girl didn't fit into my father's plan.

"I eventually went to work for my father's company and became everything he dreamed of. I married the daughter of one of his co-workers. We had a son within a year, bought a house and began living the all-American life. Things were good on the whole. I can't say they weren't. I grew to love my wife with a familiar, safe kind of love. She was a good woman, the best really." Eric paused and looked out the window. He said the next sentence so softly I almost didn't hear him. "She died from cancer nine months ago."

"Oh God, I'm so sorry."

"Me too," Eric whispered. We sat in silence for a few minutes before he continued, "My wife was the glue that held our family together, and I've been feeling a little lost without her. This trip fulfills a promise I made to her. I swore I'd try to find common ground with our son, so I figured I'd start by introducing him to the King of Rock and Roll." Eric laughed, obviously embarrassed about sharing more than he intended to with a virtual stranger.

"So you were never in love with your wife?" I asked.

"I didn't say that. I loved my wife more than anything in this world. You see, my love for Rose was like fire. My love for Georgia was glowing embers. Both were what I needed when I needed them."

"What happened to Rose?"

"I don't know. My one regret in this life is-"

"Leaving her."

"Yes."

Beside me, Stella was crying.

Chapter 13: Stella

"Are you crying?" Jess asked irritated.

"Yes," I blubbered.

"Why?"

"Because it's so sad."

"Stop it."

"I can't. Besides, I'm not the only one. Maggie's crying, too."

"Get our bags," Jess ordered. "Let's go. We're finally here."

The lobby of the Fifth Street Plaza in Columbia, Missouri, was filled with people who apparently lived there year round. A shirtless, toothless man stared at me while he scratched his crotch. The desk clerk stood behind a cast-iron counter shielded by bulletproof glass.

"I like the whole prison décor they've got going," said Jess.

"Must have known we were coming."

Marion was rambling at us again. "The hotel manager, Mr. Bigsby here, has asked me to remind everyone to heed the warnings on your room doors. Do not, under any circumstances, open your door for anyone—especially people claiming to be hotel employees."

"Marion," said Char, "what kind of shithole have you checked us into now?"

"That's a very discouraging comment, Char. Mr. Bigsby said everything is fine if you follow all precautions listed on the room doors. There is also a longer list of safety tips posted on the bathroom mirrors."

"May Elvis protect us all," prayed Brother T.

Jess and I found our way to Room 202. I entered, mace first, with Jess covering. We did a quick inspection. Other than the green and brown wallpaper, everything seemed fine. With that settled, I rushed to the bathroom to take care of business. I dropped my pants in front of the mirror and turned around.

Still there.

"Is the blue moon rising?" Jess taunted through the door.

"Shut up! Go find Elvis. I'm sure he's lurking around somewhere."

"Oh, Stel. C'mon. I'm sorry. I won't laugh anymore. Promise. We'll put our heads together and think of something."

I opened the door and demanded, "Think of what? What can be done? I have a blue ass."

"Just let me see. It's probably not that bad. I bet with a little scrubbing it will come right off."

"Are you going to scrub my butt?"

Jess crossed her arms and stood in the doorway. "No, just let me see the extent of the damage."

"Gee, thanks." I turned around to show her a tiny peek. Jess and I had been through a lot together, but this went beyond the call of friendship. I braced for her reaction.

Silence.

"Jess?" I turned around to find her clutching her mouth, tears of laughter seeping down her cheeks. After I caught her, she let it rip. "Oh, yeah," I said, "'I promise I won't laugh anymore.' You jerk. I knew I shouldn't show you. Stop laughing and get up."

"I've never seen anything so blue!"

I grabbed a stained washcloth and some soap and began to scrub with all my might. The color only seemed to brighten. Admitting defeat, I dried off and pulled up my pants. Angered by Jess's incessant laughter, I started hurling various bathroom articles at her. "So, you think my ass is funny, do you? Take that." I threw the soap. "And that!" There went the shampoo. Jess retaliated. We yanked, bit, clawed, screamed, laughed and ate soap for the next five minutes.

We created such racket that neither of us heard Marion enter our room. When we both noticed her, we screamed and fell over.

"Hey, Marion. How did you get in here?" Jess asked, pushing my leg off her. Jess got to her feet by putting her elbow in my gut.

"Ow!" I kicked her in the butt on her way up.

Marion stuttered, "Oh, I, uh, not that I was snooping, I just . . .well, your door was open and I just—"

"Our door was open?" we screamed.

"Yes, it was open, so I—"

"Jess, you shut the door didn't you?" I rolled onto my knees and jumped to my feet, but immediately had to sit on the bed as the blood rushed to my head.

"Of course, I shut it. I made sure to shut it in a place like this," Jess answered. She was looking at her tangled mess of hair in the mirror.

Marion began, "Well, it was open, so I just came in to tell you—"

"Do you suppose someone opened it?" I asked Marion.

"I don't know. I just know that your door was open when I came by to tell you—"

"How long have you been in our room?" Jessica asked.

"Not long," Marion answered a little too quickly. Her face flushed, "Not long enough to hear anything. I mean, no, I don't mean anything by that." Marion looked at the floor, the television, the 'Dogs Playing Poker' poster above the bed. "Not long," she repeated. "About five minutes. I tried to get your attention, but you were, uh," She gestured to spot on the floor where she found us. "Well, about five minutes."

"Five minutes," I exclaimed, "We've been here about fifteen. That means our door was left wide open for at least ten minutes! Jess, we've got to check our stuff." We ran to our bags and started rifling. Money, camera, camcorder, journal—we rattled off the checklist and returned a volley of yeses.

"What a relief," said Jess.

Marion agreed, "Yes, that's good. You'll want to keep your door locked." She took a big sigh. "I'm trying to tell you the VFW is holding a free soup and sandwich feed tonight followed by Bingo. They are taking donations to help raise bail money for Joe Turner."

"Who's Joe Turner?" Jess asked, stuffing her clothes back in her suitcase.

"Some local kid. Anyway, everyone agreed it would be a nice gesture if we went."

"Oh, sounds good." I answered for the both of us while I folded my clothes and put them back in place.

"Good. We are meeting in the lobby to walk over together. Safer that way. The plan is to meet at 6:30."

"Good," I said.

"Good. Well, I'll just be going then." She made no effort to leave.

"Can we help you, Marion?" asked Jessica.

"I was just wondering…"Marion said and ran her hands over her blazer, trying to smooth the wrinkles set in by two days of wear and one night on a bus. "You're not going to put these little mishaps in your article, are you? I've never had anything like this happen before. And I can assure you, from now on, the tour will run smoothly." She stood up straighter and tried to act like she had some control over the latest chain of events. The dark circles under her eyes, accented by smudged mascara, indicated otherwise.

I felt for our disheveled, yet proud and determined tour guide. "We wouldn't dream of it."

Jess was wearing her cat smile. Marion didn't know whether to believe us or not, so she just smiled and made her way to the door. As she did, a thought occurred to me.

"Hey, wait a minute." I was suddenly very aware of my blue butt. "You said you weren't here long enough to hear anything, which probably means you heard everything, which means now you know our little secret."

Marion began to squirm. "No, really I wasn't here that long." She seemed absolutely mortified, which confirmed my suspicion that she knew about my butt.

"Marion, tell the truth." We moved in on her.

"Well, I, uh... I suspected earlier, but didn't want to say anything. It's not like I have a problem with it. It's nothing to be ashamed of." She said in a sort of patronizing simper.

"Ashamed of?" I asked. "Well, I'm not. It's just I don't think the whole tour needs to know. Agreed?" *Wait a minute*, I thought, *she suspected earlier?* Does that mean she heard us in the cornfield? What if other people heard? What if Don...oh dear.

"Agreed," said Marion. She was already backpedaling for the door.

"Okay then. Well, see you in a bit." With that settled, Marion made a quick exit, leaving the door open in her haste. I headed for the door, saying over my shoulder, "If we're meeting at 6:30, we only have an hour. You showering first or am I?"

Jess's cat smile was a full-blown cynical leer. "Oh honey, why not together? Save some time."

"Sorry, not until we're married." I shut the door and locked all five bolts.

#

We arrived late, so everyone was waiting. As we made our way down the iron grid staircase, all conversation shrank to silence. It might have been my imagination, but it seemed that everyone was staring at my butt.

The tables at the VFW were set up cafeteria style with the kitchen at one end and a dance floor at the other. A portable stage, table, chairs and lotto-roller were set up in the open space. We had our choice of chicken or egg salad sandwiches with chicken or cheese soup. After selecting chicken salad with cheese soup, Jess and I sat at one of the tables.

No one joined us.

"Do you think Marion told?" I asked.

"Who knows? Who cares? This gives us time to write our article without everyone telling us how to write our article." Jess unwrapped the paper cuff from her napkin and flatware. "Man, I'm starving."

"I'd die if everyone knew about my blue butt."

"So, die and get over it. Let's start with profiling Mary." Jess settled her napkin on her lap and opened her notebook on top of her knife and fork. "We still don't know much about her." However, we didn't get far before Bingo started. Two elderly gentlemen approached our secluded end of the table.

"What are two of the prettiest ladies doing sitting by themselves?" said the first geezer, who had eyebrows overgrowing his eyes.

"In the middle of a good conversation," I answered.

"Well, we love a good conversation," continued Bushy Brows. "May we join you?"

I glanced at Jess, but she shrugged. I decided I could set aside my aversion to locals this once. "Sure."

"Well, thank you. You know, your daddy must have stolen the stars from the skies and put them in your eyes."

I managed a small laugh and rolled my starry eyes. Unable to work, Jess bought ten Bingo cards to monopolize her attention. The conversation with the elderly gentlemen was a combination of I-remember-whens and pick up lines. They attempted to woo Jess by telling her she had the fair skin of an angel. My irritation rose to the tipping point when Bushy Brows mashed his dentures and said, "You must be tired—because you've been running through my dreams all night."

"Look, Gramps, you're cute, but I've had a long day, so if you don't mind..."

"Oh, I don't mind," he said not getting the point. I exhaled slowly and started counting to ten.

Jess realized I was about to morph, so she intervened, "Gentlemen, thanks for your company, but my friend and I need to focus on the game, so if you'll excuse us."

"Oh, big Bingo players are you?" they asked.

"Oh, yes," Jess assured. "We're serious about Bingo."

"B-11," the announcer cried.

"Yeah, real intense," I agreed, swiping a card from Jess.

"Well, Bud, in that case we'd better leave these young ladies alone." They rose slowly, shuffled across the room and started chatting with a couple of old ladies.

"I-21." Jess stamped a square of her card.

"Thanks, Jess. I was about to lose my cool."

"Theme of the day, it seems."

"G-58."

"Give me a break, Jess. It's not easy having a blue ass."

"Does it itch?"

"Bite me."

"N-36."

A deep voice asked, "Say, miss, if I become your knight in shining armor, will you be my Genevieve?"

"Oh, piss off already, you disgusting old fart!" I turned on my wannabe seducer, wielding my card-stamper, only to find myself attacking Don.

He put his hands in the air. "Hey, sorry, I was just…" He shrugged his shoulders. "Whatever." Then quickly walked away.

"No, wait. I'm sorry, I thought…" I trailed off. He was already halfway across the room. I watched him pretend to read the war plaques on the wall. Disappointment and self-loathing sat in my throat as I continued to stare at his broad back.

"Jess, just shoot me. My one chance to talk to him and I ruin it. His cheesy come on threw me off. I mean, why did he say that? Was he joking? It doesn't make sense."

"And you've made perfect sense every time you've tried to talk to him."

"Exactly! We're hopeless. It's like the gods are trying to keep us apart."

"O-63." The announcer's eyes were on us.

"Stel, don't cause a scene," Jess murmured.

"Don't cause a scene? Why not? What do I have to lose? I just called the man of my dreams a disgusting old fart. Now we'll never marry and I'll be stuck with you for the rest of my life."

"Thanks, but no thanks."

Jess thought I was joking, but a part of me knew I wasn't, that part of me causing this tightness in my chest. I've started to believe I'll never have someone who'll call in sick on Monday just to lie in bed with me all day and watch *The Deadliest Catch* re-runs. And not because I won't find him. I'm sure I'll find the one. But I'll say something stupid or make an ass of myself and scare him off. Then I'll have to watch as he falls into the arms of another woman who may be more beautiful, but won't be able to make him laugh like I can.

"B-3."

"What did he say?" I asked, coming out of my self torment.

"I believe he said sorry and walked away."

"No, not Don, the announcer," I clarified.

"Oh, B-3."

"B-3! Yes, Bingo! I have Bingo!"

The announcer leaned closer to the mike. "Well, let's see, miss." I read back my Bingo and he declared me the true winner. I collected my crocheted potholder and returned in glory to the table. Jess scowled.

"What, Jess? That's how the game is played."

"Just because you've made a wreck of your love life doesn't mean you have to ruin my fun."

"I won fair and square, you petulant old hag."

"You swiped my lucky card."

"Jess, get real. It's the only thing that's gone right for me all day."

"Whatever," she said and grabbed her purse and journal. "I'm going to find Mary. Try to get a story out of her or at least get her reaction to Brother Thomas's sermon." She looked at me before flippantly saying, "We are on an assignment after all," and walked away.

"Jess," I shouted, but she kept walking. *Sore loser*, I thought. Like I need a reminder of what's at stake.

As I glanced around the room to find someone to talk to, I noticed Don was still by himself. He was wearing a striped button down shirt rolled up to his elbows over stonewashed jeans. *Fine, I'll get a story*, I thought. I'll get Don's story. That'll show Jessica. I started to make my way across the room. I could already feel the blood rush to my face, but I was determined.

However, Char intercepted me. "So, you won Bingo? Good for you."

I didn't know if she meant it or not, but being desperate to make things right by her, I grabbed the olive branch. "Yes, I can't believe it. I never win anything."

"Me either," she said, but quickly corrected herself. "Before this trip anyway." We both laughed nervously. I thought, *I guess this is how we say sorry.*

"What did you win?" Char asked.

"A potholder." I held it up for her.

"Oh, that's nice. Crocheted even."

"Do you want it?" I thrust it in her face in my eagerness to be friends.

"I couldn't."

"I insist. Really. I don't cook. Go ahead and have it." I put it in her hands and let go, so Char was forced to take it.

"Well, thanks."

"You're welcome." See, we can get along so nicely.

Lenny joined us, "Say, are you two going to the bar with everyone else?"

"Sure," answered Char.

"What?" I asked. Lester's question suddenly brought my attention back to my original quest to talk to Don. I desperately looked for him, and when I found him, the bottom fell out. He was talking with Maggie, Billy and Tansy again. I turned my focus back on Lester before my emotions made their way to my face. "What did you say?"

"A bunch of us are going for a nightcap at the Corner Tavern."

"Is that the name of the bar or are we going to a tavern on the corner?" I asked.

"Uh, I don't know." Lester was flustered. I didn't mean to sound aggressive, and I really didn't care about the stupid name of the bar, I was just pissed off at the situation.

"We can just follow everyone else, I guess," said Lester.

"Of course. Sure. Let's go," I agreed.

We turned toward the group when I was assaulted by the Elvis and Priscilla wannabes.

"Hey Stella, take our picture," said Vince.

"What?" *Why is everyone in my face*, I thought. *What the hell is going on?*

"We got all dressed up so you could take our picture for your article," Vince explained. "Don't we look like the famous couple?"

"Wow," I said aloud. "You do." And they did. Just like Elvis and Priscilla on their wedding day. It was almost creepy. I dug my camera out of my purse and did as commanded.

"Be sure to write what a very successful, very happy couple we are," quipped Ella. She glared at me through narrowed eyes and repeated, "Very happy."

"I know you're very happy, and I'm very happy for you." I said through a smirk of my own.

"Okay, that's all we wanted," Vince said, then drew Ella into his arms. "Come here. You are so hot dressed as Priscilla, you know?" She giggled, and they started making out.

It was too much for me. Abruptly, I left the group and started marching to the ladies room. Damn Char for thwarting my objective and canoodling me out of a potholder. Damn Lester for being annoying. Damn Vince and Ella and their damn happy marriage. Damn Don's bad timing. And damn myself for being so damn stupid!

I hit the door hard as I entered the restroom. What's wrong with me? Why can't I be normal? I covered my face with my hands. I knew I was overreacting, but that didn't stop the pounding in my heart nor the tears in my eyes. It's probably due to the lack of sleep from spending last night on a bus fearing for my life. Or maybe it was a release of emotions from embarrassing myself by calling out Don's name in my sleep, attacking Char for making fun of me, throwing a crate on Elvis's head, managing to dye my ass blue, and then calling Don an old fart. It has been a busy day, even for a travel journalist. I leaned on the sink and took a few deep breaths.

"Are you okay, sweetie?" asked an elderly lady. She held out a wad of toilet paper.

I took it gratefully and pressed it into my eyes. "Thanks," I mumbled. "I'm okay. It's nothing."

"Doesn't seem like nothing to me." She put her arm around me. "What's wrong, dear? C'mon now."

Isn't it strange, when you're upset, all it takes is one act of kindness—someone expressing genuine concern for you, even if that someone is a complete stranger—to make you come completely undone.

I gave up and let the tears flow. "I have a blue ass," I said between sobs because I couldn't think of anything else.

"It's okay, miss," she said, patting my back. "These things happen all the time."

Chapter 14: Jessica

Happens every time. Stel has one too many pink martinis and passes out. Then I'm left dragging her sorry blue ass home. I knew Stella was going to pay for the way she, Char and Lester were throwing them back last night.

"I said, get up!" I grabbed her arm and pulled her half out of bed. She slid the rest of the way on her own and landed on the floor in a lump.

"Mime up..." she mumbled and reached for the phone.

"Who are you calling?"

"No one." She tried to hang up the receiver, but missed. It flopped to the ground and started beeping. "Where's the alarm?"

"What alarm?" I asked, stepping over her to replace the receiver.

Stel whined, "Stop the ringing. Must stop the ringing." She looked under the bed.

"What ringing? There's no ringing. There's no alarm." Stel was crawling to the bathroom, and I called after her, "While you're in there, jump in the shower. We're supposed to meet at Perkins in half an hour."

Stel got as far as the bathroom threshold, groaned and put her head on the tile floor.

I should have stopped her binge, knowing I'd be the one to deal with her, but she was so upset last night, I let her go. "C'mon, Stel. Let's go." I bent to help her up.

"Just leave me. Save yourself."

I hoisted her over the side of the tub. She still had her clothes on from the night before, but that didn't matter. They needed to be washed anyway. They still held the smoke, beer and bodily secretion smell from the Corner Tavern. I turned on the shower.

The cold water hit Stel in the face and she screamed. She reached for the knob and missed. She hit me next. "Back, devil woman. What are you doing?" At least both eyes were open now.

I threw a washcloth at her. "Giving you a bath. You stink."

"Get out of here. I can do this. I can shower myself."

An hour later, we arrived at Perkins. We weren't the only latecomers due to the wild night. Even Eric couldn't pull it off; his clothes weren't pressed and his face showed three days growth.

Marion introduced us to Ted Ewald, our replacement driver. Poofy white hair framed his timeworn face. I guessed he was in his early fifties, judging from the age spots on his hands. His manner was friendly and open, and he answered our questions eagerly.

"No, I've never participated in open combat. I was too young for the World Wars and too old for Vietnam." His voice was pleasant and soothing.

Char was the hard case, as usual. "Do you carry a gun?"

He laughed, a great jovial laugh that made everyone smile. "Ma'am, I don't even carry mace." He winked and his blue eyes twinkled. "I find a nice smile usually disarms most people. Plus, I don't have anything anyone would want. If I do, they're welcome to it." He turned to Marion and pulled out a pack of gum. "Would you like a piece? It's fruity." Marion smiled and pulled the last piece.

"Well, folks, if there's no further questions, I suggest we get going," said Billy, taking command of the situation. "We have a lot of ground to cover today."

Spirits high, we loaded the bus and waited for Ted to lock the baggage compartments and join us. Cybill only chugged twice before coming to life.

Marion handed everyone a revised schedule. "As you can see, I've had to eliminate two days from our time in Memphis. Instead of six days, we'll only have four. I also had to limit our stops along the way to just two more sites. The first is Martha's Memorable Mansion of Majestic Music featuring her extensive collection of Elvis pins. We'll see Martha's Mansion today, and spend the night in Springfield, Missouri. The second is Riley's Rock n' Roll Bar where some of America's finest rock 'n' rollers have played. It's right outside Memphis."

The college boys began snickering. Luc handed me a new schedule and whispered, "Check out Marion."

Dressed in her usual Donna Reed dress with a flared skirt, I couldn't discern any major difference. Harulu and Sachi started laughing from across the aisle. "Hey, Marion!" Matt stood up and made his way down the aisle. "I was wondering if you would pose with me for a picture." Luc and Marcus flipped open their camera phones.

"Now, son, you need to remain seated while the bus is in motion."

Matt was blocking my view of Marion. "Please? It'll only take a second."

"Oh, all right, but then you must return to your seat."

"Now give me a big smile," Matt prompted. She grinned as the flashes popped.

Char hooted while Sister Mary cried in dismay as everyone on the bus immediately saw the joke. Stella and I burst out laughing. Matt's eyes watered as he walked back to his seat. Marion was confused by everyone's reaction. Sister Mary took pity on Marion and informed her the gum Ted had given her had turned her teeth black.

Marion covered her mouth with her hand and ran to the bathroom.

At the front of the bus, Ted laughed, one hand slapping the steering wheel. We couldn't help our own amusement, even after Marion exited the bathroom with a look of wounded pride. Somehow that made it even funnier. For the next hour she kept her mouth clamped shut.

We stopped at a gas station for a quick refuel. For a mid-August day, the air was surprisingly mild. Tansy announced it was going to rain soon.

Char rolled her eyes as she exited behind Tansy. "You know that for a fact, huh?"

Tansy eyed Char. "I can smell it."

Char sneered at Tansy's departing back. "With your nose stuck so far up in the sky, I'm not surprised,"

Marion returned to the bus with a toothbrush in hand. She smiled, her pearly whites once again pearly. With the efficiency only a tour guide possesses, she shooed everyone back on the bus. Ella dug into her bag and pulled out a can of Pringles. She giggled at something Vince said when she popped the lid and a fake snake hit her in the chops. Ted had struck again.

And again. And again. He switched Maggie's lipstick with one that turned black, put super fizzing tablets in the pop bottles of Marcus, Luc and Matt, placed a whoopee cushion under Char's seat and rigged the seat of Brother Thomas to whip back and forth until Brother T got sick. By the time we stopped for lunch at McDonalds, we were a little tired of our prankster. Bossman insisted Ted join us for lunch. We'd be damned before we'd let him out of our sight.

I approached the McDonald's counter and stared at the glowing wall of food. I wasn't hungry until I inhaled the signature smell of grease and salt. "What can I get for you, miss?"

Sweet Jesus. At the register, giving me a lop-sided grin from under a red visor, was Elvis.

"Well," I drawled, trying to sound casual. "I would love one of your salads." I checked his nametag. "Sam."

"Which salad would you like?"

"Do you have a chef's salad?"

"Dressing?"

I was losing it. Who was he? Why did he keep popping up? Did Ursula put him up to this? But I just stared until Stella jabbed me in the ribs.

She spoke slowly, over-enunciating every word. "What kind of salad dressing do you want?"

I blinked. If God were kind, the floor would open up and swallow me. I stared at it, hoping for a miracle. "Oh, uh, ranch," I said and smiled at Sam. "And could I get a Diet Coke with that?"

"Sure. Will that be all?"

"You know, you look very familiar. Have we met?"

"Uh, no, I don't think so."

"Any brothers?"

"Only child."

I leaned on the counter and smiled at him while Stella paid for both our meals. When she was done, she took my arm and led me away. She shoved me into a booth. "What are you doing?"

"Stella! It's him. It's Elvis, again!"

"Yes, hon, I know. But we can't grill him when you're leaving a puddle of drool on the counter!"

"You are a fine one to talk! You've been drooling over Don this whole trip."

"Pull yourself together. At least Don is a possibility in the romance department. I've spent more than ten minutes in his presence and he doesn't change his name and job every time I see him."

It was just like her to get all defensive about her crush-of-the-month. I nibbled on my salad. I tried to check on Sam, but he vanished into the back of the restaurant. I needed to see him. I needed to talk to him. I needed his story. There's a time for eating lettuce and there's a time for action.

I plotted my mission. An "Employees Only" door stood about twenty feet away, about eight feet past the ladies bathroom. I scanned for obstacles. An obese woman moved towards the loo. Perfect.

"Where are you going?"

"Cover me, I'm going after our story."

Chapter 15: Stella

"You're going after our story?" I asked. Jess didn't answer, but quickly walked to the bathrooms. I wondered who could be in there and what she meant by 'cover me.' I returned to my Big Mac with a shrug.

"You know, McDonald remind me of Etsu," said Midori, sitting to my right.

"Me remember, too," said Sachi. "Summer of 1977…"

I forgot about Elvis, Jess and the pounding in my head as I sunk my teeth into greasy goodness and listened to the Japanese trio stumble down memory lane.

"No, 1978," Midori corrected.

"You both wrong," said Harulu. "1982. I remember very hot summer."

"No, 1977 because Etsu take job at big college," said Sachi.

"Oh, you right," Harulu and Midori agreed, and the story continued.

"Like I say, Etsu at big college in 1977," Sachi looked at me as she told the story. Apparently I wasn't hiding the fact I was ease dropping.

"Etsu take us to big college for visit," added Midori. "And for lunch."

"Friends for life, remember," said Harulu and the three ladies shared a laugh.

"Like you and Jessica," said Sachi, winking at me. I could only nod in agreement because my mouth was full of French fries.

"That summer so hot," said Harulu.

"Etsu drive to McDonald for lunch," added Midori. "On road to McDonald, Etsu drive over cat."

Sachi added, "It squish all over."

"Oh gross," I said and almost lost my appetite. Almost. I took a long pull on my vanilla shake.

Harulu continued, "We feel sad. We no want leave cat in road for kid to find. Kid be very sad."

"Etsu say put cat in garbage. But no garbage. So we put in car trunk." Sachi looked proud.

Harulu explained, "We plan to dump kitty on highway."

Midori joined the conversation. "We go to McDonald. But it very hot. Remember? Summer of 1977!"

I winced. Jessica still hadn't returned from the bathroom. I envisioned her cornering Tansy or Maggie, drilling them with questions and threatening to go through their luggage if they didn't tell her what she needed to know.

"Kitty smell bad. We put cat in shopping bag and leave on hood of car. Then we go inside to eat." Harulu took a bite of her chicken sandwich.

"We sit by window to watch car," said Sachi.

"We see old lady walk by our bag," said Midori.

"She look around," said Harulu.

"She look at bag," Midori said.

"She look around," repeated Harulu.

"She look at bag," repeated Midori.

"Then she take bag," said Sachi.

"No way!" I exclaimed.

"Yes!" all three said in unison and laughed like they tricked the lady into taking the dead cat on purpose.

I hung on every word, but the trio continued in Japanese, forgetting I couldn't understand. Sachi realized this and switched back. "Oh so sorry! I say she come inside and order Big Mac. Then she sit at table."

"Then she look around," said Harulu.

"She take bite," said Midori.

"She look around," repeated Harulu.

"She take bite," repeated Midori.

"Then, she—" Sachi tried to continue but couldn't because she started laughing. The other two joined. Sachi tried again, "She . . .then she . . .she—"

"She what?" I practically shouted.

"She look in bag," said Sachi before bursting into laughter.

"She scream so loud," Midori wheezed.

"So funny," said Harulu.

It took a while before Sachi could continue. "The lady, how you say? Fall over?" She looked at me for help.

"She fainted?" I offered.

"Yes, fainted! Lady fainted. So men in ambulance came and take her to hospital," said Sachi.

The three ladies looked at each other before saying together, "Men also take bag with cat!" Again, they erupted in laughter, and I joined in. Tears were running down my face. Imagine the thief trying to explain to the doctor why she was carrying around a bag containing a dead cat.

"So funny!" said Harulu.

"So many funny memories," said Midori.

"Friends for life!" declared Sachi.

"For life!" cheered Harulu and Midori.

At that moment, I heard my friend-for-life scream from the kitchen. "I'm not letting you go until you tell me who you are!"

Oh, shit, I thought, *she's got Elvis.*

Chapter 16: Jessica

"Stella, help me! I've got Elvis!"

Elvis, a.k.a. Sam, struggled against my bear hug. "Lady, let me go. I'm not Elvis. Are you crazy?"

"Do you think I'm stupid? I know Elvis when I see him. I'm not like the others." I wrestled Elvis to the counter. Looking up, I met the disbelieving stares of the other patrons. At last, I would have witnesses.

Stella stepped between me and the group of bewildered onlookers. "Uh, nothing to see here, folks," she said to the crowd. "Just to back to your burgers and fries." She reached over and grabbed my hair. "Let go of him right now!" She yanked and my grip slid until all I had was his shirt. Buttons pinged the floor and stainless steel surfaces in the kitchen. In a moment, they were all that remained of Elvis. He had fled.

Forlorn, I stared at the shirt. "I was so close."

Sounds of someone gagging moved the crowd's attention from me to Ted. He was choking. Marion rushed to his side. "Ted? Ted, are you okay?"

Ted's coughing became more violent as he stood up. The coughing ceased as Ted's eyes rolled back into his skull, and he collapsed on the floor. Everyone screamed.

Big Billy pushed his way towards the counter bellowing, "Call 911! Call 911!" Sachi, Midori, and Harulu quaked, and Sister Mary prayed. Tansy started to cry while Char bitched out the waitress for serving bad food.

A situation like this called for the clear-headed, the quick thinker, the First-Aid certified—the situation called for Marion. She rolled Ted onto his back and checked his jugular. "A strong pulse," she announced. She tilted his head back and pried open his lips. She put her ear over Ted's mouth.

Ted stuck his tongue in Marion's ear, giving her a nasty version of a Wet Willie. Marion was on her feet in a heartbeat, screaming. She grabbed a dirty napkin and wadded it into her ear. On the floor, Ted rolled in laughter.

"Gotcha!" he cried.

The group's concern turned into anger. Several customers and some employees joined us, including the store manager. His face was crimson.

"Sir, that wasn't funny. Now I have to explain to the ambulance it was all a hoax. This group has disturbed my other customers and employees. If you leave now, I will not press charges." Flecks of spittle flew from his mouth.

Embarrassed by Ted's behavior, I filed out with the others. I was angry with Ted for causing such a scene. Customers and employees glared at me as if I'd planned the event and encouraged it. I was guilty by association, and damn, that pissed me off.

There was a lot of grumbling as the tour boarded the bus in record time. As we drove away with Ted hunched over at the wheel, a wailing ambulance pulled into McDonalds. Marion seemed to sense the mood of her passengers, and since she was still coping with having Ted's tongue in her ear, her answer was to pop in a movie.

"Group, I think now we need some quiet time. Our next video on the list is *Girl Happy*." She paused, ready to go into her usual introduction about numerous need-to-know facts, but looked around the bus and stopped herself. She turned to the DVD player and various Elvis movies next to it, selected the right one and popped it in. She sat down and stared out a window.

A pretty girl with flowing red hair pranced onto the screen. Her tiny bathing suit was ill equipped for her body, specifically her breasts, as she frolicked up to join two other girls and three men on the beach for a rousing game of volleyball. I looked for Elvis, but he wasn't one of the guys. I lost interest and turned to watch the passing scenery.

"Hey, Marion. I don't think this is *Girl Happy*," said Lester. "At least this isn't how it starts."

His announcement brought everyone's attention back to the flickering screens. As we watched, the three girls collapsed on a beach blanket, exhausted after their thirty-second volleyball game. The guys proceeded to remove the girls' bikinis. On screen it was a scramble to remove clothing. On the bus, it was a scramble to turn off the DVD.

Across the aisle, Maggie gasped and covered her mouth. The three college guys whooped it up as the beach scene turned into an orgy. Marion pushed at the buttons, but only succeeded in fast-forwarding the tape. I became mesmerized by sex at super speed. Shouts of "Turn it off!" overpowered those of "Keep it on!" and I looked around guiltily, hoping that no one saw me gaping at the porno. Beet red, Stella stared at her shoes as though diamonds were glued to it. The little old ladies worked on their afghan. Char, Elliot and Lester looked on with frank amusement. Sister Mary buried her head in her hands. Don stood up behind us and tried to turn off the screen closest to her, but finding no switch, he covered it with a jacket.

The screens went blank. The noise died with the action, except for the laughter. Big Billy and Eric returned to their seats, but Marion stood mid-aisle, breathing like a marathon runner, fists clenched and face slowly turning purple as she listened to Ted's chuckles. Marion closed her eyes and picked up the microphone.

"I've had it with his pranks!" Vince bellowed.

"I'm afraid to open my bag," announced Maggie.

"I'm afraid to use the john," retorted Brother Thomas.

"I say we call for a new bus driver!" yelled Char. Her decree was answered with several assents.

Marion held up a hand. "I know we've had our fill of Ted's jokes, but we simply cannot risk losing any more time.

At the rate we're going, we'll be in Memphis for only four days. Despite it all, Ted has managed to make up some lost time."

Ted glanced in the rear view mirror. "It was just a couple of pranks. No harm done!"

Marion whirled on him, "Sir! These jokes of yours have stopped being funny for some time now. One or two was fine and perhaps acceptable, but these pranks are becoming embarrassing for the passengers. Not to mention your last stunt was completely against the rules of the company and could get you fired! One more prank and I will do everything to see that you are!"

Ted fell silent, eyes glued to the road. Billy moved to his side and began an earnest, but quiet conversation, trying his best to smooth over the situation like usual.

Several moments later, Marion turned back to the group. A false smile spread across her features. "All righty then, gang! I think we should…" Marion trailed off no longer able to keep up pretenses. Abruptly she sat down and stared out the window. Everyone turned to their own quiet means of passing the time.

"So," Stella ventured. "I suppose we should talk about these Elvis sightings."

"It's Ursula," I said, wringing Sam's shirt in my hands as though it where the Sea Bitch's neck.

"What?" Stel asked.

"Isn't it obvious?" I shouted.

"Shhh, calm down," Stel admonished. "Jess, this isn't like you." She put her hand on top of mine.

I yanked free, but gave up Sam's shirt. "I know. It's usually you causing a scene."

"Thanks," she said. I could feel her glare.

"Sorry," I apologized. "But these Elvis sightings are really getting to me. It has to be Ursula."

"Why do you say that?" Stella can be so blind when she doesn't want to see the truth.

"She wants us to fail, so she sent Elvis to torment us, spy on us, and throw us off the story."

Stella rubbed her temples. "Okay, I can see where you're coming from."

"Think about it, Stel. She hasn't even called. And you know why? She doesn't have to because she has Elvis."

"But how would she know where we are? We are way off schedule, and these Elvi keep popping up at random."

"Elvis is following us!" I shouted. A few people were staring. I realize I've started to sound like them. "I mean the man she has hired to play Elvis is following us."

"Uh, okay," Stel said slowly, but I could tell she still wasn't convinced.

"C'mon, Stel. It's either my theory or we are crazy."

"True," she finally acknowledged. "Speaking of crazy...we should get rid of the evidence." She walked to the back and put Sam's shirt in the trash. When she returned she said, "If you're right, we can't let Ursula win, so we better work on the article." However, I was too agitated to write, so I simply handed her my journal so she could read what I had written so far.

#

She was ten years old, and her parents were dead. Car accident. Everyone was sorry. Her only living relative was a great-aunt who lived in Toledo with a house full of caged birds, and she couldn't possibly care for a child she did not know.

This was how Mary Brickel came to live in St. Anthony's Home for Children. It was a formidable collection of brick buildings, set upon a network of sidewalks, hemmed by a few flowerbeds. The only grass was the few pristine square feet to either side of Mother Superior's front door. Mary Brickel began her life at St. Anthony's by standing in this grass, and plucking the heads off of Mother Superior's roses. Their thorny stems, clutched into a bouquet, were the beginning of a ten-year rebellion.

She sneaked the cook's cigarettes and smoked in the confessional. She tormented the smaller kids and stole their snacks, and made them play pranks on the sisters. She skipped class and talked about kissing boys just to rile up the nuns.

St. Anthony's was entirely self-contained. You slept there, ate there, went to school there and prayed there. Rewards for excellent grades and good behavior were day trips to the world beyond the brick labyrinth; Mary, however, rarely got to leave.

You learn in orphanages that prospective parents generally like young children. If you're over the age of two, the chances of your being adopted are cut in half and decrease with each year. Foster parents rarely took on a 'problem' child.

So St. Anthony's became her home.

Dorm rooms on the fourth floor were the most coveted rooms simply because they had views of the outside world. You could see over the tops of trees and houses. When the wind was just right, you could hear music playing. From those windows, you could plan your escape.

Mary modified her behavior so she could join one of the day trips, and within twenty minutes she had split from the group and found her way to K-Mart. She walked up and down the bright aisles of colorful plastic toys, the racks and racks of new clothes. The manager called the police, and within the hour Mary was sitting at Mother Superior's desk, sullenly not explaining herself.

You could tell the day of the week by chores. Weeding on Mondays. Lunch duty Tuesdays. Laundry on Saturdays. She longed for the world that did its chores any time it wanted to and skipped them if it didn't. St. Anthony's was a prison for people whose only crime was being unwanted. The unfairness of it was so potent, a bile taste hung in the back of Mary's throat for months at a time.

One day she poured green food coloring in the holy water. She had to scrub the basement floors as punishment. Now the basement of St. Anthony's was the kind that mystery novelists write about. Just when you thought you've finished, you find another room. She was cleaning out a large storage room when she discovered a closet that wasn't a closet. It was a passageway that led to a locked storm door. The forgotten door led to the alley and freedom. She couldn't believe it. She had been handed her very own secret to guard.

The best time to slip away was between three and six in the afternoon. That was free time, in which students could do homework, play, read or catch up on prayers. Unless you had dinner duty, which happened once a week. So Mary would sneak outside and explore the neighborhood; and for once, someone wasn't telling her which side of the street she had to walk down.

The orphanage was located on the edge of St. Michael, Minnesota. She would walk through all kinds of shops. She would linger as long as she dared before slipping back to St. Anthony's.

One day as she was walking through the neighborhood, she heard music. She followed it to a set of speakers set up outside a record store. The bins of records were captivating—so many different artists. St. Anthony's students learned next to nothing about music except what was in the hymnals. The owner let her listen to any record she wanted, and Mary started coming just to help sort stock. After the fourth visit, she was offered a part-time job for fifty cents an hour, whenever she wanted to work.

It was in this store that Mary discovered Elvis. Or Elvis discovered her. She fell in love with his voice and his words. She read all sorts of articles about him, and saw a man with whom she had a great deal in common. She would listen to the giggling girls who would come into the store to buy his music, and she knew they didn't understand him at all. Not like she did.

Mary fell in love with Elvis. She smuggled pictures of her beloved to her room and tacked them in the back of her closet. Emboldened by love, she walked two miles to the movie house to watch a re-release of *Follow That Dream*. She was late getting back and had to miss dinner, but no one scolded her, and sleeping with an empty stomach was a small price to pay for dreaming of Elvis as she had seen him on the big screen.

Her secret changed St. Anthony's for her. She became nicer to the younger kids, her grades improved and she started taking pleasure in the sturdy architecture and comforting routines. The sisters assumed she was just growing up, and never questioned her motives, since she would turn down any chance to go on a day trip.

Mary was seventeen, and for two years her secret had given her access to the world she would join on her next birthday. At eighteen, orphans left with two hundred dollars and a job interview. She planned to go to Memphis and get a job in a music store. She would use her stipend and her wages from the record store to purchase a cross country bus ticket. She would somehow meet Elvis, and their common interests would do the rest. Mary and Elvis, bound in a way neither had ever experienced with any other human being. She would become the wife whom Elvis always needed, the one who truly understood him.

Then came the day when everything changed. She sneaked out of St. Anthony's in high spirits. Not even the August heat could squelch her excitement, and she stopped for an ice cream cone on her way to work. Standing in line, she noticed several girls crying and an older gentleman was shaking his head. "Serves him right," he said. "See what that kind of lifestyle leads too?" Mary asked one of the girls what had happened. And that's when Mary discovered her Elvis was dead.

She held up a newspaper with a huge headline: "Elvis Dies of Heart Failure." It knocked the wind out of her, and she sat on a bench outside reading and rereading the headline.

A touch on her shoulder. A police officer asking if she was all right. That's when she realized she was crying. Worse, she realized the sun was setting. She had been crying on that bench for over two hours. The cop recognized the symbol stitched on her clothing as St. Anthony's, figured her for a runaway and brought her back.

The sisters were beside themselves when Mary showed up. Sister Maria escorted her straight to Mother Superior, moaning the whole way, "You were being so good!" She sat Mary in a chair while Mother Superior railed, asking questions, making accusations. Later, Mary couldn't remember a word she said. She had sat in her office with tears pouring down her face. And that was answer enough for Mother Superior: this wasn't just a miscreant breaking the rules again. Something was really wrong. But Mary couldn't explain. How do you explain your love for Elvis? Because of him, she could endure the worst simply for a chance at the best.

For three days Mary stayed in her room mourning the loss of her first true love and her sense of freedom. Occasionally a concerned sister would check on her, but she couldn't talk. On the fourth day, she went for a walk and found herself in the chapel.

It is amazing, the places you become connected to when you're a child. Pieces of them latch onto your soul without you being aware of it.

Mary paused and tried to hold back her tears. As she sat in the chapel, she felt God's love wash over her, telling her everything was going to be okay. And she finally forgave him for taking her parents. She forgave her parents for leaving her all alone. And she forgave the Sisters for not understanding.

And all of a sudden, she knew that St. Anthony's was right where she needed to be. For the first time in seven long years, Sister Mary was home.

Chapter 17: Stella

"I want to go home," I said, once again choking back tears. This was turning into quite an emotional trip.

"What?" Jess asked, coming out of her reverie.

"This piece you wrote about Sister Mary is really good." I handed her journal back.

"It's nothing really," said Jess. "Just something I jotted down after talking to Mary last night. She has a moving story." She tucked her journal into the seat pocket in front of her.

"Jess, I'm serious," I insisted. "I know you're a good reporter when you're hot on the trail of a breaking news story, but this softer, creative side is something different. You really captured Mary's loneliness, and then her relief when she finally finds a place to belong."

"It's nothing really."

"Jess, I'm trying to give you a compliment."

"Oh, is that what you're doing? Well, thanks."

I punched her in the arm. "You're welcome, geez. Did she ever tell anyone about her crush on Elvis?"

"She confessed to her Mother Superior."

"What did she say?"

"That's the reason she's on this trip: to do a bit of soul searching. Mary wonders if maybe there wasn't another purpose for her on this earth. It's very complicated."

"Hmmm, interesting," I mused.

"Well, if you ask me, you inherit your own trouble." Char interrupted our conversation with her pessimism. "I'll bet when she gets back, she'll find she's been excommunicated!"

"Nice outlook, Char," I said without turning around.

"You'd be surprised how often the worst does happen!" Char insisted. "I've got more first hand knowledge of the crap that happens to people than anyone else on this bus. I'm a hair stylist, and the stuff people tell me could turn your highlights pink."

Jess and I just laughed at Char and rolled our eyes. Unbidden, Char moved into the vacant seat across from me and continued to educate us on the ways of the world.

"There are times when you're just walking down the street, minding your own business, and the world crashes into you like a speeding produce truck. Just like what happened to Emily Jenkins's cousin's boyfriend. He was walking down the sidewalk and bam! A truck pulls out of an alley and mows him down. Knocked him right out of his boots."

For some reason, her story was even funnier to me given the fact she was wearing purple sweatpants with iron-on lace around the collar and cuffs. She had to be roasting; it's August.

"So you never know what's going to happen," Char continued. "I figure that the worst is usually going to happen and nine times out of ten, I'm right. Like when Jackson Miller's widow let that Bobby Newport move in with her. I told everyone he'd use her for a while, then rob her blind. Sure enough, three years later, her house was burglarized. The police said it was another guy, but I knew it was that Bobby character. I even tried to do my civic duty and reported him to the police, but they wouldn't believe me."

"Imagine that," Jess whispered.

"Which just goes to show what the police know. The only one who's any good is my son, Jeremy."

"Your son's a cop?" I asked. I don't know why this surprised me, but it did.

"Yes, he just made lieutenant," Char said proudly. "Not bad for a twenty-six-year-old. But all the rest of them need a good sound beating, if you ask me. Or don't ask me. I don't care—I'll tell you anyway."

And she did.

"I found out it isn't the drug dealers and murderers you have to look out for; it's the police. You see, three weeks ago, I was taking a cab ride home from a friend's costume party."

"This ought to be good," I whispered to Jess.

"It took place in the biggest dive in the city. Anyway, I left around eleven and the cab driver was probably the biggest idiot to walk the face of the planet. It took him three minutes to get lost in the worst part of town. I kept trying to tell him he was lost, but he wouldn't listen. Then he just pulled over and told me to get out. The asshole!"

I had to smile at this. I could just see Char yelling directions at the cab driver—'You big dipshit, you're going the wrong way'—until he gets pissed and kicks her out. That cab driver was my hero.

"So there I was, all dressed up, minding my own business, with no cab in sight," Char continued. "I started walking, trying to find a payphone or store that was open so I could call the police on that SOB. I passed some unsavory looking characters. All these people kept giving me dirty looks, like I had no right to be walking down the street. I just kept my head held high and glared back. I ain't afraid of no one." She slapped me on the shoulder to emphasize her point.

"Hell no, I bet you ain't," I said, giving her the kudos she wanted. After all, I wouldn't want to meet Char in a dark alley.

"Then I noticed this guy across the street checking me out. It wasn't a good look; it was like he was measuring to see if my dead body would fit in his trunk. He started walking towards me. I slowed down. He stopped and waited for me to get closer. At first I thought I should cross the street to get away from him, but then I got pissed. Who the hell was he? I carry mace and a purple belt in Tae Kwon Do."

Bullshit, I thought.

Char dropped her voice to a dramatic whisper. "So I keep walking and he keeps leering. I'm getting creeped out. We got within an arm's distance from each other, and he *winked* at me. That's when I decided to defend myself before he had a chance to attack and rape me."

"So what did you do?" Jess asked.

"I kicked that bastard right in the balls!" Char was so damn proud of herself.

Jess and I burst out laughing along with the back half of the bus. Apparently we weren't the only ones caught up in Char's story. Furthermore, I noticed Char was very aware she had an audience. She continued her story in a much louder voice for the benefit of the rest of her fans.

"And when I do something, I do it right. My kick caught him unawares and he dropped to his knees, squeaking like a mouse. I kicked him in his junk twice more for good measure. Then I kicked him in the ribs and started beating him over the head with my purse. When he was on the ground I found my mace and sprayed that leer right off his face. I kicked for my life and screamed for help."

This was too much. Jess and I were dying at the thought of Char kicking the crap out of some poor guy walking down the street.

"Remind me never to cross paths with Char in a dark alley," said Matt, and the rest of his gang agreed. Everyone else shook their heads.

Char took this as a compliment and continued, "Down the block a bunch of guys explode from this van. I'm thinking, here comes the other members of the rapist's gang, so I turn and start running, screaming bloody murder. But I'm in my heels, and a couple of the guys tackled me. I thought for sure my next stop was their trunk. Know what they do instead?" Char asked.

"No," I couldn't imagine. I caught Don's eye for a split second before he looked away. I tried to bring my focus back on Char.

"They put handcuffs on me and read me my rights. I figured these guys were the cops and they were arresting the wrong person. So I tell them the other guy's who they want, get with the program, you know? But they tell me to shut up. I tell them I was an innocent bystander. They tell me the guy I attacked was an undercover police officer."

"No way," said Jess. "You're making this up."

"I am not," Char insisted. "I swear to you on my life. I just about crapped my pantyhose right there on the street."

I smiled at Char's delicate way with words. I wrote in my journal, you'll never read the phrase 'I about crapped my pantyhose' in a poem by Emily Dickenson, but for Char Larson no other line quite captured the moment.

"I told the police over and over I was just minding my own business when this weirdo approached me. That's when they informed me I was being arrested for prostitution and assaulting a police officer. Humiliating, let me tell you."

"I'm sure," I said. "I mean, I've never been arrested on prostitution changes, but I can imagine."

"I know," said Char taking me seriously. "And all I had done was walk down a street in a seedy neighborhood—no, all I had done was get in a cab. No one would believe my outfit was a costume. I couldn't wait for my one phone call. I was going to call a lawyer and sue the pants off these clowns. I told the jerk that drove me to the station to contact my son, who just happened to be a lieutenant. I'll never forget the look on his face when he checked and found out there was Lieutenant Jeremy Larson.

"So I get home and sleep for hours, and wake up to the phone ringing. I won this trip from my son's favorite diner. Great timing, I thought. A nice vacation to help me forget my problems for a while. And here I am with all of you. So you see, shit happens, and it's usually worse than you'd ever imagine."

She added for the benefit of those who were listening, "Stick that in your pipe and smoke it."

Chapter 18: Jessica

She had to be blowing smoke up our asses.

"So the cops thought you were a prostitute?" asked Luc. The college boys were sitting in the seats ahead of Stel and me. At Luc's questions, all three turned around to face Char.

"Yes," answered Char.

"And now you're facing assault charges because you kicked an officer in his nads?" asked Don from two rows back.

"Yes."

The college boys started laughing first, but soon the whole bus was in an uproar. Eric wiped tears from his eyes, and Maggie doubled over in laughter.

"It's not funny," said Char, now irritated by our laughter. We were obviously not taking her predicament serious enough.

"Yes, it is," wheezed Lester, who snorted while laughing, making the rest of us laugh harder. I thought I was going to wet myself.

Char tried to ignore us as she glared out the window, silent. We knew she was hurt, but we couldn't stop laughing. The thought of Char as a prostitute was too unbelievable.

All of us were too caught up in Char's story to notice Cybill sat idle in a steady stream of traffic. Char brought it to our attention, "Why don't you all stop laughing and tell me why we aren't moving?" she shouted over the din.

With Char's question, we became aware of drivers blaring their horns, cars whipping around Cybill, and people giving us the finger. Our eyes traveled to the front of the bus where Ted lay with his arms and head resting on the steering wheel.

"Mr. Ewald?" Marion quickly moved to his side. "This is no place for a nap. You need to wake up!"

"Oh great, another prank," announced Brother Thomas, crossing his arms.

Marion sent Thomas a withering glance, but didn't argue with his statement. After receiving no response from Ted, Marion placed her lips inches from his ear. "Ted!" she yelled. "You had better not be joking around. It's dangerous to sit in the middle of a freeway. You need to wake up!"

Everything happened at once. As Marion crouched beside Ted, she held onto the steering wheel for balance, which caused the wheel to turn toward her. This caused Ted to slide off the steering wheel. With a shriek, Marion lifted her hands to stop him from falling on her, but his weight proved too heavy. Marion ended up in the aisle, pinned to the floor by Ted's body. Her shriek turned into a full-throttle scream.

When Ted's foot left the brake, Cybill rolled into traffic with no one at the wheel. Everyone began screaming at once.

"Guys, we're moving!"

"We know!"

"Someone get him off me!"

"We gonna die!"

"Get him off me!"

Cybill didn't roll too far before clipping a Porsche Boxster, which rammed a Dodge Neon, which took out part of the guardrail.

"We've stopped," said Lester.

"Does anybody hear me? Hello! I'm stuck under Ted!" Marion was becoming hysterical.

Brother Thomas and Lester were closest. With help from Billy who rushed to the front, they extracted Marion from beneath a motionless Ted. She looked ready to puke.

Billy put his fingers on Ted's neck. "No pulse. Does anyone know CPR?" Marion did, of course, but she was in no state to help.

Tansy screamed, "For God sake, someone please help him."

At Tansy's cry, Thomas and Billy turned Ted over. His face held the peacefulness of death. He wore a smile that hinted at mischief. I wondered what joke he would play on St. Peter, and whether or not he would get away with it.

"Too late," said Eric.

"No!" Tansy screamed again and began to cry. "Please, please someone help him." Her face was white under her layers of makeup. Billy moved to his wife's side and tried to comfort her.

I thought Tansy's reaction was a little over the top considering Ted has only been our driver for a day. Then I immediately felt bad for not feeling worse about his death.

Brother Thomas lifted his hands to the sky. "May Elvis have mercy on his soul!"

"I don't believe this," cried Char. "What kind of a cursed tour is this anyway? Two drivers go nuts and now this one's dead!"

"What, he dead?" asked Sachi.

"Yes, he's dead," shouted Vince. And in case she was having trouble hearing, he put his hands to his neck, stuck his tongue out and made gagging noises.

"Please," Billy begged, holding his wife, "have some respect."

"I'm trying to help them understand."

"I think they get it."

"We'll need an ambulance for the body," Eric announced. "And we should probably call the police."

"They're already here," announced Char, folding her hands on top of her purse, looking reading to beat them down if they tried anything funny with her. The cruiser pulled beside us, lights flashing. A policeman in Ray-Bans knocked on the bus door. I looked around and noted the uncertain looks on everyone's faces. The cop knocked again and Lester responded, stepping over Ted to reach the handle. The door hissed open and the policeman climbed aboard.

Stella groaned, and I realized why. The policeman was Elvis.

"Not you! Get out of here!" I yelled.

This Elvis was different. He had his cop face on, and when he turned in my direction, I was looking straight into the face of GI Tulsa McLean.

Stella jabbed me with her elbow and smiled at the officer, "She's not feeling well."

"It looks like you've been in a major accident…" He trailed off as he caught sight of Ted. His face grew even more suspicious, and his hand drifted to the revolver strapped to his hip. "What's going on here?"

Marion burst into tears. "Ted is dead!" she wailed, flinging herself into the cop's arms.

Officer Elvis wrapped one capable arm around her and pulled off his glasses with his free hand. His baby-blues eyed everyone before landing on me. "Would someone please tell me what happened?"

Since he was staring at me, I answered. "He died."

"I can see that, ma'am. Mind telling me how?"

"Don't know. He just died."

"When?"

"Don't know."

"You don't know? The driver of your bus just up and dies and you don't know when or how?" He paused and I felt guilty even though I had nothing to do with Ted's death. At least, I hope not. At this point I can't be certain of anything. I'm talking to Elvis for Christ's sake. "I find that hard to believe, ma'am, so I'm going to ask you one more time and you'd better be completely honest with me because if you're hiding anything we'll find out. How did he die?"

"I didn't do it. Why's everyone looking at me?" I was hardly the most likely suspect in this cast. But the combined effect of a dead body and the presence of a cop left everyone a little bewildered, me included, and if the cop asked me my bra size I would probably tell him and volunteer my pants size, too.

In the end, the person who came to my defense was Char. I was never so grateful for her brassiness.

"You leave her alone, you hear? We don't know how he died and that's that. Let the coroner decide. We're innocent, and if you try to hold us back with a hundred questions we can't answer, you'll have one hellcat on your heels. My son—"

"Calm down, ma'am," Officer Presley interrupted. "I'm just trying to understand—"

"Oh, don't you tell me to calm down. My son—"

The second person to recover was Mary. "We were listening to a story," she said, glancing at Char. "We didn't notice the bus had stopped moving."

"No one on the bus knew Ted croaked until he fell on Marion," continued Char.

Loud, angry voices drew my attention out the window. A second cop, presumably Elvis's partner, was having a hard time calming the owner of the Porsche. The cop finally turned and walked toward Cybill with the angry driver still yelling.

"Hey, Sullivan!" called the second cop from Cybill's first step. "Everything all right?"

"Better radio for an ambulance, Jack. We've got a body."

The partner stepped inside to check it out.

"It's probably heart failure," said Elvis. "Just call it in."

Fifteen minutes later flashing lights surrounded the bus. "Don't you just love a man in uniform," I murmured to Stella.

"Take it easy, Jess. This one will arrest you if you rip off his shirt."

"Ladies and gentlemen, we need to speak with each of you, but we can do that at a hotel instead of the middle of the freeway. Amazingly, your bus didn't suffer any major damage in the collision. Just a couple of dings in the front fender. She's a tough old bird."

"Yes," Marion blubbered. She had been crying the whole time. "Cybill is a good bus. Yes, a good bus for us."

Officer Elvis stared at Marion before clearing his throat, "Okay then. The bus should make it into town. Phillipsburg is only another thirteen miles. Once you get to your hotel, you'll meet Detective O'Mally, who—"

My stomach did a somersault. "You're not coming with us?" I asked. *Oh no you don't,* I thought. *You're not getting away until I get some answers.*

"I'm sorry, but I have to return to the station to—"

I was thinking frantically. "I, well, we would feel better if you were the one we talked to." I tried my best to play the damsel in distress, hoping to appeal to his manly ego.

"Yes, you've been with us from the beginning," said Tansy with a display of unexpected support. Several of the members nodded.

"I'll see what I can do, but it's really O'Mally's ballgame from here on out."

#

Officer Linda arrived and drove us the thirteen miles into town where we checked into a Marriott, one of those veritable Taj Mahals of a hotel, the kind with working toilets and hot water. I could hardly wait to see my room. Stella and I let out a sigh of bliss at the sight of the two queen beds, one for each of us.

"Stella! I need help! We're supposed to meet downstairs in five minutes and I look like crap. Elvis can't see me like this! Help me pick out an outfit." I upended my suitcase onto the bed.

"What about this?" Stella lifted up a blue shirt with palm trees.

"Are you insane? I can't see him looking like a tacky tourist. Why did you pack that shirt for me anyway? I don't even wear it at home."

"Ursula said to blend. To become one with the Elvis fans. And speaking of that, what do you think? Are we going to include today's adventures in our article?"

I seized shirts, held them up, cast them down again. "Yes, it'll be the best part. We're putting it all in. Truth in journalism. Isn't that our motto?"

"But we told Marion we'd smooth over the rough edges. She's sure to read what we write."

I snorted. "After it's published. Besides, any more days like today and she'll end up in an institution. She'll never know."

Stella abruptly stopped digging through clothes to glare at me. "You are a cold hearted wench."

I rolled my eyes.

"Here." She held up my light blue sundress.

I eyed it. "Do you think it's too obvious?"

"No. It's just what you need to look fragile and heart-broken."

"Perfect." I stripped out of my grungy outfit and slid on the dress. I looked in the mirror. "Just the right amount of cleavage," I told my reflection. Stella spritzed me with some perfume and gave instructions, while I styled my hair with a wide brush.

She said, "Signal me if you get Elvis to talk. I want to be close enough to record the conversation."

"Hell, no!"

Stella eyed me as she exchanged her t-shirt for a peasant's blouse. "We need documentation. This may be the only time we have with Elvis."

"Don't worry. I'll get him to talk" I wanted a wind-blown look, and shook out my hair.

"You look alluring. Now let's go allure."

I slipped the tape recorder into my purse and we made our way to the conference room. Several pizzas were stacked on one table along with canned soda and paper plates. We helped ourselves to the impromptu meal and settled in among our fellow passengers.

Facing us was the handsome doppelganger and an older, more weathered cop who I figured for the detective. The two waited in silence for the rest of the tour to trickle in. I tried to look alluring as I inhaled pizza. I made eyes at Elvis, disguised as Officer R. Sullivan. He tried to act as if he was more interested in watching the door than me, but I perceived this was a ruse to throw off his boss.

"This is Detective O'Mally," Elvis announced after everyone arrived. "He's here to help."

"Thank you, Sullivan." In appearances Detective O'Mally held his own against Elvis. He was older, true. Say late forties, early fifties. But his square jaw line, tan skin and piercing hazel eyes still held their sex appeal. I imagine his slender body was built from a strict regimen of running every morning at dawn and a diet of steaks and steamed vegetables. He did not eat any pizza.

"First of all," O'Mally began, "I just wanted to let everyone know this is just an informal meeting. We're not here to charge anyone with a crime. It appears to be a natural death. We would just like to know a little about what was happening prior to your noticing your driver was dead."

Billy, our self-appointed spokesman, set down his paper plate and stepped forward. "We were listening to a story, officer. So we didn't notice the bus wasn't moving or that Ted was in trouble. When we became aware of the situation, at first we thought it was one of Ted's pranks. Then we thought maybe he'd fallen asleep at the wheel or something. Marion went to wake him and that's when he fell out of his seat and landed on top of her. We pulled Marion out from underneath and turned Ted over. That's when we realized Ted was no longer with us." Billy put his hand on Tansy's shoulder while she sniffed and picked at her pizza.

The detective eyed all of us. "Is this what happened?" Feeling inexplicably guilty, we nodded. "Well, your story does answer a couple of questions. I'm sure this has been a rough day. How long was he your bus driver?"

"Just for today, Detective. He replaced Helix after he ran into the cornfield," offered Maggie.

"Your original driver abandoned you? In a cornfield?" Both Detective O'Mally and Officer Sullivan found this interesting.

"Oh, no, Helix wasn't our original driver," corrected Maggie. "He replaced Gus, who left us to pursue his destiny."

The two cops looked as though they were going to start asking many, many questions but wondered if the paperwork was worth the time. O'Mally lifted his eyebrows and flipped through a battered notebook.

"Did anyone know how old Ted was?"

"Mid-fifties," guessed Eric.

"Try seventy-three," O'Mally said. "Look. Why don't you all try to get a good night's sleep. We'll be in contact tomorrow morning."

"We going to continue tour?" asked Midori.

"We'll let you know tomorrow," said O'Mally. The group grumbled and got up to leave.

Stella reached into my purse and switched on the recorder. Then she gently shoved me in the direction of Elvis. "Get him talking, but don't come on too strong. I'll leave you two alone so he doesn't feel cornered."

I took a few deep breaths and approached Elvis. "Uh, excuse me, officer? What's going to happen to Ted?" I surprised myself with that almost intelligent question.

"Well, we're trying to locate his family. His body will be released once the autopsy is completed." Elvis tucked his notepad under his arm.

"Autopsy? But we told you everything."

He smiled at me. "It's a formality. For the death certificate. We need to know if he was sick or if he was just old."

"Oh." I blushed. "I guess I'm feeling guilty for not noticing sooner that Ted was in trouble. Maybe we could have helped him."

Officer Presley put his hand on my arm and I almost swooned. His look turned philosophical. "It was his time."

"Officer?" I murmured, staring into his dreamy blue eyes.

"Yes?"

"What does the 'R' stand for?"

He blinked and dropped his hand from my arm. "What?"

"The 'R' on your badge." I pointed to the letter.

"Red."

#

"Red? That's it? That's all you got?" Stella asked when I returned to our room.

"No, that's not all." I quickly crossed the room in my excitement to share what I'd discovered, but the sight of Stella's bed made me stop short. She sat cross-legged in the center of the bed surrounded by candy bar wrappings, mini bags of chips and a pile of crumpled papers. For pajamas, she wore men's boxers with a white tank top. She had tied one of her fashion scarves around her head like a bandana.

"Stella," I said as I approached more slowly. "What are you doing?"

"I'm writing!" she announced and threw her hands up in victory.

"Writing? Good. What are you writing, our story?"

"Uh, no."

"A side piece to our story?"

"Nope." She wouldn't look at me.

"Then what?" I snatched her journal out of her hands. I could see she'd torn out several pages, failed masterpieces I assume. On the page labeled 'Journal Entry #13' was a sketch of what looked like her and Don on a unicorn. The Stella caricature's boobs were busting out of her eighteenth century dress, and the Don caricature's white shirt was torn to reveal an exaggerated six-pack. Stella's drawing was the cover of some cheap romance novel. I didn't even say anything. I just gave it back and looked at her.

"You like it?" she laughed.

"No." I did not. "And what's all of this?" I indicated the junk around her.

"Inspiration. Food for the soul. A cure for writer's block."

"This isn't a cure for anything. It's a disease."

"No, it's wonderful. Here have a Twix." She handed me one and ate the other, then ate mine when I didn't take it. "I emptied like twenty dollars in the vending machine at the end of the hall," she said with food in her mouth. "I got one of everything and two of my favorites. Here look." She thrust a bag of half eaten Funyuns in my face. "I haven't had these in years. I don't even know what they are made of, probably not even a food source but something concocted in a lab, but they taste so good." She finished the Funyuns by stuffing them all in her mouth.

"Stella, listen to me." I sat on the bed and took her hands in mine. "You don't need junk food to cure writer's block."

"Yes I do."

"No you don't. You're a good writer. The Incident had nothing to do with your writing. You took someone at their word when you should have secured another source. That's it. It happens in journalism. Lesson learned. It doesn't change the fact you're a good writer." I picked up her journal again. "And you don't need Don to save you." I tore out Entry #13 and threw it away.

"No," Stella protested. "I don't want him to save me. I want him to protect me, to hold me." She pulled the comforter up to her chin and fell back against the pillows, sending candy wrappings everywhere. "I'm a fragile bird."

"No, you're a pig," I said and started picking up the trash.

"A fragile pig then."

"Stella, stop it." I yanked the comforter off her face. "You're acting crazy, now just stop it."

"I'm crazy. You just spent an hour interviewing Elvis."

"That's right!" I grabbed my purse and started digging for the recorder. "Stella, you're not going to believe this."

"Did he confess to being Ursula's mole?" She jumped out of her bed to sit beside me on mine.

"No, I've discarded that theory. There's no way one person could be a busboy, a farmer, a bartender and a state trooper. But something cop Elvis said made sense to me." I put the recorder between us. "Stel, I think I know what's going on, but I want you to listen to see if you come up with the same thing." I clicked on the recorder and held it up to our ears.

First we heard Stella say, "Get him talking, but don't come on too strong. I'll leave you two alone so he doesn't feel cornered." Then sounds of my footsteps as I walk up to him. Someone coughing. Then we heard Char say something about keeping the leftover pizza. Someone laughing. We heard Billy ask Detective O'Mally about Ted's funeral arrangements. An indiscernible noise…

We kept listening, but we never heard me ask any questions. And we never heard Elvis answer. I put the recorder on the bed. We both stood up and stared at it like it was possessed while it continued to play background noise.

"I don't get it," I said at last.

"Why aren't you talking?" Stella asked.

"I was. I did. I talked to Elvis for an hour."

"Why can't we hear it? Was the recorder too muffled in your purse to pick up your voices?"

"No, it picked up every other noise. You can hear people talking from across the room. You can hear chairs squeaking for Christ's sake. You just can't hear my conversation with Elvis."

"Why not?"

"I don't know!" I shouted. My heart was pounding. I started pacing the room. This didn't make any sense. My interview with Elvis was gone. My mind was racing, but coming to no reasonable explanations. It kept circling around one fact. "Stella, I think we're dealing with some sort of mystical force. Think about it. Everywhere we go, Elvis magically appears!"

Chapter 19: Stella

"Jess, it's not going to magically appear!" I called after my friend-for-life as she continued to march down the sidewalk. We were trying to find Dennys. We turned left out of the hotel when I know we should have gone right. We were supposed to meet the rest of Sun Tours at ten, and now we're-

"Late by twenty minutes," Marion snapped when we finally arrived.

Jess shrugged her shoulders and offered a lame, "We turned left."

Marion's beady eyes focused on me. I said nothing. *Don't make me show you my blue ass,* I threatened silently. After a long stare-down, Marion allowed us to take our places at breakfast. We slipped into a booth opposite Matt and Marcus.

"What'll ya have?" a waitress asked.

I grunted again. Jess interpreted, "She'll have coffee and a cinnamon muffin. I'll have coffee and a strawberry waffle. Thanks."

Jess and I weren't the only latecomers. Lester, Char, Ella and Vince were still missing. The honeymooners arrived. Ella ignored a stone-faced Vince. Lester made a spectacular entrance. Decked in a black leather jacket halfway unbuttoned with no undershirt, Lester strutted into the restaurant, his leather pants squeaking with every stride.

When Char arrived, disgusted because she turned left and got lost as well, Marion just shook her head and began her spiel. "Well, once again our new driver will be joining us shortly." She started to pass out fresh copies of the itinerary.

"Save it. I want my money back!" barked Char. Her morning detour did nothing for her usual foul mood. "This tour is a joke."

Marion pointed out, "Char, you didn't pay anything. You won this trip."

"That's not the point."

"What exactly is the point, Char?" interrupted Brother T. "I mean, do you love Elvis or not, you know? Isn't this inconvenience just a small price to pay to see the homeland of the King? Won't all this be a distant memory when we stand in awe at his palace? Tell me the truth, my sister, are you just a fair-weather follower or are you a true believer?"

Char rolled her eyes and ordered eggs, bacon, sausage, short stack, juice and muffin from the impatient waitress.

"Thank you, Thomas, for reminding us of our purpose and where our priorities should be. We should be grateful for this opportunity." Marion was back in full swing. "Okay, then, I've revised the itinerary again. I'll just take a few minutes to point out some of the major changes while we wait for our new driver."

The words 'new driver' sent a shudder of horror through the group as we envisioned what kind of freak would appear. Knowing Marion would rattle on for hours, I settled in. I stared out the window and plotted how I would get Don to talk to me. I openly stared at him. He was sitting two booths over with Lenny. Marion had Lester's full attention, but Don's eyes were following his fork. He plunged it into a glob of syrup, picked it up a few inched and let the molasses dribbled back onto his plate.

The sun warmed my face through the glass. Slowly the room grew dark. I don't know how long I slept before the door to Dennys opened and the ringing bells woke me. A man entered looking like a throwback from *Shane*. He sauntered to the counter, and the host pointed him in our direction. He approached Marion slowly. When she turned around, he removed his hat and bowed. Several liver spots showed through a comb-over of red fuzz. He had pasty white skin and albino blue eyes.

"Oh," Marion said as she blushed. "Well, you must be Mr. Neeley."

"Yes, ma'am," he said with another graceful bow. "Stanley Norman Neely at your service." In classic cowboy etiquette, Stan removed a rose from his right shirt pocket and handed it to Marion.

"Oh, how nice," Marion gushed. "Everyone, this is Mr. Stanley Norman Neeley, our new driver."

"You may call me Stan."

"Oh, okay Stan," Marion giggled.

We could tell by her flirtations Marion approved of Stan. His gentleman's charm had made her a quick win, but the rest of us would be a battle. As a collective, we stared at Stan hoping our laser vision would illuminate any evidence of ailment or lunacy. No way were we going to be trapped on that infernal bus again. You could fool us once or twice or, in this case, three times, but never again.

"Have you ever been convicted of a felony?" Char asked.

"Look who's talking," whispered Luc.

"No, ma'am. I've never been in trouble with the law," Stan answered.

"How old are you?" asked Eric.

"Fifty-three, sir."

"Can you prove that with a birth certificate?" pressed Eric.

Marion intervened, "Eric, I hardly think that's necessary."

"It is."

"It's okay," Stan assured Marion with a wink. "I bring a copy of my birth certificate and Social Security card everywhere I go."

"You do?" asked Maggie. "Why?"

"Just in case I need to skip the country," Stan said then laughed at his joke. We were not laughing.

"Why would you need to skip the country?" Don asked, and eased his cell phone out of his pocket.

"I'm only kidding, sir. Like I said, I've never had any trouble with the law."

"Did you serve in any wars, especially Vietnam?" asked Vince.

"Well, Vietnam was never officially declared a war, you know."

"Of course, I know that," Vince snapped, angered at being corrected in front of everyone. "Just answer the question."

"No. I did not."

"How is your health?"

"Fine."

"Define fine."

"Fit as a fiddle, no problems."

"How is your mental health? Any depression, mood swings, homicidal tendencies?"

"Absolutely not."

We went on and on, sautéing him for another ten minutes. At last, we consented that he was acceptable, as if we had any other option. Even then, we loaded the bus with trepidation.

#

Our first and only attraction of the day would be Martha's Memorable Mansion of Majestic Music, located in Aurora, Missouri, a small town to the west of Springfield. Twenty minutes into the trip, I concluded Stan was all right, liver spots and all. Hell, we couldn't hold that against him. It's not like he has a blue ass.

"Why you smiling, dear?" asked Sachi.

She was leaning over the back of the seat, so when I looked up, we almost bumped noses. "Oh, nothing," I replied. "Just a funny thought that went through my head."

"Oh," she said. "I have funny memory. You want to hear?"

Before I could respond, the Japanese trio was running down memory lane in both Japanese and English. I listened politely not minding the fact I didn't understand most of what they were saying. Jess scribbled frantically in her journal, her new Elvis theory I'm assuming after last night's mystery with the recorder.

"We have so many good times," said Sachi. "We even have a secret call."

"A secret call?" asked Jess, finally closing her notebook and blinking as if awakening.

"Yes, and we tell you two because you like us—sisters. But you no tell anyone," said Midori.

"Okay," we answered.

"Promise?"

"Promise."

"Okay." They huddled closer and we could smell their medicine breath. "Whenever you in trouble," said Harulu, "You give this call…"

Sachi took over and whispered, "Cawcaw, cawcaw." The noise was something like a crow in heat.

"It our signal all these years," explained Midori.

"Cawcaw, cawcaw. Just like that," said Sachi.

"Much louder though if you in trouble," added Harulu. "But quiet now because it secret."

"Cawcaw, cawcaw," called Midori. "You try."

Jess and I looked at each other, shrugged, and whispered the sacred call. "Cawcaw, cawcaw."

"No lower," Sachi admonished.

"Yes, with more punch," added Harulu.

"Cawcaw, cawcaw," we tried again.

"That it," all three said at once.

"Now remember, when you in trouble—"

"What are you doing?" Tansy popped her head into our group, interrupting Harulu.

"Nothing, nothing, nothing," mumbled the trio.

"Oh. Well, we need to decide on a song for the contest." After Lester's performance at Harvey's Hangout which ended the bar brawl, the members of Sun Tours decided to have an Elvis karaoke contest, girls against guys. Marion even scheduled it on her itinerary for tonight when we end the day in Springfield.

The occupants of the bus had shifted seats, aligning the girls at the back and the guys at the front with the exception of Marion who would never relinquish her director's chair. Besides she was enjoying Stan's company.

"We need to come up with something awesome," said Tansy.

"Right," added Mary. "I was thinking of one of Elvis's faster songs like, 'That's All Right' or 'Hound Dog.'"

"What about 'Good Rockin' Tonight'?" asked Maggie. "It's always been one of my favorites."

"We should sing 'Don't Be Cruel,'" suggested Char.

No one said anything. Nobody was up for an argument with a hurricane. In fact, we were nodding our heads in agreement. Her tyrannical hold of the group pissed me off, but I didn't have the energy to fight her. I was saving myself for Don.

For the next two hours we talked of nothing else but the contest. Maggie had some great ideas for the choreography. She wanted to give everyone a chance to use their own talents while maintaining a unified dance. Tansy and Char volunteered to be in charge of the costuming. Ella occasionally helped Vince with his shows, so she volunteered to set up the lighting, and Sister Mary said she would help Ella. Midori, Sachi, and Harulu said they wanted to be in charge of hair and makeup. We pretended not to hear them; we'd find something for them to do later. Jessica and I jumped on the costuming crew.

Before we knew it, we arrived at Martha's Mansion of Memorable Majestic Music. Aspens lined the lane, sheltering us under a sun-streaked canopy of leaves. The end of the drive circled a pond. We stopped at the elaborate entrance, and as we disembarked, a butler approached the bus and greeted each of us.

When we entered the mansion, we stood in the foyer frozen in sheer amazement. Everywhere we looked we saw Elvis looking back at us. Gemstones and mirrors hung in the spaces that weren't covered with a poster, picture, pin or costume. An enormous chandelier caught the gemstones and mirrors, lighting up the room in a brilliant display of color. Elvis's gospel songs played softly from some hidden sound system.

"My Elvis," breathed Thomas, tears shown in his eyes. "We have found Heaven!"

"Oh, fun!" said Harulu.

Slowly we became aware of a presence in the room other than the butler. We adjusted our eyes to the glare of the lights and saw a stunning woman dressed in a white ball gown filigreed with gemstones. She floated to our group and introduced herself as Martha.

"No, surely you are an angel," Brother T gasped. I imagine he had searched for this place all his life.

Martha smiled. Even her teeth sparkled. Up close, we could tell she was an older woman, but aged no less gracefully than Jackie Onassis or Liz Taylor. Her fading blonde hair fell in giant curls down her back. She was speaking and it was like music from a harp.

Until she hit a wrong note.

She was explaining the history of the mansion when it happened. "The mansion was built by the Woodfords in the early 1800s. The exact date of completion is unrecorded. In 1933, the family lost po-po-po-po-possession of the property during the De-De-De-De..."

"Depression?" Marion timidly offered.

"Yes, Depression. Thanks," the angel answered. She struggled to continue, "The land was turned over to the state where it remained for for-for-for-fort..."

"Forty?" Sister Mary tried.

"Forty-four years," Martha continued. "In 1977, my father, a ba-ba-ba-ba . . ."

"Banker?" Bossman jumped in. The oracle turned into a vocabulary game.

"Banker from New York, bought the land for a winter home. Or so mom and I thought. The first night we moved in, da-da-da-da—"

"Dumbo!" exclaimed Midori, happy to contribute.

"My father shot himself in the den. Then, before I grasped what happened, my mother followed suit." Martha paused. "I never knew wh-wh-wh-wh—"

"Why," gasped Tansy.

"Yes."

It was tragic. All of it; yet, her fragile imperfection made her more perfect. We leaned forward encouraging her to continue if she could.

"For days, no, weeks after I just lay in bed wondering what to do. Then one night . . ." she trailed off lost in the memory, and we all wondered why she was telling us any of this.

"What happened?" Marion asked.

"He came to me," she answered with one of her gemstone smiles.

"Who?" asked Maggie.

"Your father?" Lester asked.

"Elvis."

The group sighed. Of course. Jess and I rolled our eyes.

"It was August 20, 1977. I didn't even know he was d-d-d-d—"

"Dead," I said and Jess gave me a warning elbow in the ribs.

"Dead. I had been so wrapped up in my own grief that I never noticed the passing of the King."

"That's if you believe in that publicity stunt," corrected Marion.

"Of course, Marion, of course," Brother T soothed. "None of us really believe he's dead in that all encompassing sense of the word. Please go on, Martha."

"Elvis walked up to my bedside and brushed my tears from my face. Then he kissed my lips. Oh, it was so tender and sweet. I knew he understood my pain, having lost his own mother. Then we made l-l-l—"

"Love," Maggie said and everyone giggled like high school idiots.

"Yes, made love all night long. In the morning he told me I was to build a shrine to his memory. That way he would never leave me." She paused before admitting, "I haven't always stuttered. It happened after Elvis's v-v-v-vis-vis-."

"Yes, of course! Oh, you are an angel!" Thomas said as he leapt toward her and made to kiss her cheek. Then reconsidered, grabbed her hand and slobbered all over it.

Martha turned, and with Thomas on her arm, she floated into the other rooms. We followed like a herd of sheep. As we passed from room to room, I noticed Mary seemed jealous of Martha. Mary was less radiant and more withdrawn than usual. Brother T had spent most of the trip trying to convert our formidable nun. Mary had feigned disgust, but now that Thomas' attention was on someone else, she seemed put out. Or else she was jealous of Martha's all-night lovemaking with the King.

Elvis's image appeared on coffee tables, end tables, dining tables, lamps, beds and bathtubs. I became dizzy with Elvis heads swirling in all directions. I ducked into what I thought was a closet. I discovered it was Martha's bedroom when she brought the entire tour into the tiny space.

I pointed to the framed pictures on her bedside table and asked, "Are those your favorite pictures of the King?"

"No," Martha answered, confused. "That's Parker, the neighborhood boy who cuts the grass and brings my groceries. He is like a son to me."

Everyone stared at me like I was stupid. I glanced at Jess and she nodded.

I left the mansion, needing to catch my breath and steady my head. I walked through the garden and sat on a bench by the pond. Soon Jess joined me. We sat in silence for awhile before I wondered aloud, "Do you think we keep seeing Elvis because we want to see him, we're looking for him in a sense?"

"Everyone on this tour is looking for him, and they can't see him when he's right before their eyes."

"Not really. They're not looking because they already found him."

"What?" Jess sounded annoyed. I was being too philosophical for her comfort.

"They're Elvis fans already," I explained. "They've already decided which attribute of Elvis—his life, career and death—earns their undying devotion. Until this trip, you and I really didn't care for Elvis."

"Don't say that too loud," Jess warned. We looked at the Mansion to check on our fellow tourists. The bus was parked on the opposite side, and through a tangle of yellow roses, I saw Don get on.

"Well, that's kind of like my new theory," Jess began, but I was already off the bench.

"Okay, good. Love to hear it, but I got to go," I shouted over my shoulder.

"Stel!" Jess yelled after me, but I was on a mission.

I pushed through the garden, faster and faster, happening upon Elliot and pushing past him, too, until I stood within the circle of exhaust fumes and the beast's heavy musk: hot metal and ancient upholstery. I took a deep breath to gather my courage, then climbed the stairs inside. Don was sitting in the very last seat in the back of the bus. I almost chickened out at seat fourteen, where Jessica's notebook still lay open, but kept going.

"Is anyone sitting here?" I asked, knowing the answer. He always sat alone.

"No," he said, looking at his hands folded in his lap.

"I'm sorry about calling you a perverted old fart the other night at Bingo," I said in a rush. "I thought you were someone else."

"That's okay, happens to me a lot."

"Girls call you a perverted old fart a lot?"

"No," he laughed. "They think I'm someone else." His face darkened.

Okay, I have no idea how to respond to that, I thought. I sat down in the seat next to him, although it felt too close and very awkward now that neither of us was talking.

"What did you think of Martha's Mansion?" I asked, changing to a lighter subject.

"Impressive," Don answered, looking out the window. "Although . . ."

"Although what?" I asked.

"Although, I don't see what the fuss is all about," he said, looking out the window.

My heart leapt! "Me either," I gasped. If only he'd look at me.

"I mean, it's not like he's that good looking. There are plenty of better looking guys out there."

"Oh, really?" I teased. "Like who?"

He turned and stared into my eyes.

"Like me."

The blast hit me with a gale-like force. His breath stunk like a sewage treatment plant. The foulness took my breath away and caused my eyes to water. I coughed, trying to jump-start my lungs, but the stink surrounded me. I turned to the side only to inhale the smell of toilet and exhaust. There was no escape.

"I mean, I'm hot. I know that. Women throw themselves at me, but I would never sleep with a woman postmortem and make her erect a shrine to me."

I felt like he was sitting on my face and every word was an egg fart. What did he eat for breakfast? Curdling in the stench were his words themselves, arrogant, conceited words. In the front of the bus were footsteps. I looked up and caught a thumbs-up sign from Jess. I tried to think of ideas to leave.

"Other people are getting on the bus; maybe I should find my seat again," I said. "I think Jess is waiting to talk about our article now." I started to rise, but he pulled me back onto the seat.

"I know you better than you think I do."

"What is that supposed to mean?" I asked aloud, and thought *now that's just creepy*. Again I started to rise, and again he grabbed my hand and pulled me onto the seat.

Don leaned close and for one terrifying moment, I thought he was going to kiss me. Knowing sudden death would probably result, I tried to pull away, but he slipped his arm behind my back.

"No wait," he whispered and his maggoty garbage can breath washed over me. "Let me start over."

Oh, Cupid, you are a vindictive bastard! This was my last thought before everything went black.

Chapter 20: Jessica

Everything was clear.

We would write a Pulitzer Prize winning travel article. I would find and expose the fake Elvi populating the Midwest. Stella would get her man.

I watched as she turned her face away from Don. Probably trying to be coy. I've tried to school her in the fine art of flirtation. It looks like my lessons are taking hold. I smiled and turned my attention to the front of the bus where the college boys were getting on.

"Yo, what's up?" asked Matt, dropping into the seat beside me.

"Nothing," I answered.

Marcus and Luc took up flanking positions. This was obviously a planned attack. I knew by the way they just stared at me that they wanted my attention, probably to share their Elvis story. I sighed a bit irritated and let the silence become uncomfortable, feeling no desire to break it. I really wanted to jot down my impressions of Martha's Mansion.

"So what did you think of the Mansion?" I asked, finally giving in.

"Cool," said Luc.

Marcus echoed, "Yeah, man, way cool." I'm sure he pretty much goes along with whatever Matt and Luc suggest. He held himself like he was uncomfortable in his own skin. His Scandinavian heritage made his cheeks perpetually red, which was adorable really.

"Martha was hot," said Matt, but clarified after a pause, "you know, for an older lady." The other two laughed in agreement. Then worried he offended me, Matt added, "So are you of course."

"Of course," I said. Easy big fella.

"And you're not that old." Mat was really flustered now. "I didn't mean-"

"I'm old enough," I said, meaning too old for you. But to be honest, I was a bit flattered, if amused, by Matt's fumbled flirtations. He was a good looking kid. He tried really hard to pull off the 'I-don't-care' attitude and look of a California surfer with his torn Bermuda shorts and retro 'A-team' t-shirt. Mr. T was plastered tightly to Matt's chest. *Heroes for hire*, I thought and smiled. I loved that show.

"Anyways, the Mansion was like trippin,'" continued Matt, getting back to the subject.

"Trippin," I echoed and wrote in my journal while saying aloud, "Martha's Mansion of Memorable Music was totally trippin' according to our young college students."

"You know, we're not just dumb college students," said Matt. "We know more about Elvis than probably everyone on this tour except Marion."

Knowing I'd wounded his ego and wanting to make it up to him, I said, "I know. In fact, your point of view might put an interesting angle on our article." And I surprised myself by actually meaning it.

My comment was the invitation they were waiting for. At once they started telling me about Elvis, and why he's still the King.

"We go to the University of Minnesota in Minneapolis," said Matt, taking the lead as usual. "That's where we met. The one thing we have in common is Elvis—"

"Yeah, that guy knew his shit!" Marcus interjected.

We had to pause the interview while Cybill warmed up, lifted off and shot down the road.

"We host a radio show dedicated to Elvis: the man and the music," Matt continued and leaned across the aisle. "We also run an Elvis web site. This is our first time to Elvis

Week. We are writing a daily blog about the trip and posting them to our site. We have quite a following actually."

"Hey, do you want to use some of our blogs for your article?" offered Marcus.

"Uh, sure maybe," I said. "So, you host an Elvis website? Tell me more about that."

"The main focus of our site is to show Elvis is alive and well. He lives on in spirit, in the hearts of those who love him. You would be surprised by who visits our site. People from around the world, people who barely speak English, absolutely love Elvis! The man is a phenomenon second to none. And it's not just older people either. People my age and younger have heard and understood the magic of Elvis."

"That's what I don't get," I stopped writing to ask. "I mean, you guys weren't even alive when Elvis was a hit."

"Neither were you and you're a fan," said Marcus.

"Oh, right. But I mean…" I trailed off. For a moment, I forgot to be an Elvis fan.

"Elliot asked me the same question," Matt saved me. "Why would someone my age have such a profound respect for a man who died before I was even born. Why don't I listen to bands that shape and influence my generation? My answer is, Elvis did influence my generation. He challenged the image of rock n' roll, of dancing, of what it was to be cool."

"Elvis was an individual with a dream, and that is something everyone can identify with," said Luc who had been quiet up to this point. He was more tempered than his counterparts. His French accent and cool good looks made him the eye candy of the bunch.

"When people think about Elvis, they think about images," Luc continued. "There is the rebellious King of rock and roll, the womanizing movie star, and the older, heavier drug addict. People know he shook things up, but that it is all on the surface. What most people don't know is, he spent most of his life being very scared about the future, he had to beg to be heard, and he grew up in poverty. He was just a man with a dream that got so big; he had a hard time dealing with it." Luc put is hand over mine to stop my writing and make sure I heard his final point. "He was a man who did great things, yes, but underneath it all, he was just a man."

"I don't know what to say," I admitted. "You guys really do know Elvis."

Matt smiled, "Anyways, we just wanted to talk to you about the reason we are here in the first place - Elvis and his power to bring people together."

#

I was settling in for a nap when Stella flopped into the seat beside me. "Don't ask any questions, because I don't want to talk about it." She reached for a pillow and reclined her seat the half-inch it allowed.

"But it looked like things were going so well."

"I don't want to talk about it." She shut her eyes and pretended to sleep.

"But what happened?"

"Nothing. I don't want to talk about it. Can't you see I'm sleeping?"

I let her be. She'll tell me when she's ready. She probably embarrassed herself again. When I woke from my nap, the bus was five miles from Springfield. (It only took us two *days* to arrive.) On the up side, Marion booked a convention center for what was supposed to be our fourth night's lodgings. On the down side, the convention hall appeared to be vacant. A total of three vehicles sat in the acre of parking lot, including Cybill. Somewhat uneasy at the noticeable lack of patrons in the height of tourist season, we unloaded.

Large pillars supported an enormous canopy over the entrance. The double glass doors were open, admitting the cool breeze. A massive chandelier hung from the ceiling of the foyer and illuminated the curving three-story staircase, which was open to the lobby below. Signs directed guests to their rooms, three conference rooms and two banquet halls.

Another sign stated the gym was located next to the pool and sauna. Nice digs—a hotel built with old money.

A lone clerk stood behind the check-in desk, a mahogany museum piece that blended with the deep red carpet. Marion spoke with the clerk, who wore a charming smile and assured Marion everything was in order.

The clerk lifted her head higher and called to the group. "I'll be here at the desk tonight, so feel free to ring me if you have any problems. Your rooms are in the east wing. Go to the second floor and follow the signs. Also, Marion asked for the use of one of our convention rooms." Marion postponed the karaoke contest until tomorrow after Maggie begged for time to practice. The clerk continued, "I'll unlock the door to Swan Room, which is just off the lobby. You will have the use of it until one a.m. The kitchen is currently closed, due to some renovations. Any questions?"

I was anxious to explore. Maggie informed everyone the men would practice for the contest in the Swan at eight and the women at ten. Stella and I made our way up the impressive stairs and followed Billy and Tansy's lead down the hallway. The search for Room 288 led us past windows overlooking the pool, down several hallways and through a set of fire doors. My joy in a staying at a resort dimmed as I pondered its vacancy.

After reaching a second set of fire doors, I finally voiced my opinion. "Uh, does anybody else find it strange that, in a nearly deserted hotel, we are staying in the rooms farthest from the lobby?"

Tansy shrugged her shoulders. "The clerk did say they were renovating. Maybe they're still working on the closer rooms."

When we reached 288, we found a casual yet elegant room. It was a suite with an overstuffed sectional couch and a large TV. A writing desk faced the windows and another with computer hookups faced the wall by the door. A breakfast bar stood in the corner opposite the television. The bathroom had a Jacuzzi and a separate shower. Stella and I grinned as we fell onto the two queen sized beds found in a room adjacent to the lounging area.

Marion came by to make sure the room was satisfactory.

"Way to go, Marion," I said.

She was looking better since Stan joined the crew, as radiant and perky as the day we met her in the P-n-P parking lot. "Thank you. And did you enjoy your time at Martha's?"

We hesitated. "Oh, yes. It was quite a place."

"Isn't it? I look forward to it every year. Did you get lots of pictures?"

Shit, did we get pictures? "Um, Stel, you took pictures, didn't you?"

"You had the camera."

Shit.

"That's okay. I thought as much." Marion shrugged pleasantly. "It's overwhelming the first time, so I made sure to take lots, and so did Lester. Between the two of us, there should be some good shots."

"Thanks," I mumbled.

"Feel free to order take-out from any of the brochures on the desk. Just have them deliver to the front desk. The clerk will take care of the bill and will ring your room when it arrives."

We thanked her and she left. The door fell shut. "*Did you get pictures?*" Stella mimicked. "I didn't think so, because you girls are a couple of idiots."

"She has a point, Stel. We've become distracted."

Stel flipped through the menus on the desk, but she was staring right through them. "Okay. No more Don. No more re-appearing Elvis expose. That will have to wait until we go down in travel writing history. It's strictly work from here on out."

"No more Don? Really? That bad, huh. Want to—"

"No. What do you want to eat? I'm starving."

I let Stella's abrupt change of subject pass. A couple of beers would open her up. "How 'bout Chinese?" Her favorite—a slam dunk. The restaurant said there was a forty-five minute wait, and in the meantime, Stella and I set out to explore the cavernous hotel.

"Jess, do you notice anything odd about this place?" Stella asked as we made our way up a flight of stairs.

"You mean besides the fact we are the only people staying here"

"Yeah, makes you wonder..."

The same red carpet found in the lobby lined the floors of the hallways and also crept halfway up the walls in a bizarre form of wainscoting. At midpoint, there was a strip of dark red wood, which gave way to ornate wallpaper. Small brass lamps, attached to the wall between each room, cast an eerie haze over the hallway. The more we explored, the creepier it felt.

"This place is straight out of a horror film."

Stella nodded. Imaginations running wild, we cautiously made our way down to the end of the hallway. As we rounded the corner, we ran into Char and Lester.

"What are you doing here?" we all asked simultaneously.

Char recovered first. "We're checking out the Twilight Zone."

"So are we," Stella said. "Which way is the lobby?"

Lester and I laughed. Char smiled. When she wasn't scowling, she had pretty eyes. "The lobby is back the way you came," she said. "Two lefts, down the stairs and a right."

Shocked by her pleasantness, Stella and I were too dumbstruck to thank her. Lester saved us. "I'm hungry. Did you order take out yet?"

"Yes," I said. "Chinese."

Char smiled again. "We ordered pizza, but I'd kill for a good egg roll."

Unsure if her comment was innocent or a veiled threat, I gave her the benefit of the doubt anyway and invited them to join us. "I'm sure there's enough to go around," I said. Stella and I volunteered to pick up their pizza with our Chinese and meet them back at Char's room. By the time we made our way through the maze of hallways and found the lobby, our food was sitting on the counter.

The clerk looked up and smiled. "May I help you?"

"That's our Chinese."

"Is it? Your names, please."

"Jessica and Stella."

"Room number."

"Room 288."

The clerk checked her computer and the take-out ticket to verify the match. "Okay. The Chinese is for a Jessica Bernard and Stella Smith registered in room 288. You are correct. Well, then, here you go."

"Thanks," I said. "We also need to pick up the pizza for Char Larson in 276."

"I'm sorry. I can't let you do that."

"Why not?" I asked and gave Stel a look that said, 'What the hell?'

"Rules. How do I know you'll deliver the food to the proper recipient? What's to stop you from eating it yourself?"

I gave her my one-arched-eyebrow look. "Other than I'm not a fat cow?"

Sensing my growing hostility, Stella jumped in. "You can call Char and get her permission."

"Rules are rules! And the rules state each customer must pick up their own food."

"Well, how do you know I'm not Char? How do you know we are who we say we are?" I asked.

"Good point." She grabbed the Chinese out of my hand.

Stella looked at me, I looked at Stella. Then Stella snatched the Chinese back, and I lunged across the counter for the pizza. Recovering both, we high-tailed it from the lobby. "Crazy bitch!" I shouted over my shoulder.

Stella giggled as we began our journey back to our room. "Jess, sometimes I just can't believe what comes out of your mouth."

I smirked. "Stella, sometimes you have to let them know how things stand."

"Do you remember how to get back to our room?"

I raised my box. "Don't worry. If we get lost, we have provisions."

#

"Are you going to eat that?" Char pointed to my chow mien.

Removing the fork from my mouth, I looked at my half-eaten dinner. "It's all yours."

"Great. Thanks. Need to keep my energy up for dance practice tonight."

Shortly before ten, Stella, Char and I worked our way back through the labyrinth and joined a group of waiting women outside the Swan Room. The doors to the hall opened and the guys drifted out. Several looked sweaty and a little tired. Billy wasn't with the group of men, and come to think of it, I didn't see Tansy waiting with us either. I wondered how they managed to escape the contest.

Don walked towards Stella, but anticipating his move, she turned around to face me. Over her shoulder, I saw Don stop and stare at her back. After a moment, he walked away.

I shook my head in disgust. Stella caught my reaction. "Don't start with me, Jess. We have more important things to worry about than men." She stomped into the hall.

I had to hand it to Maggie; she knew her stuff. I was expecting little more than herding cats, but Maggie was a true professional. Wearing yoga pants and a matching tank top, she divided us into the task groups we established on the bus. She moved effortlessly from group to group giving instructions.

"Costumes, we need to think about what we can pull together from what everyone has in their suitcases. Lighting, more than likely the bar won't have a spotlight, so your job will be to find the best spot in the bar to use as our stage. Sound, you'll need to prep the DJ with our songs. I've selected three."

Maggie was in her element, and I couldn't help but be impressed. "Maggie, you're a real pro," I said. "Have you done this before?"

"In another life," she said. Her face darkened at the memory, but she shook it off and clapped her hands, "Okay, ladies, back to work."

Tansy arrived just before we started the dance routine. She said she fell asleep while watching TV, but I noticed she was flushed and out of breath.

"I'm sure she was sleeping," I said to Stella.

Stella laughed and punched me in the arm, "Grow up."

"Feet together, slide, hold one, two. Then back three, four. And repeat." Maggie talked us through the dance routine. "No, Char, slide to the right–you're right."

"Well shit," muttered Char.

The rest of us tried our best to keep up with the fast paced routine. Maggie gave each person a small part that contributed to the whole production. Under Maggie's drill sergeant like guidance, we learned our parts in under fifteen minutes. We had the ten-minute routine down in one hour. By midnight we felt confident we could really put on a show.

"Now remember," Maggie said, "the key to any show is you have to sell it." She clasped her hands in front of her chest as she spoke. Although she wasn't shouting, her voice was loud—she knew how to project. "If you are on stage having fun, then the audience will have fun. If you mess up, mess up with flair. No one will mind, and sometimes the mess-up is better than what you rehearsed." She clapped her hands. "Okay, ladies, that's all for now. Get some rest, and thanks for your hard work."

Stella and I stayed behind to help Maggie put the hall back in order. I bundled up the stereo's power cord and Stella tucked the vinyl CD case under her arm. We pushed the chairs and tables into place and flicked off the lights, while Maggie told the clerk we were finished. Together, tired, satisfied, we made our way back to our rooms.

I could already feel the effects of the exhausting practice in every inch of my tired body. Glancing at Stella and Maggie, I knew they felt the same. Yet we were all smiling.

When we reached the end of the first hallway, I glanced back over my shoulder. "Hey, guys, check it out." From where we stood, the chandelier seemed to be floating in the doorway at the end of the hall.

"Cool illusion," said Stella.

Maggie frowned. As we stood looking at the chandelier, I noticed the first set of hallway lights were dark. Then the second set of lights from the doorway went out.

I froze. I could feel Stella and Maggie's fear, as well. A shiver ran up my spine. As we continued to watch, the next set of lights clicked off. I suddenly found myself unable to breathe. By unanimous decision, the three of us did an about-face and resumed our journey down the hallway—this time, with the speed and focus of track stars. A fourth set of lights went dark. The lights were going out as fast as we passed them. A yawning hole of blackness opened up behind us.

"Faster!" I screamed.

The darkness was right on our heels and I could feel it tickling the back of my neck. We pressed forward, panting, slowing only to push open a fire door. Each time we slowed, I looked over my shoulder at the pursuing gloom.

From somewhere in the pulsating dark came a long, drawn-out wail. For two hallways it chased us. My Grandma Bernie would have called it the voice of a banshee, whose shriek foretold death. I could almost feel my highlights turning white as it streamed behind me.

Miraculously, we made it to our hallway without getting lost. The darkness overtook us when we slowed for the second set of fire doors. I could feel its weight on me. Stella fumbled with our key. I screamed, "Hurry!" Maggie ignored her key and pounded on her door for Mary. We tumbled into our rooms and slammed the doors behind us.

Stella and I leaned against the door, gasping for air. I realized that I was clutching the stereo with white knuckles. I forced myself to put it down.

"What the hell just happened?"

Stella shook her head. "I don't know." She straightened and, being a braver soul than I, peeked through the door's eyehole. "I don't know," she repeated, "but the lights are back on."

"What?" I pushed her aside and took a look for myself. Sure enough, the hallway lights blazed. Fortified by what I saw, I opened the door. The eyehole wasn't playing tricks. I stuck my head into the hallway and saw Maggie's head. We looked at each other. Then, not saying a word, we went back inside our respective rooms and locked the doors.

Stella sat on the couch. "Jessica, I think I know what's going on."

I nodded, anticipating her theory. "I think I know, too." The cold, the chasing lights, the long moan, they could only mean one thing.

"The crazy bitch at the front desk!" we both said at once.

"She had to do it."

"Of course. She saw us leave when Maggie told her we were done," Stella said, flopping onto her bed.

"And she had the motivation and the resources," I added.

Stella started laughing. "I bet she watched us from the security cameras. That had to be a sight. What a couple of idiots. What were we thinking, the place was haunted?"

"Well, this hotel is creepy and almost vacant," I defended and slipped under the covers. I was too tired to even wash my face or brush my teeth. "Plus, we keep seeing Elvis."

"True," Stella yawned and crawled into her bed fully clothed.

I set an alarm and switched off the lights, but I didn't close my eyes. With everything running through my head, I just couldn't sleep.

Chapter 21: Stella

I just couldn't sleep, not with everything running through my head. At 5:00 a.m. I gave up and decided to go for a run. I tried to be quiet, but it didn't matter. Jess was awake, too.

"Where are you going?" she asked.

"For a run. Can't sleep. Want to come with me?"

"No," Jess answered. "I prefer to keep staring at the ceiling."

Once outside, I took a deep breath of fresh morning air. Not being an early riser, I rarely see this side of day. I took a few more breaths before I started jogging down the street. I really should get up earlier. The day is so peaceful, quiet and full of promise.

Our hotel was in an older part of Springfield, so I ran a few blocks past run down apartment complexes, old strip malls with only a couple of stores remaining and derelict gas stations. When I reached Burger King, I turned around since I didn't have much of a view. However, I was looking for an excuse to cut my run short. My body was feeling the effects of too many sleepless nights, a bad diet heavy on the alcohol and too much stress. By the time I reached the convention center's parking lot, my lungs burned and head throbbed. I leaned against Cybill and tried to catch my breath.

At first I wasn't certain, but I thought I heard voices coming from the other side of the bus. Then I heard the latch of the luggage compartment give, and I knew some other members of Sun Tours were up. Billy and Tansy by the sounds of it. I rounded the bus to see what they were up to. Of all things, I was not expecting what happened next.

It was Billy and Tansy, but my mind could not comprehend what they were doing. It looked like they were dumping ice on top of a body bag. I screamed. Then Tansy screamed and rounded on me, ready to attack. I ducked out of instinct and missed her kick to my head by that much.

"Stop!" I yelled. "It's me, Stella."

"Sweet God in Heaven," exclaimed Billy, slamming the door to the luggage compartment closed. "You scared us darn near out of our wits."

"I scared you? What the hell are you two doing?"

"Nothing," they both said in unison.

"Don't bullshit me. I saw a body in there!" I started to back away. My heart was pounding out of fear, not exercise. "Now you have two seconds to tell me who it is, why you killed him, and why he's in the luggage compartment before I call the police."

"You will not," ordered Tansy, again moving to come after me. For a second I thought I was going to end up in the luggage compartment.

"Stop, both of you, please," ordered Billy as he stepped between us. "Stella, let me explain."

I waited but didn't let my guard down. Every muscle was tense.

"We didn't kill anybody." Billy rubbed his face in exhaustion.

"Then who's the stiff?"

He hesitated for a minute, then admitted softly, "Ted."

"Bus Driver Ted?"

"Yes, Bus Driver Ted. He died at the wheel, remember?" Tansy said. "We didn't kill him." She started to cry.

Strangely enough this news was only slightly comforting. "But why did you stuff him in the luggage compartment?" I asked.

"We had no choice," Billy said in defeat and pulled Tansy into his arms.

"Billy, you're not making sense."

"Well, first of all, my name's not Billy Butler. We're not who you think we are."

"That's obvious."

"Don't," choked Tansy.

"I have to," Billy answered. "The game is up."

I'm prone to thinking, and usually voicing, the most random thoughts at the most inappropriate times. Billy, or whoever he is, stood on the verge of telling me his real name, why he hijacked the dead body of a former bus driver and threw him in the luggage compartment. But all I could think was *why did I pick this morning to go for a run?*

"My name is Percy Nelson, and this is my wife, Anastasia." At least they're married, one less lie.

"My friends call me Stacy." The woman I knew as Tansy held out her hand as if we were meeting for the first time. I shook it, no sense being rude.

"We own Sun Tours."

"What?" I shouted. "You're telling me you own this tour?"

"Yes," said Billy. I already forgot what he said his name was. He had the look of a kid who just found out Santa Clause doesn't exist. "We run several tours throughout the US. We're taking each one undercover to see how things are going. Obviously our Elvis Week tour needs major work."

"Uh, yeah," was all I could say. But there was still one little problem. "So you own Sun Tours. Fine. Still doesn't explain why you put Ted in the trunk."

At the sound of Ted's name, Tansy started crying again. Even Billy's voice was husky when he explained, "You see, Ted, no Theodore, was more than an employee to us."

"We were the only family he had," stammered Tansy. "Ted never had any children, so he sort of adopted us or we adopted him. Whatever the case, he's been part of our family for the last fifteen years. He was like a father to me." She sat down in the middle of the parking lot and let go. "And we killed him!"

Billy squatted beside his wife and cupped her face in his hands. "Honey, we didn't kill him. He was just old."

"But we brought him out of retirement."

Billy looked up at me. "After Gus, so help me God, and Helix, who's still missing in action, I called on the one driver I trusted, Ted."

"And the stress killed him," wailed Tansy.

"There, there, sweetie. We've been over this." Billy was rubbing her back. The two huddled together on the pavement. "We can't blame ourselves."

I hated to break up the love fest, but there was still that one problem. "So you own Sun Tours. Fine. Ted was like family. Fine. I'm sorry I keep bringing this up, but please, for the love of God, tell me why he's in the luggage compartment!"

Standing, Billy finally explained, "Ted died broke. He didn't take advantage of the company life insurance. And over the last few years, he gave away everything of value, saying, 'You can't take it with you.'"

"He was just that kind of guy, you know," said Tansy, getting to her feet.

"Ted named me executer of his will," continued Billy. "I'm in charge of carrying out his last wishes, which are to be buried beside his parents in Bald Knob, Arkansas. The problem is, it's a lot of money to bury someone these days. There's the mortician, casket, headstone, flowers, organist, funeral home fees, etc. And it's even more money to transport a body. It was going to cost twelve thousand just to transport Ted from Phillipsburg, Missouri, to Bald Knob. And you can see my business isn't going so well, so I did the only thing I could think of: take Ted to Bald Knob ourselves."

"It's fitting really," Tansy added. "He loved this bus so much, you know."

It's not fitting, it's creepy, I thought.

"So there you have it. Now you can call the police," said Billy. "You have some exciting material for your article."

True. But looking at the two pitiful souls, I knew I couldn't do it.

"Billy-"

"Percy."

"Whatever. I'm not going to call the police, and I'm not going to put this in the article."

"You're not?"

"No."

"Why?"

I sighed. "Because you're trying to do the right thing. And frankly, I just want to get to Memphis so I can write this damn article and go home. Calling the police will be another delay, and we are already two days behind schedule. So, here's what I'm going to do. I'm going to help you."

"You are?" Tansy flung her arms around my neck.

"Yes," I choked, "It's against my better judgment, but yes."

"How?" asked Billy.

"Well for starters, you should have had him burned."

"Oh my God!" screamed Tansy and doubled over as if she was going to puke.

"You're sick," shouted Billy.

"I'm sick? You've been hauling around a dead body on some damn sight-seeing tour!"

"At least I didn't torch the guy like you're suggesting."

"Geez, Billy, I'm not talking bonfire and weenie roast here."

"Oh my God!" Tansy shouted again.

"Please, have some respect," Billy ordered.

"I'm sorry. I meant you should have had him cremated. That would have made transporting his remains easier."

"Oh, I didn't think of that," said Billy. "Say, that's what we should do."

"Unfortunately it's too late for that." I started to pace, thinking.

"Why?" asked Billy.

"We can't exactly pull up to a crematorium in a tour bus and say, 'Hey, we've got a body in the trunk. Mind if we use your facilities?'"

My thoughtlessness brought another, "Oh my God," from Tansy.

Another reprimand from Billy, "Stella, please."

And another apology from me, "Sorry."

"But what we can do," I continued, "is buy some dry ice." I popped the luggage compartment open to confirm my suspicion. I was right, Ted was floating in the melting ice. I quickly shut the door as the smell made me gag. Good thing I haven't eaten yet. "Dry ice will preserve him better in this heat."

"Should we go now?" Billy asked. "We bought this ice from the gas station down the street."

"No, they probably won't have dry ice. Plus, everyone will be up soon. We can't risk being caught by any more members of the tour." I couldn't help but become excited by the conspiracy of concealing a body. I was proud of my take charge attitude.

"Here's what we'll do," I said. Billy and Tansy huddled around me. "We wake everyone up. Tell them we're going to Bald Knob to attend Ted's funeral. When we stop for breakfast down the road, we'll go buy dry ice-"

"And air fresheners," Tansy added.

"And air fresheners," I agreed, "while everyone else eats. Sound like a plan?"

"Yes," Tansy shouted, sticking out her hand palm down.

"Let's go!" Billy put his hand on top of Tansy's.

I put mine on top as well and yelled, "Go, team, go!" We laughed and started walking briskly toward the hotel entrance.

"So our identities are safe with you?" asked Billy.

"You'll always be Billy and Tansy to me." We laughed again. I couldn't believe how upbeat we were given the situation. "Does Marion know who you are?"

"No, we've never met face to face. She was hired by a recruiter, and we've always corresponded over phone and email."

"So Jess and I will be the only ones."

Billy and Tansy stopped suddenly. "What do you mean you and Jess? You promised not to tell."

"And I won't. Jess doesn't count." I mean, really, think about it. "I tell her everything. But don't worry. You can trust her." Billy and Tansy didn't seem so sure, but I didn't give them a choice. I was already walking through the front door. "Plus, we'll need her for damage control."

#

Forty-five minutes later, I met the co-conspirators in the lobby as planned with Jess in tow. I had to give it to my soul sister; she took the news of Ted's whereabouts and our plan all in stride.

"We have to tell Marion" I said.

"She already knows," replied Bossman, rubbing his eyes.

Marion was slumped in the lobby chair, scribbling on her clipboard. "Ted. Ted. Ted. Dead. Dead. Dead," she chirped like an insane Dr. Seuss.

"What did you say to her?" I asked.

"I told her something needed to be done about Ted that would probably interrupt the schedule. That's when she wigged-out and hasn't been coherent since."

Marion began tearing her itinerary into tiny shreds. Then she threw the pieces above her head and giggled as the confetti fell about her. *Okay*, I thought, *we'll just deal with Marion later.*

After a few minutes, the sleepy members of Sun Tours joined us in the lobby. Bossman took charge of the impromptu meeting. "My friends and fellow Elvis lovers, today presents us with another challenge on our way to see the King. However, I'm sure we'll rise to this challenge just like all previous, emerging even stronger in our devotion to Elvis and all that is right." He sounded like he was taking lessons from Brother T.

"Get to the damn point!" Char bellowed.

"Char," said Thomas, "I'm beginning to seriously doubt your faith, you know. Elvis didn't like women who used foul language."

"I just want to know what God-awful adventures Billy Bob has in store for us today," Char retorted. Sister Mary's lips pressed to a line, but she was too gracious to correct her.

"Everyone, calm down." Bossman resumed control of the meeting. "This is the plan. On our way to Memphis, we will detour to Bald Knob to attend the funeral of Theodore Roosevelt Ewald, Jr., better known to us as Ted."

There was some grumbling and discussion amongst the tour, until Billy said, "Look, Ted doesn't have any family." He looked at his wife who was blinking hard. "Outside of a few close friends, this tour was all he had. Now we can continue to Memphis or we can take a moment to honor a kind and gentle man, knowing this tour gave him some of the last laughs of his life."

Everyone was silent and stared at their shoes. I looked at Jess and wondered what are we going to do with Ted's body if they don't agree?

Finally Thomas saved our necks, "My brothers and sisters, at times like this we have to ask, what would Elvis do?" With that, everyone agreed to the change in plans and felt guilty for arguing in the first place.

"Good!" Bossman clapped his hands. "Let's load up. Cybill is ready. Uh, Marion, why don't you get everyone onboard and Stan and I will do the honors with the luggage."

Marion perked up. "Bye-bye, Dead Ted. Bye-bye."

We stared at her for a moment, then Jess ordered, "Okay, everyone load up."

We stopped for brunch at IHOP, where we told the non-conspirators to eat without us. "We have a couple of errands to run," Bossman assured them. Then we grabbed Stan by his cowboy belt and told him to follow us.

"Stan, we need you to drive us, remember?" Bossman asked in an amplified voice.

"But, Marion?" Stan asked.

"She's fine," I assured him, watching the woman in question walk away with Tansy, who stayed behind to guard the home front. "She would want you to take care of us in this hour of need."

That almost convinced him. "But…But…" he stammered.

"Don't ask any questions. Just get back on the bus and take us where we need to go." Jess always favored the direct approach. Stan gulped and nodded, then swaggered to his rusty steed.

At Food Lion, we blindfolded Stan, bought twenty pounds of dry ice and twenty bags of regular ice, paid with cash and insisted on carrying the bags ourselves. After Ted was sufficiently iced, we headed back to IHOP, right on schedule. Billy, Jess and I breathed a temporary sigh of relief.

The tour was waiting in the parking lot when we arrived. "Everyone done eating?" Bossman asked, looking at his wife for assurance. She shook her head slightly, giving a there's-trouble-ahead signal.

"No, we didn't eat!" snapped a now functional Marion. "We discovered something you did this morning, and it made us lose our appetites."

Bossman looked at me. I looked at Jess. She looked at me. I looked at Bossman. He held up his hands. "Marion, calm down. Please everyone. Let me explain. It had to be done."

The group gasped. "It had to be done?" Sister Mary sounded like she was being strangled.

"What kind of sick-o are you?" shouted Char.

"I'm just trying to honor his last wishes. I know I should have told everyone, but it's such an awkward position to be in."

"What are you talking about?" Marion asked.

"Ted, of course. Aren't you upset because of Ted?"

"Oh, no. I'm over that. I've revised the schedule in my head and I'm fine. The tour must go on. I agree with you about Ted. We should honor the last wishes of a great man, after all he sacrificed for the tour. I'm talking about Harulu, Sachi and Midori."

Bossman frowned. "Who?"

"The three little old ladies. You do remember them, don't you?"

"Yes," replied Bossman.

"Do you remember the last time you saw them?"

A loaded question with only one safe answer. Hedge. "Uh, they're inside, aren't they?" I guessed.

The group was silent.

"Where are they?" Bossman asked.

"Nice of you to ask," huffed Marion. "You left them back at the hotel!"

"I did?" exclaimed Billy. "Oh, golly. I didn't mean to. Marion, you have to believe I didn't do it on purpose. I thought we had everyone. I'm real sorry. Well, good thing we haven't gone far. Let's go get them."

"Don't bother," quipped Lenny.

"What?" Now we were really confused.

"Apparently, they wandered around town, found a retirement home and have decided to stay. No need to come back for them, they assured me," said Marion. "I found this out after ten phone calls and enlisting the help of the police! Do you realize this is the second police involvement regarding this tour? We might as well ask them to escort us to Memphis!"

"No!" Bossman practically leapt forward and grabbed Marion. "No need to, ah, trouble the officers anymore."

Marion wasn't listening. "But that's not the worst of it," she sobbed. "The ladies informed us they…that they…oh! I can't. I can't say it!" She turned and started blubbering in Tansy's arms. Sister Mary patted her shoulder.

Eric took over for our distraught guide. "Apparently they never liked Elvis. Not one little bit. They shared the same view as my father–that Elvis was a gyrating, vulgar man. They weren't supposed to be on this tour. They were meeting another lady to take them on a tour of Sunset Living when they claim Stella assaulted them and forced them on our tour."

"I was trying to help!" I explained. "I thought they were just confused."

"Of course. We all thought they were a little off." Eric reassured me. "They told Marion to tell you, it's okay. They forgive you. And you must remember the secret call. I hope you know what that means. Anyway," Eric turned back to Billy, "they said they've been trapped on this tour and being left behind is a delivery from God!" His statements caused the whole tour to once again become enraged.

"Can you believe it?" asked Luc.

"Isn't it awful?" wailed Ella.

"The blasphemers!" raged Brother Thomas.

"Never liked Elvis? What's not to like?" asked Lester.

"The blue-haired bitches," proclaimed Char.

Bossman didn't say anything, just hugged his wife like a great disaster had just been thwarted. I shook my head and murmured sympathetic phrases to the affronted passengers. Jess followed suit.

"Unbelievable." I turned to Jess for support.

"Outrageous." She grabbed my arm.

"That's just…I don't know what it is," I babbled.

"I know what you mean. How could they live with themselves, not liking Elvis?" Jess pronounced this loud enough for several members to overhear and elicited appropriate responses.

"No kidding. What a shame," I added.

"Well, good riddance to bad rubbish!" The group agreed with Jess and boarded the bus.

Jess and I followed, our hearts pounding. If the tour ever found out we weren't exactly Elvis fans ourselves, we'd be dead. I felt like a robber hiding in a police station. Danger lurks everywhere. And there's no escape.

Chapter 22: Jessica

'There's no escape. Death comes for us all,' I wrote in my journal.

"And some ride to their grave in the belly of a bus," whispered Stella who was reading over my shoulder.

"Stop it," I said, but laughed. "Let's do some work. I'm going to visit with Elliot. The college boys gave me a lot to think about, and I want to see Elliot's point of view. Why don't you start up a conversation with Maggie."

"Yes, ma'am." Stella obeyed.

I moved to the front of the bus and took a seat across from father and son.

"Can we help you?" asked Eric.

"Actually, I wanted to hear Elliot's impressions of the tour," I said.

"Oh, that won't be necessary," said Eric. "I've already told you why we're here."

"Yes, but I'd like to get Elliot's take on things," I clarified. I couldn't tell if Eric was being protective or dismissive of Elliot.

Eric conceded and turned to his son, "Maybe you could give us an outsider's perspective."

"I'm not an outsider," Elliot argued. He sat on the inside next to the window and never took his eyes off the road.

"You know what I mean. Someone who doesn't appreciate Elvis," clarified Eric.

Elliot turned on his father. "I bet it never crossed your mind I just might have something worthwhile to say."

Maybe this wasn't such a good idea, I thought.

"Now, son, you watch your tone with me."

Elliot looked at me and pressed on defiantly. "Let me start off by telling you something about myself. I'm a normal kid, just like most kids I know. I go to school and hang out with my friends. I like music and sports. And I have problems like any other kid. My mom was really good at mediating between my dad and me, but she's dead now." He announced it with such force, I winced.

"My dad and I are having problems because we don't talk," Elliot continued. "He gives orders and I obey, but we don't talk. We don't know how to communicate. At least that's what my counselor thinks."

Elliot turned to his father. "Yes, dad, I said counselor. I've been going to talk to the school psychologist for about eight months now. I'm doing it because mom's death is really hard." Elliot paused. The muscles in his jaw flexed as he fought for control.

"I'm just so mad," Elliot whispered, and the tears which were building in his eyes spilled over. He turned away and quickly brushed them off. He stared out the window for a long time. I didn't know what to say, so we just sat in silence. When he finally continued, his voice was thick with emotion. "I'm mad at Mom for dying, even though I know she didn't do it on purpose. I'm mad at myself because there wasn't anything that I could do to help her. I hate feeling helpless."

Then Elliot looked straight at his father, and all the things he needed to say came tumbling out. "And I'm mad at you, dad. You shared more with Jessica and Stella, two virtual strangers, than you ever have with me. I'm your son. You've never talked about 'Nam or a long lost love. And you refuse to talk about Mom's death. You've shut her out with the efficiency of the businessman you are, but that's not going to work this time. I need to talk about it. I need-" Elliot broke off, unable to go on.

I felt uncomfortable being part of this family feud, but I couldn't make myself leave.

Elliot continued venting. "The best part about my counselor is she listens to me, really listens. She doesn't automatically judge everything I say or do as being stupid or the product of a rebellious youth. To her, I'm a person.

"I think that's the hardest thing for you to realize, Dad." Elliot's voice softened. It was no longer an attack, but a plea. "I'm a person with my own ideas, feelings and wants. It's hard for me to think of you as being this big rebel. You seem so eager to not rock the boat. Your story made me wonder what you were like when you were my age."

Elliot remembered I was still there. "I picked up a book about Elvis when my dad told me we were coming on this trip. Elvis was a rebel, but here's the thing: he didn't mean to be. He was just a kid who liked music. He stuck to his guns and sang the way he wanted to even though he was ridiculed. Many adults believed Elvis would destroy the youth of the nation. In truth, he was a misunderstood, God-fearing man. I admire Elvis's tenacity. Too bad his fame overpowered his passion.

"I don't know if this trip will accomplish its purpose. I don't know if Dad and I will ever be able to communicate. I do know that because of Elvis, I understand my father a little more. Maybe one day he will understand me."

Chapter 23: Stella

We didn't understand.

Until noon on day seven, Stanley Norman Neeley was the best thing that had happened to Sun Tours. He scoured the bus until it shone. Even the shit-colored Elvis sparkled. Mountain Spring Air Freshener sedated the commode. We could see through the windows again. He safely navigated through traffic, handling Cybill's antics with ease. Best of all, he and Bossman got along well, and for the most part he kept Marion giddy and distracted.

It was marvelous. Stan was the perfection of efficiency and cleanliness. Our hero, a true cowboy. If asked, we would have sung his praises to the mountaintops. We almost felt smug in our choice for driver number four. The fact that we didn't have a choice is beside the point.

Then came noon.

Granted, we should have remembered this tour was cursed from the onset. We should have remembered we were two steps from the Devil the whole time. Or at least remembered the Devil has a wicked sense of humor.

The happy people of Batesville, Arkansas, shot from work to lunch to work on a busy interstate with Cybill in the crossfire. At first, no one noticed. There was nothing to notice. The traffic grew heavier, but Stan glided Cybill along. The tour members drank in the sun through the gleaming windows. Some read, some napped, some listened to music, some chatted with their neighbors and all anticipated lunch at a cafe twenty minutes down the road. To the unsuspecting minds, we were peacefully making our way to Bald Knob to attend Ted's funeral, oblivious to the fact he was riding along.

Two miles ahead, a car sideswiped another car and caused a minor collision. Traffic became grid locked and Cybill slowed to a crawl, then to a complete stop. We sat back and prepared to wait it out, immersed in the heat mirage over the highway.

After ten minutes of absolute stillness, Stan broke the tranquility by screaming, "Go! Go! Go!" He flung his arms out to the side, pumped them over his head, then out to the side again. He looked like a cheerleader on crack. Stunned by Stan's bizarre chant, conversation ceased and all eyes focused on the driver. Stan repeated his cheer. Then he ripped off his seatbelt, stood and did it again. Before anyone could move, Stan opened the door and leapt off the bus. He darted through cars and trucks to a construction site in the far right lane. Without comment, we witnessed Stan jerk a long piece of rebar out of a worker's hands and pole-vault over the guardrail, disappearing from sight.

We didn't scream. We didn't cry in dismay. We didn't even blink. We simply shrugged and resumed our various activities. Only Marion reacted to Stan's episode of road rage. She muttered *bastard* under her breath and started in on her itinerary with a red marker.

Without any discussion, the tour decided to sit it out. Cars began honking, but it didn't matter now. A tank could run us over and we wouldn't flinch. We were never going to see Graceland.

Bossman moved to the front. "I suppose I'll drive."

A few miles down the road, Billy caught my eye in the rear view mirror. He jerked his head wanting to talk. I leaned in. "Do you think Ted's okay?"

"He's dead, Billy. What do I have to say to get that through your head? It's not like he can become more dead."

"I'm worried about his body."

"Well, what do you–Oh, shit."

"What?"

"You're being pulled over."

"What!?"

"Just pull over."

"No, I can't! They'll find Ted." Billy was starting to panic.

"You want to get involved in a high speed chase with the police when you're driving a bus? This isn't *Speed* and you aren't Keanu Reeves. Pull over!" Knowing I was an accomplice in the whole body snatching, unwilling yes, but guilty nonetheless, I tried to keep a clear head. "You were probably speeding. Just pay the fine, and we'll be on our way. They'll never know."

The August heat and humidity had done a number on our empty stomachs and flagging spirits. Cybill was starting to smell, a weird, moist smell that was worse than Don's breath.

"License and registration, please." gagged the officer.

"What did I do, Officer? Did I do something wrong? What did I do?"

"Calm down," I hissed, and looked at Jess for support. She just shrugged.

After examining Bossman's license, the officer asked, "This isn't a commercial license. I need to see your commercial license."

"I…I….I…" I hit Billy on the back of the head.

"I don't have one," Bossman screamed and held out his hands as if ready to be cuffed.

"Then explain to me why you are driving this bus."

Billy just stared open mouthed at the cop.

"We lost another driver," said Marion.

"How?" the cop turned his attention on our guide.

She shrugged. "Ran away."

"Why?"

"It happens."

"Well, I'm sorry to hear about that, but this gentleman can't drive. He doesn't have the appropriate license."

"What are we supposed to do? I don't have a plan! Do you think I have a plan for this? Who thinks they will need five drivers for one tour for Christ's sake?" shouted Marion, throwing her arms in the air.

"I'll see what I can do." After filling the dispatcher in on the situation, the policeman requested Jasper. Then he turned back to us. "Do you know you're leaking something?"

"No!" Marion gasped.

"Yes. The whole back of the bus is practically afloat."

"What?" The tour members went to the windows to check it out. A pool of water surrounded the back of the bus.

"Maybe we should call a mechanic," suggested the officer.

"Oh, no, Officer!" Bossman stepped forward with a salesman smile. "I just remembered we're having a bit of trouble with our johnny."

The policeman smiled. "Really? I just remodeled my bathroom. I can take a look at it for you."

"Oh, you don't have to."

"No problem." The policeman made his way to the bathroom, Bossman unable to stop him. I was right on the policeman's heels. As he opened the door, I pretended to fall, knocking him into the bathroom. He stumbled forward and the toilet erupted–just as I hoped.

Apologizing over and over again did not appease the now Smurf-colored policeman. He left in a huff, forgetting to issue Billy a ticket.

Victory.

Jasper arrived and drove us to our motel without question. Catastrophe avoided, I sank back in my seat.

#

My name is Frazin, and I'm the Ice Princess. My glass slippers make a clean crunching sound as I walk the frozen meadow. My white fur-lined cloak keeps me warm as my breath produces ghosts in the air. I smile with delight as a gust of wind sends diamonds of frost flittering through the trees. My kingdom is perfect.

As if summoned by my blissful mood, my male fairies appear and dance around me. I laugh as I watch their blue, naked bodies bounce in the snow.

The earth trembles and fear stabs my heart. Something is amiss. I become aware of singing and the warmth of the sun. On the horizon is my nemesis, Dorthaw, Keeper of the Spring.

My fairies flee. I rush at Dorthaw, desperate to save my crystallized kingdom. "Stop!" I shout, standing on the edge of what remains mine. Before me lies a jungle of vines and flowers. It's hot and messy.

My chest is heaving with anger. Dorthaw sits proud on his valiant white steed, his defiant chin thrust forward in challenge. My body begins to tingle. I drop my cloak. I will woo him with my beauty. I will use my charm to tease him into submission. My kingdom shall rule.

I step seductively into his territory. His singing satyrs part as I approach this arrogant knight. The gemstones of my sheer gown catch the sun.

He smiles, pleased with my appearance. Soon he will be mine. His iron will is already starting to cave to my wishes.

He takes my delicate, up-stretched hand and effortlessly lifts me onto his stallion. I trace my fingers over his chiseled chest. I lean my body close and whisper, "Dorthaw. Have you come to tangle with me again? Do you think that is wise? Why can't we be lovers?" I smile waiting for him to answer, to tell me he's my slave.

When he speaks, flames shoot from his mouth, engulfing my head. My charred face begins to crumble in the wind. Dorthaw drops my decapitated body and rides away, as his satyrs break into "Love Me Tender."

I woke up on the bus alone. I felt my face, still intact. I went to find the others.

Our dismal group had checked into The Lariat. Bossman stood guard in front of the luggage compartment. "We need more ice," he whispered as I passed.

#

At the Kincaid Funeral Home, I herded everyone inside giving Bossman cover.

Jess appeared moments later, flushed from having helped unload Ted's rotting corpse from the luggage compartment.

"How's Ted?" I asked as we bowed our heads for the opening prayer.

"Still dead, but thanks for asking." Jess whispered.

Brother Thomas gave the eulogy, a local minister added the appropriate pomp and circumstance, and everyone sang hymns.

The members of the tour were the only spectators save one: a shrunken lady about two hundred years old. She wore all black with a mourner's hat and veil on her head. At first, we thought she might have been an old love of Ted's, but the preacher informed us she is Crazy Sue Jones, their professional mourner. She believes every life should be properly grieved when gone. She wailed like Ted was in the torrents of hell and only her tears could quench the fire. The Rev said she started her career twenty years back and this was her 198th service.

Graveside, Sister Mary said a final prayer for Ted. Jess and I sang "Oh Danny Boy." And that was about it. We stood in awkward silence while we tried to think of something nice to say, but we really didn't know him that well. Billy and Tansy couldn't say anything without revealing their identities. So we just stared at each other.

I caught a mischievous look from Jess. "What?"

"The dance."

"What?"

"The dance. Tonight. For Ted."

"Yes! Tonight's the night!" Maggie said.

"For Ted!" everyone exclaimed.

"But we're not ready! Are we?" I asked.

"'Course we are. We just need to find a few finishing touches for the costumes," said Maggie.

"That could take hours," I argued.

"What? You women aren't ready? What a surprise!" taunted an eavesdropping Vince. "We've had our act together for days now."

That was all it took. Ella leapt to her feet. "Two hours," she announced, glaring at Vince. "That's all we need." The gauntlet was thrown.

"That's right," said Tansy. "You meet us at the Circle B Bar and Lounge across the street at ten sharp."

"And shine up those asses 'cause they're gonna get kicked!" yelled Char. "C'mon girls. Let's go."

#

Ella and Maggie set things up with Trudy, the owner of the Circle B. She was only too happy to loan her establishment and called a couple of radio shows to tell them of the impromptu contest. She would pack the house, she promised. Jess, Mary and I set the lights and cleared the stage.

We wore our funeral black, decorated with colorful scarves. We finished our preparations in time to run the routine twice. The men had yet to straggle in, and we had been ready for show time since nine.

Maggie's face appeared in the mirror behind us. Her expression chilled my heart. Maybe she thinks we're terrible, but has been too timid to say anything.

"Girls, no, women. No, friends. This trip hasn't been exactly what we expected."

We turned around. She raised her hands, and clasped them in front of her.

"None of us expected this Elvis Extravaganza to include disappearing maniac bus drivers, dead bus drivers, freaky hotels....This tour has pushed us to our limits. For some of us, it has confronted us with emotions we thought we'd banished with the rest of our history. But the one thing Sun Tours has done is to solidify a sisterhood between us. Oh, we have our differences," she said, looking at Tansy and Char. "But when the shit hits the fan, we're still here, standing hip to hip. It's beautiful. It's a testament to a woman's spirit. You've worked hard, my sisters. You've made me proud. Kick those legs high and let's box some balls!"

Empowered by Maggie's bizarre, yet fitting, pre-game speech, we roared, "Let the battle of the sexes begin!"

Ted, if you could only be here for this—your practical jokes will be missed.

#

The bar was packed. By a flip of a coin, the men went first.

Other than Vince, Lester, and Thomas, they didn't even bother with costumes. The trio was dressed to the hilt in Elvis-wear. The others simply unbuttoned their shirts to expose their chests in a sorry display of baboon-ism.

Vince grabbed the mike. He curled his upper lip, spread his legs and wiggled a knee, then winked at the DJ. Vince crooned "Any Way You Want Me" with the rest of the boys providing backup in a sort of swaying barbershop nine-tet. It was apparent Vince wasn't used to sharing the limelight, as he constantly sang over top of his accompaniment. He knee-jerked his way around the stage, finger-shooting all the women in the audience. Ella was downright pissed at the flirting.

When Vince's song ended, Lester stepped up to "That's When Your Heartaches Begin." The DJ slowly turned up the music until it all but drowned out Lester's wailing. The bar did a booming alcohol business during those three minutes.

Don was a showstopper. He picked up after Lester to sing "I Want You, I Need You, I Love You." His voice wasn't bad, but he held his audience by stripping off his shirt. His backup stripped off theirs, as well. This elicited screams from the female viewers and a few of them crowded the stage. I rolled my eyes.

When the guys finished, we hesitated. Maggie called a quick meeting. "Should we go on?" she asked.

"I don't know," said the kind-hearted Sister Mary.

"That performance was so pathetic, to go on would be like beating up the school wimp," muttered Char.

"Hey guys!" jeered Vince. "I think the chicks are afraid to go on."

"That's it!" retorted Char. "It's time we put these ya-hoos in their place."

And we were on. The DJ prepped Elvis's "All Shook Up," "Don't Be Cruel," and "Hound Dog." We danced for two measures as a group, drawing most of our moves from the Elvis classics: *Jailhouse Rock*, *Blue Hawaii* and *Spinout*. Then for five measures, two women stepped to the front and did their thing while the rest provided backup. We alternated solos and choruses throughout the rest of the songs.

With our sparkling scarves and slick moves, we were better than a Las Vegas act. The crowd went wild. Then something magical happened. As "Hound Dog" howled to a finish, the DJ switched to "Blue Suede Shoes." The audience joined in. Soon we were all over the bar with everyone dancing. We cut a rug through every Elvis song the DJ had. He popped in "Milkcow Blues Boogie." Compelled by the bipolar magnetism of the sexes, everyone paired off.

Across the room, I saw Eric pull Maggie into an unabashed embrace. She flushed, but drank it all it. She caught my eye and winked. I nodded my head and smiled. The victory was hers, tonight was her night.

In the wake of recent events, I forgot to tell Jess about my conversation with Maggie. I started to walk toward Jess, when Don grabbed my hand. He twirled me to him. I huffed and spun away. He circled me and I slid between his legs.

We took out our angst in song. He flung me over his head, around his back, around and around in his arms. As "Boogie" hit a feverish pitch, Don threw me on top of the bar. I ran to the end and jumped into the air.

It did occur to me mid-leap that Don might not catch me, but it was a little too late to change my mind. As I descended towards the floor, two arms wrapped around my waist and guided me to the ground.

I was laughing. I don't know why, but I was. As I looked around, so was everyone else—laughing, hugging, and kissing. A strange thought occurred to me: *Elvis did this.*

The music returned to Elvis's "Can't Help Falling in Love." The notes floated over the loudspeakers. I realized Don's arms were still around me, his heart thumping near mine. With his face pointed away, I inhaled the sweet aroma of man. We began to dance without saying anything. I lay my head on his chest and closed my eyes. Suddenly I was met with visions of blue fairies melting, their cries torturing my soul.

"No!" I pulled away. "You're Dorthaw, and I just can't do that."

Chapter 24: Jessica

"Don is Dorthaw?" I asked as Stel rubbed her eyes.

"Yes. In my dream. But then we were dancing-"

"I know. You two looked like you were having fun."

"We were, but then I remembered he torched my head, so I walked away," Stella said as if this made perfect sense.

"He torched your head?" I asked.

"With his breath. In my dream. So I called him Dorthaw and walked away."

"First you . . .then you . . ." I sighed. "And you wonder why you're still single." Stella frowned and I couldn't help but laugh at my hapless friend. "Come on. Get up. I want to show you what I've been working on." I sat at the chinsy desk by the window, with my notes fanned out in front of me. We had more story than we realized.

"What time is it?"

"Ten," I said.

"Ten?"

"Yeah, Marion let us sleep in."

"Of course, why not?" Stel whined.

"We're supposed to meet in a half an hour," I said. "So we have to hurry. But first, I want to show you what I've been working on. So hurry and brush your teeth."

"Yes, mom." Stella obeyed, but came out of the bathroom before she was finished. "So, what do you have?" she asked with the toothbrush dangling from her mouth.

"Okay," I handed her my outline. "So we talk about the events and tourist sights we've seen so far. We'll add Elvis Week if we ever get to Memphis. But we focus the article on the tour members. You know, how Elvis has touched each person."

"Maggie!" Stella shouted, toothpaste flew from her mouth. She ran into the bathroom to rinse her mouth, but quickly returned and started digging for her journal. "I can't believe I keep forgetting to tell you." She thrust her journal in my face, open to Entry #19.

"What's this?"

"Just read it." She was jumping out of her skin. "It's what I wrote after my conversation with Maggie. I wanted to tell you right away, but with Stan's disappearance, Ted's funeral and the contest, I forgot. You're not going to believe it."

#

Maggie's parents are successful. Not your average successful, but your wildly, ridiculously, so successful it's not fair successful. They own A Stone's Throw Productions, which boasts a long list of box office hits and Oscar winning films.

Maggie's brother graduated from high school early at sixteen and completed his business degree at Stanford in three years, not four. He has taken the family business from Independent production house successful to Miramax contender.

Maggie's sister is beautiful: tall, blonde, thin, perfect. She has appeared in commercials practically since birth and now commands two million for every leading role.

Then there's Maggie. She came along as a mistake fourteen years after her sister. As a child, she heard her parents describe her as common, average. And in this family of overachievers, this was unacceptable, an embarrassment at movie premiers and glitzy parties.

They tried to squish the mediocrity out of her. They enrolled her in dance classes, hired a voice coach, started acting lessons. She had a distinctive voice and an onstage presence, but she lacked passion. Her heart wasn't in it and it showed. Eventually her parents gave up, and their obvious disappointment stung.

So Maggie rebelled, as anyone would. She dyed her hair black, started doing drugs and focused on being expelled from a record number of schools in one year. After her third expulsion and a particularly devastating confrontation with her parents in which her mother said Maggie really didn't belong in the family, Maggie left. She stuffed some clothes in a duffle bag, hopped a bus and cried all the way from LA to Vegas.

Shortly after starting as a cocktail waitress at the Flamingo, Maggie met the man who would change everything. He'd come to Vegas looking for something as well. He saw through her tough veneer to her fragile sense of self worth. For six months, nothing could separate them. They talked about their future like it was a given they would always be together.

Then they decided he needed to go home to make peace with his father, so they could build a solid future. That was the last she ever saw of him. She moved shortly after, and in the confusion, lost his address, so she couldn't write to let him know she was still out there, still thinking about him.

A few months later, Maggie took a part as a showgirl at another casino to make more money. She worked for eight months before the director started harassing her. When she didn't give him what he wanted, Maggie was fired. She tried to get another job, but the director blackballed her to other directors, claiming she had a drug problem. She had been clean since coming to Vegas.

Desperate and needing to eat, she began waitressing in a topless bar. When she heard girls talk of making five thousand in a weekend stripping, it wasn't hard to switch. She figured she had nothing left to lose anyway.

Maggie had a goal. One hundred thousand dollars and she would quit the business altogether. She'd go to some obscure little town and open a coffee shop or bookstore.

She managed to save seventy grand in three years through great dancing, loyal fans and a good broker. However, Maggie was three years old in the business, she wasn't the fresh young thing, and word was out all she did was dance. You wouldn't believe how damaging that could be to a career in stripping. She didn't have another three years left. She didn't have one year. She needed out now.

So Maggie did what she swore she wouldn't. She took an offer to star in a porno for twenty-five thousand dollars– the hardest and worst thing she has ever done. She sold her soul for a ticket out of town and the chance for a new life. She left all of her possessions, threw her clothes in the backseat of her Cadillac and got the hell out of town, vowing to forget everything that happened in Vegas. Everything, except him.

He was the one thing that sustained her when it seemed she wouldn't make it. She would lie in bed at night and think about this amazing man who saw the real Maggie and accepted her for who she was. He didn't make her feel common, average, invisible.

Maggie never married. She had a series of lovers, but no one could measure up to him. Then by random chance or maybe divine providence, twenty-three years later, she opened her newspaper and there he was. He was being honored as one of the city's who's who in business.

Maggie took a chance and reached out. Yes, he remembered her and would love to meet, but it was a tough time. His wife had just died. He was having trouble with his son. Maggie almost gave up. Then he suggested Sun Tours Fourteen-Day Elvis Extravaganza. Maybe she could help with Elliot. Maybe they could recapture what they lost.

You see, we know her as Maggie. But in Vegas, Eric called her Rose.

"No way!" I shouted when I finished.

"Yes!" shouted Stella.

"Maggie is Eric's long lost love?"

"Yes!" she shouted again. "They planned this trip to see how Elliot would react."

"And how is he reacting?" I asked and gave Stella back her journal.

"Not very well," Stella said.

"I can imagine."

"They haven't told him the whole story, who Maggie really is to Eric, but Elliot senses something between them and doesn't like it."

"Oh, shit," I said looking at the clock. "We're late."

We gathered at Dixie's Diner for a Southern-style brunch. I spotted two open chairs at a table and pulled Stella over to sit with Char and Ella. I noticed Vince pouting two tables away. Trouble in paradise. I shook my head at the antics of the honeymooners. Vince stared miserably at his coffee and barely raised his head when the waitress came around to take his order.

Char laid her book aside. "Come on, kid. Let three experienced ladies help you with your love life." I shot a surprised look at Char. Maybe last night mellowed her out. Or maybe she's just a morning person.

"I don't know what you mean," snapped Ella, getting up from the table. "Can't I sit with the girls for a change without people thinking there's a problem with my marriage?" She stomped over to Vince who looked as surprised as we were by her table hopping.

"Well, excuse me," said Char.

"Don't worry about it," reassured Stella. "I made the same mistake."

I was thinking of a way to lighten the mood when Don showed up. He looked beat up, hung over and wrung out. He sat at a table by himself, ordered and snuck a look at Stella when he thought no one was looking. But I was looking.

"Speaking of someone who needs help with their love life…" I started.

Stella looked at me, then at Don, then back to her plate. "Yeah, see, I really don't want to talk about it either."

"What's this?" Char asked, but I shook my head. I guess we'll leave Stella alone for now. Char followed suite. "Looks like our new driver is here," she said. "There's a pool going on how long he's going to last. You in?"

I twisted in my seat. "Where is he?"

She pointed. "Over there, eating breakfast with Marion."

I craned my neck to get a good look at freak number five and nearly swallowed my tongue. Stella did a classic double take, too. At Marion's shoulder was Elvis, calmly sipping a cup of coffee.

"Of course," was all I said. At this point, I wasn't even surprised.

"I give up," Stella echoed my sentiments.

"You know," Char said, "from this angle he sort of looks like a young Elvis." She shrugged and returned to her omelet.

Stel and I stared at Char, then at each other. Then, because we just couldn't take it, we burst out laughing.

"He does," insisted Char.

"We know," said Stella. "Believe me, we know."

We quickly finished our breakfast, raced to our rooms and threw our stuff in our bags to stand first in line by Cybill.

Elvis took our bags. "Now, a pretty lady like you shouldn't look so sad," he told Stella in that whiskey and Southern Comfort voice. "Come on, give me a smile."

Stella gave him a look of total confusion and frustration that said, *who the hell are you?*

"That's better." Elvis turned to me, I grinned broadly. "Now that's what I like, a woman who shines!"

As the rest of the tour climbed aboard, I noticed Marion checking things off on her clipboard. She picked up the mike and addressed the group. "Hi, everyone, I'm sure we are all excited. Today we will finally reach Memphis!"

Maybe it was the last seven days of hell, but for some reason her announcement was met with skeptic silence.

Marion pressed on, "I just wanted to introduce our new bus driver, Aaron." Again, her words brought silence as the other passengers stared at the man behind her. I wasn't surprised at the lack of response. If she'd presented an alien, there wouldn't have been a ripple.

Bus Driver Elvis, a.k.a. Aaron, took it in stride. He reached for the mike. "Hello, folks, I just wanted to say it's nice to meet you. I'll be your driver for the rest of the tour. If you'll just put your faith in me, we'll have a smooth ride from here to Memphis."

We wore expressions of disbelief. He didn't know Cybill. I think it was the college boys who started laughing first, but soon it grew in waves, rolling over us as we responded to our new driver's claim of a "smooth ride." He reached for the key. I braced myself for the earthquake. It took Cybill four tries to get a sufficient growl going, but the shaking wasn't as bad as before. Everyone laughed again. Aaron grinned, finally getting the joke.

"I'll be right back," he yelled over the noise. He opened the door and stepped outside. I stood up and watched as he walked to the back of Cybill.

"What's he doing?" asked Eric behind me.

"He's opening the engine hatch," said Matt from the back.

I imagined Aaron's head disappearing inside the she-devil. I held my breath, wondering if this would be when we parted ways. But instead of the death and dismemberment I imagined, Cybill suddenly stopped shaking and her growl quieted into a purr. Murmurs of amazement came from behind me. Aaron climbed back aboard. "All fixed," he announced with a crooked smile. Cheers shook the bus as our new hero sat down and proceeded to find the correct highway to take us away from Bald Knob. My heart swelled with pride.

I settled in for the ride. *So we're actually going to reach Memphis today*, I thought and pulled out my notes.

The college boys moved to the seats across from Don, two rows behind me and Stel. We heard Matt ask, "So you're a model?"

And Don answer, "Yeah."

"Cool," said Matt. "I bet you get loads of hot chicks."

"Yeah, really hot chicks," added Marcus.

"Give me a break," Stel whispered. "Are you listening to this?"

"Yes," I answered. "And so are you."

"Whatever."

Don laughed at the younger boys. "Uh, not really."

"C'mon, don't hold out," urged Matt.

"As a profession, modeling isn't bad," Don continued. "You do meet lots of beautiful people. You travel to exciting locations. You are paid money, sometimes lots of money, to let people take pictures of you. It's hard work at times, really long hours, but not a bad life. However, it's a lonely life.

"You're never in one place long enough to get to know anyone. Plus, I've never been good at relationships. I shy away from people because I have what is called halitosis, or chronic bad breath. I can take a pill that helps, but sometimes I don't. Sometimes I just want to see how people will treat me without it.

"I had almost convinced myself that a life alone isn't so bad, until I logged onto a forum called Braggarts and Bullheads."

"Oh, dear God, no," Stella gasped.

"What?" I whispered.

"Nothing."

Don continued, "The forum started with a few nerds who had nothing better to do than hurl Shakespearean insults at each other over the Internet."

"Shakespeare?" asked Matt.

"Yes, you could say I admire Elvis for the same reasons I admire Shakespeare. Both had a unique style and awe-inspiring talent. Although their individuality brought them ridicule and hardship, they persevered and won the everlasting devotion of many generations.

"You see, my dad died when I was young, so it's been Mom and me my whole life. She's an amazing woman. She teaches 17th Century Poetry at Notre Dame. And she's part of a secret society." Don stopped to laugh. "They meet in a society member's cellar where they drink wine and discuss all things Shakespeare. I remember going to these meetings. I would sit in a corner and listen, first to the rhythm of the language, and later at what it meant, and then at their insights. I grew up surrounded by intellectuals.

"Anyway, this forum is great. There are even prizes for the one who comes up with the best insult. We talk about other things as well. The members of this group are practically the only friends I have.

"There's one in particular who has become my best friend. It started when we shared our favorite sonnet with the group. Hers is Sonnet 130. She wrote she would marry the man who sent this sonnet to her in a Valentine because then she would know he loved her for her and not her appearance. In other words, she wants to be loved in spite of her flaws. I guess that's what we all want. I asked for her address, but she told me, 'Not on your life. You are probably some freak or stalker.' And that started our friendship."

Stella doubled over. "I think I'm going to puke."

"What? Why?" I asked. Then all of a sudden I remembered. "Oh my, God. Don is Mr. eHarmony."

Stel just nodded. Without thinking, I turned around to look at Don. He stared at me like he was expecting my revelation. In fact, I suspect he was telling this story for Stella's benefit and not the college trio.

"Turn around." Stella hissed and pulled on my elbow.

I sat back down. "He knows we're listening."

"Brilliant." Stella covered her face with her hands.

"We talk about everything, important things and not so important things," We heard Don continue. "We could be talking about our views on death and euthanasia and in the next sentence be debating the last episode of *Lost*. We've never met, but I can tell you she takes her coffee with cream and sugar, still has a crush on Luke from *Dukes of Hazard*, and believes low-carb is a horrible thing to do to food."

That's my Stella all right. At this point, she was an interesting shade of purple.

"The women I've dated have been models or model material. Until recently, I had never seen this girl's face, but the more I got to know her, the less that mattered. And I know it doesn't matter to her because she's never even asked for a picture. For the first time, a woman likes me for me and not what I look like.

"I've never felt so free as when I'm with her. Yet I'm not with her. But here's a secret."

"What?" asked Marcus.

"I've made a vow to find her. I told her I'm going to prove to be the stalker she's always suspected. And when I track her down, I'm to say: 'The October rooster crows at noon.' And she will reply-"

"The November nightingale sings at midnight." Stella whispered the line with Don on cue, but the college boys didn't hear.

"Way cool, man," said Matt. "Kind of lame ass code though."

"You'll have to let us know how it goes when you find her," said Luc, probably the romantic of the group.

"Oh, I will," said Don. I'm sure he was staring at the back of Stella's head. Stella was staring at the floor.

"I hope she likes Elvis," said Marcus.

"She's his biggest fan."

Chapter 25: Stella

"His biggest fan," Jess snickered. *She's so immature.*
"Just shut up," I warned.
Thankfully Cybill saved me from dealing with either Jess or Don. She started spewing white smoke from her back end. Aaron noticed it first from his side mirrors. "Ma'am," he said to Marion. "I believe we have a problem."
"No," Marion argued. "We don't have any more time for problems. There are no more problems allowed."
"Well, I'm sorry," said Aaron, "but we have smoke coming from the engine. We'll have to pull over and check things out."
"No," Marion insisted. "You will keep driving to Memphis. We are only about forty minutes away!"
"I'm sorry, ma'am."
Jess and I got up to investigate along with Don, the college boys and everyone else at the back of the bus. Yes, we definitely had a problem. As I craned my neck to look out the windows, I realized Don was standing right beside me. And he wasn't looking out the windows.
I turned to face him. "I'm not talking to you," I said and returned to my seat.
Aaron pulled off the highway at the next exit and came to a stop at a Marathon gas station. Everyone filed off the bus to see the damage.
"What's wrong?" asked Marion.

"Blown radiator hose from the smell of it," said Aaron. Several of the men nodded in agreement.

"Can it be fixed?" Marion asked. "Like right now."

"We'll need a new part," said Aaron.

Billy was already walking toward the entrance. "I'll check with the attendant about a mechanic or auto parts store."

I ran to catch up with Billy. "At least we don't have a body in the trunk to worry about," I said trying to lighten the mood.

Billy smiled, but his face held defeat. "Yeah, but I'm done. I'll have to give everyone a refund after this, and that will be the end of Sun Tours."

I tried to think of something encouraging to say, but my thoughts were interrupted by a desperate need to pee. So we walked silently into the gas station and parted ways.

Latrinaphobia: the fear of toilets. I'm twenty-six years old and afraid to take a piss. I never thought an automatic toilet would be something to fear, but it is. This one is especially dangerous. Its Clorox Blue is the color of the deepest parts of the ocean. My ass has faded, finally, and no way do I want to risk re-coloring. But I do have to pee.

I leaned against the cool stall door. Maggie is the ex-porn star Rose, who was once the love of Eric's life. Billy is the owner of Sun Tours, which is about to go under. Elvis is driving our bus and only Jess and I know. Don is… Don is… I didn't want to think about it.

"Are you okay?" Jess asked.

"No, my eyeballs are floating."

"What?"

"I have to go and I can't."

"Estelle Marie Smith, pee right now." Her voice came from right behind my stall door. "You'll be fine. Here, I'll show you there's nothing to be afraid of." She entered the stall next to me and simultaneously started to pee and talk. "Stella! Our article is going to be great! First we find out about Maggie and Eric. Now Don is the guy you've been talking to online. Did you see that coming? I was blown away." I didn't answer. She finished peeing. "Now about Don, you know I love you and care about your feelings, but you can't abandon me for Don now that you know who he is and vice versa. We need to focus on the article." She flushed, washed her hands and returned to her post outside my stall door. "If he's so rich he can visit you when we're done."

"Do you have a point, Jess?"

"I'm just saying, don't go berserk because Don is your email love. I don't think our careers can handle a display like that."

"Fine. Jess, I need your help."

"Now? With what?"

"You can't say anything and you can't laugh. I'm relying on years of friendship here. I got some ointment from Rite-Aid and the tube says I need to cover evenly. And I need to do it now."

"Are you asking me to look at your ass?"

"Yes."

"I'm not looking at your ass."

"I need to cover evenly!"

"I don't care. I'm not looking. Use the mirror."

"My legs would have to be seven feet tall in order to see my ass in that mirror. Please. This isn't easy for me either." I pushed open the bathroom door and checked under the stalls. "Come on, while the coast is clear." With my pants around my ankles, I came out butt first.

"You missed a spot," Jess said. "It looks like Australia."

"Where?"

"Left cheek."

"There?"

"No. Higher."

"There?"

"No! Just give me the damn cream." Jess stuck her hand in front of me.

"Okay, but if you tell anyone…"

"Like I'm going to say I rubbed cream on your ass." She grabbed the ointment and slapped a liberal amount onto

Australia. And that was how, at that precise moment, Don walked into the restroom and came to meet my ass, and Jess's hand rubbing it vigorously.

"Oh shit, I'm in the wrong…" Don froze when his mind registered the scene in front of him. "Never mind."

Jess froze as well while I shrieked and bunny-hopped back into the stall.

"Stel has a blue ass," Jess explained.

"Jess! Don't… I… Shit! What the hell are you doing in here?"

"I'm going now." Don quickly retreated, and if I had to guess, I'd say the look on his face was more hurt than shocked.

I considered drowning myself in the toilet. "I'm not getting back on that bus, Jess."

"I'm not spending any more time in this bathroom."

"But what am I going to say to him? 'I'm sorry you had to see my blue butt? I'm sorry I called you Dorthaw. My shrink thinks my condition can be cured with lots of medication and shock therapy. Then I might be able to handle a relationship. Jess!" I wailed. "What's wrong with me?"

"I have no words for you. You are beyond my help."

#

Back outside, we discovered no one in town had a radiator hose that would work for our old bus. The part would need to come from Memphis, which would take several hours. Then several more hours to fix it, so we weren't going anywhere today. Stranded once again, this time in Levesque, Tennessee.

I wonder if Elvis fans are more polite than most folks or if we've just accepted the fact we are never going to see Graceland. Whatever the case, no one shouted in anger about our situation like I would expect. Or maybe it was Marion who kept everyone's tongue in check. She didn't say anything. She couldn't. Her face was red, eyes were full of tears which she ferociously fought back, and her hands were constantly patting her hair and straightening her blouse.

Equally as depressing was the sight of Tansy and Billy. Husband and wife clung to each other and stared at the bus. Their business was failing right before their eyes, and there wasn't anything they could do about it. My heart went out to my friends, and I immediately forgot about my own troubles.

Without much comment or complaint, each member of Sun Tours grabbed their bags and began walking down the sidewalk to the nearest motel—the Rockin' Oasis Inn, a "Honeymoon Hideaway" as the brochure boasted. It also rented by the hour making it one of those kind of places. The desk clerk informed us the only rooms available were two honeymoon suites, and it was Mary's idea for all the men to stay in one room, and all the women in the other.

Marion set out looking for a copier for some road-trip activity, and said we were free for the evening. In my head danced visions of Marion flapping her arms real fast, flying all over town, then diving through the ceiling of some office supply store. Given her state of mind, this scene wasn't entirely impossible.

So Mary, Maggie, Ella, Char, Tansy, Jessica and I checked into Honeymoon Lodge, room 16. It was decked out in a nasty shade of orange-red, down to the rose-colored, heart-shaped, vibrating bed. All seven of us set down our suitcases, gave the room a once over and stared at each other, thinking *now what*?

"This is some bullshit," Char said.

Sister Mary sighed, and Maggie tried to save the day. "Hey, it is what it is," she said. "Let's make the most of it."

"How?" asked Ella.

"I say we go get some junk food."

"And alcohol," added Tansy.

"And alcohol," agreed Maggie. "Then find a chick flick on TV. Make it a slumber party."

Since we really didn't have a better alternative, everyone agreed to Maggie's plan. We started for the door, when Jess grabbed my elbow.

"Hey, Don told me to tell you he'd be at Applebee's if you'd like to join him and maybe start over."

I couldn't believe it. "Which way was Applebee's?"

"Just hold on," Jess said in her mom tone. "First you need to call Ursula."

"What? Why?"

"Because we need to check in, and this will be your part of working on the article before chasing boys like we agreed."

"But what am I supposed to say to the Sea Witch?"

"Figure it out," Jess said, handing me the cell phone and leaving to catch up with the rest of the ladies.

I paced the room a few times before pressing speed dial 001.

"Yes."

"Uh, Ursula. It's Stella." I waited for the Sea Witch to say something, but she didn't. "You know, Stella Smith covering the Elvis Week story."

"I'm aware."

"Of course. Well. I'm just calling to check in." I felt like a kid calling home.

"So, how's it going?" She asked in a tone that made me think she already knew, but that was impossible.

"Good, really good." Then I remembered the facts. "Actually, things are a little messed up."

"What happened?"

"It's nothing really," I said and slid to the floor. "I meant things haven't gone according to plan or Marion's itinerary that is. Or any of her subsequent itineraries either come to think about it. But it's good actually."

"Stella, you're hurting my head. Just tell me you've got a story."

"Yes, a good story. I think you'll like it."

"We'll see." And she hung up.

That went well, I thought getting to my feet. And that was just the first awkward conversation of the evening. Now onto the second.

I spotted Don at the bar just as the hostess greeted me with her chipper, "Welcome to Applebee's." I waived her off, but didn't move. I studied Don's face under the soft lights. It was such a surreal feeling to look at a complete stranger and realize I know everything about him. I know his full name is Donald which he hates, his father died when he was two, and he drinks a Red Bull for breakfast every morning. It was an even stranger feeling to realize he knows everything about me. We've stayed up until 2 a.m. chatting online, but haven't managed one coherent conversation in eight days.

Don checked his watch, scanned the room and saw me standing at the entrance. He spoke with the bartender, grabbed his drink and walked over. "We're ready now," he said to the hostess who led us to a booth.

Once seated, Don looked at me and said, "Hi."

"Hi," I said. It's as good a start as any. "I should probably explain…" I tried to think of where to begin, calling him Dorthaw or Jess's hand on my ass, but I was interrupted by the waitress.

"Hi, my name is Ashley," she said. "I'll be taking care of you. I see you're all set." She indicated Don's drink. "But what can I get for you?" She asked me, but Don' answered.

"A pink martini," he said.

Of course. *He knows my drink*, I thought. After the waitress left, I said, "This is so weird."

"I know!" Don seemed so proud of himself for having pulled this off.

"How did you know I'd be on this tour?"

"You told me, remember? Told me all about how the Sea Witch was sending you on some asinine Elvis tour."

"Oh, yeah, so you know I'm not Elvis's biggest fan," I said.

"Me either. That title belongs to Lenny. I'm here for you."

"Yeah, which is a little creepy, you know. I shouldn't even be talking to you."

"But you are," he said with a devil's grin.

We were interrupted by the waitress again when she returned with my drink and took our order.

"Speaking of Elvis," Don continued the conversation. "Do you think our driver-"

"Yes!" I shouted.

"He looks like Elvis," we said together.

I laughed. "We've been seeing these Elvis-look-alikes throughout this trip. Jess will be so relieved to find out we're not crazy."

"Well just because I see him too, doesn't mean you're not crazy."

"Thanks," I said and threw my napkin at him. He threw it back. "But seriously," I continued, "why do we keep seeing Elvis?"

"He's everyman."

"What?"

"Elvis was born into poverty on the wrong side of the tracks. As a kid, he's quiet and polite, but doesn't have many friends. He pays four dollars to record 'My Happiness' as a gift for his mother's birthday, then goes on to become a phenomenon, all the while never forgetting where he came from. So you and I are learning what Elvis means to the other people on this tour. We've known him as the international star, but now we're hearing about his humanity. So we start seeing him in the 'common' everyday people we meet."

There was a long pause while I considered Don's theory. He had a point, but I didn't want to admit it, so I just said, "Shut up."

And that's all it took to marry the image I had of my online friend with the face across from me. We spent the rest of the evening laughing and talking like the good friends we are, straight through dinner, dessert and a second drink. At a pause in the conversation, I glanced around the restaurant and noticed we were among the few patrons left.

"So has this assignment helped you overcome The Incident?" Don asked, abruptly bringing me back to the conversation. Seeing the look on my face, he apologized, "I'm sorry. I shouldn't have brought it up."

"No, it's okay. I just forgot you knew about that."

"You told me."

"Yes. Apparently I told you too much. The result of anonymity, I guess." I was tearing my napkin to pieces.

Don put his hands on mine, "So?"

I pulled my hands away, put them in my lap and stared out the window. "We'll see," I said, repeating Ursula's line. "I mean, it's going to be difficult to pull off a story about Elvis Week if we don't get to Memphis, but Jess has a plan for that."

"I'm sure you'll write a great story, but that's not what I meant."

"It's not?" I sat back in my chair and crossed my arms. This conversation was becoming uncomfortably personal.

"When we first started talking online, you spoke with such excitement and passion. It's one of the first things I noticed about you. You wrote with such force and conviction. Then it turned to indignation and anger during The Incident and ensuing fallout. But I didn't worry because you have moxy, and I knew you wouldn't back down. However, they got to you, got inside your head, because now your writing is timid and full of fear. Like you've given up and don't know who you are anymore."

He paused, waiting for my response, but I didn't like the fact I was so transparent, so I said, "Thank you, Dr Phil."

But Don wouldn't have any of it. "Stop it. I'm just wondering if you've found your voice."

Suddenly I found myself fighting back tears, but I wasn't thinking about The Incident. I was thirteen years old again, screaming at Glen and Louise, "You don't love me. You wish you never took me in. I'm just a burden." They'd always reply, "Why do you say that? Of course, we love you." But it never felt that way. Their emotions were so subdued, I grew numb. Our lives were so quiet, it was deafening. I turned to writing to make myself heard. But I didn't think anyone was listening.

"Can I get you anything else?" It was the waitress, wanting to go home.

"No thanks," answered Don. "I'll take the check, please." She had it ready, gave it to Don, waited for his card and returned quickly with the receipt.

Outside I still couldn't bring myself to speak, but that was okay. We started walking to the hotel in the easy silence when words aren't necessary. After a block, Don put his arm across my shoulders in the most natural manner, like this is what we do every night after dinner.

When we arrived at the hotel entrance, I started for my room, but Don pulled me into a hug. And I gave in, "I'm just so mad at the whole stupid thing," I whispered. "And I've messed up Jessica's life as well."

Don tucked my hair behind my ears and took my face in his hands. "It'll be okay," he said. "I promise." He ran his thumb across my cheek. "But for now, just get some sleep, okay?" Then he walked inside, leaving me to say goodnight to the night air.

#

"Hell, I'm tired of always having to keep my opinions to myself," Char was saying when I walked in the door. I assumed she was talking about the room. But Jessica's face said otherwise. On the bed was a craft kit of makeup, and suitcases were piled everywhere. "Everyone hides behind hurt feelings to avoid the truth," Char said. "Especially this trophy wife." She pointed a long fingernail at Tansy, and kept digging around in her luggage.

"Just what in the hell do you mean by that?" said Tansy, her words clipped.

"Figure it out," challenged Char.

Jess gave me a look that said: *Perfect timing.* It also said a bunch of other things that I construed to mean Mary and Maggie had chosen the perfect time to jump ship. The look didn't explain the makeup kit, however.

"Why do you pimp yourself out like that with your skimpy outfits?" Char asked the question so flippantly while she collected her face soap and toothbrush, like her comment wasn't supposed to sting, she was just curious.

Looking at Tansy's pink top, which was ill equipped to cover her abnormal amount of cleavage, and tight miniskirt, which barely covered her ass, I've often wondered the same thing.

"Is it to keep your rich hubby happy?" Char continued the attack.

"Why do you hide behind dresses the size of a tent?" Tansy replied without missing a beat. She stood two feet from Char with her hands on her hips.

What provoked this, I wondered.

"At least I didn't sell my dignity so I could be dressed up as some old man's doll."

"You bitch. You vicious, bloated bitch." Tansy practically shook with anger. "Here's a news flash: Billy isn't rich. His company's about to go under, but he keeps telling me everything is fine. Why? He wants to protect me like he always has. I owe Billy everything. He saved me from my *shit life* when every other man ran in the opposite direction. If he has any faults, it's his kindness and generosity. He'll give to anyone in need before they even ask. And he doesn't expect anything in return. He won't make you feel guilty. He just does it because that's who he is."

Char rolled her eyes and started walking to the bathroom.

"And I'll tell you another thing," said Tansy, moving in front of her. "I never cared about the money. You can shove it up your ass." She was in Char's face.

If they start to throw down, I thought, *I wonder who will win.* Tansy knows how to kickbox, but Char's a scrapper. It'll be close. I followed Jess and Ella's example: wandered to a corner and avoided eye contact.

"I hope we go bankrupt so people like you will finally believe I'm with Billy because I love him," Tansy continued. "Every day I'm confronted with another cynic who labels me a trophy wife. Do you think you're original? You can call me every name in the book, I don't care what you think of me. But don't you dare imply the only reason a woman would be with Billy is because of his money. He's so much more of a man than that." Tears filled her eyes, but she held her ground.

After several awkward moments, Char muttered, "I'm sorry."

"Why do you tear me down every chance you get? What have I ever done to you?"

Char shrugged and threw her stuff back in her bag. "If being ugly isn't enough, I don't have privilege, either." She sat on the bed. "I had a man once who made me feel like a new car. But after his test drive, he wasn't sold. All I got was abandoned with a kid." She shrugged one more time. "You've never felt the sneer of the checkout girl when you pay with food stamps. You don't know how it hurts to have no money for clothes that haven't been worn by someone else. Or what it's like to never see your son because he's too embarrassed to bring his girlfriend home to his trailer trash mom." Char shrugged a third time in a surprisingly vulnerable gesture.

Tansy sat next to her. "Actually, I know exactly how that feels." Char looked at her in surprise. "I'm going to tell you something only Billy and a few others know. But first you're going to stop being such a bitch and taking your sucky life out on me. Then we are going to make a deal."

"What kind of deal?"

"I'm going to make you my doll. I'm going to show you how beautiful you are."

"That's impossible."

"And we're going to start with your ugly attitude. Deal?"

"Deal."

They left to do some emergency clothes shopping. The rest of us emerged from our hiding spots, not knowing whether to cry, hug, give high-fives or what. I started digging through the make-up to hide my discomfort.

"What is all this stuff?" I asked. I picked up a tube of ruby red lipstick and put it on.

"Supplies for the slumber party," Jess answered.

"But it's just us," I said looking at Jess and Ella. "Where's everyone else?"

"Maggie got a call from Eric; she left to meet him and Elliot somewhere." Jess took the lipstick from my hand and applied it to her own lips.

"Nice," I said.

"Those two have been inseparable this whole trip," said Ella. She turned her back to us and started picking through her suitcase, not looking for anything in particular. "Elliot doesn't like it. You know Eric's wife just died."

"Yes," Jess and I said together. *If you only knew*, I thought.

"Where's Mary?" I asked. "Char driver her off, too?" I used the bedroom mirror to apply some foundation which turned my skin a lovely shade of orange.

"No listen to this," Jess said. "Brother T came by and invited her to dinner."

"And she went?"

"Yes!" Jess handed me some blue eye shadow that contained glitter. Obediently, I put it on.

"Speaking of dinner, how was yours with Don?" Jess asked.

"You went to dinner with Don?" asked Ella surprised.

"Yes I did, and it was lovely," I said. I found a big blush brush and started dusting Jessica's face with a fine white powder. "Jess, he sees right through me, and it's okay. We talked about everything. He asked about my writing and if I'd found my voice again." I turned Jess toward the mirror so she could see her ghostly appearance. "It's like I've known him for a hundred years."

"You couldn't have known him for a hundred years. You'd be way old," came Ella's astute observation from her position sitting cross legged in the middle of the bed.

"I was exaggerating," I said, rolling my eyes at Jess.

"I don't think I can hear this sappy talk without alcohol," Jess said. She crossed to the suite mini fridge, pulled out a box and held it up. "Can I pour you a glass of wine from a box?"

"Yes, I'd love some," I said. "Box wine is my favorite kind."

"It is?" asked Ella.

"No, I was being sarcastic."

"Well, box wine is all we've got," explained Jess. "The gas station on the corner didn't have much of a selection."

"Well, I'm glad your love life is working out," Ella said in a tone that indicated she was not glad. She rolled onto her belly and propped her face in her hands.

I took the glass of wine from Jess and tried not to think about a television show I saw exposing hotel cleaning practices. "I wouldn't exactly call it my love life."

"What would you call it then?" Ella snapped.

I'd had enough of Ella's childishness. "Look," I snapped, staring down at her, "I'm sorry if I upset you on the bus, but I apologized, and now you need to get over it. I'm very aware you and Vince are doing great."

Immediately I regretted being so harsh to her as tears filled her eyes. "But we're not," she wailed. "You were right. Are you happy now?"

"No, I'm not happy. Why kind of person do you think I am?" Jess and I sat on either side of Ella. "What's wrong?"

Ella answered, but we couldn't understand because she had buried her face in the comforter. "Yeah, I didn't get that. Did you?" I asked Jess.

"No." Jess rubbed Ella's back. "Tell us what is wrong."

Ella rolled to a sitting position. "All we do is fight."

"About what?" I asked.

"Everything. How he gives every woman attention except for me. It's like he lost interest in me after we got married." She blew her nose on the tissue I handed her. "But mostly we fight about our future. I want to start living our lives where I stay home to raise the babies, and Vince works a real job. But he wants to live as Elvis and Priscilla in Vegas."

"Didn't you talk about this before you got married?" Jess asked.

"Yes, Vince always said we should become Elvis and Priscilla impersonators because we look so much like them."

"And you married him anyway."

"I thought he was joking!" Ella's point was so obvious, I burst out laughing. "It's not funny."

"I know. I'm sorry."

"I mean really," Ella continued. "What grown man wants to spend his life dressed up like Elvis?"

"Uh," Jess and I stared at each other. "A surprising number of men share that dream actually," Jess said.

"Well, I don't," said Ella. "My marriage didn't survive the honeymoon. I'm so stupid." She cried into her hands.

"Look, it's probably not about being Elvis, but about the attention Vince receives when he's on stage," said Jess. She's so damn smart like that. "So find a way to talk, and not fight, and come up with a future where Vince can do something which provides the attention and recognition he needs, while also providing the stable, normal life you need."

Ella looked like the heavens just opened up. She grabbed Jessica around the neck. "That's it. Thank you so much!" She scrambled out of bed. "I got to go. Oh, Jessica, thank you!"

After Ella left, Jessica turned to me and said, "Stel, do you realize we've successfully scared everyone away?"

"I don't see how being the only two girls left at a slumber party is a success."

"Now we can go through their things."

"No."

"Yes." Jess tore into suitcases like a madman while I tore into more box wine. Soon the room was in shambles. More terrifying than the state of the room was our appearances. I had on an Elvis costume I found in Ella's suitcase. It was a black sequined jumpsuit like the ones Brother T is prone to wearing. Jess was wearing a shirt of Char's that went down to her knees synched at the waist by a huge plastic red belt and Tansy's spandex leggings. White tube socks pulled up to her shins completed the outfit. We also added fake eyelashes, more makeup and several different shades of nail polish to our fingers and toes.

"Funyuns!" I shouted, spotting the bag by the small microwave. "I love these."

"I know," said Jess.

"You bought them for me?"

"Of course, what are friends for?"

A lump formed in my throat as I looked at the bag of baked onions. What did I do to deserve such a friend? "I love you, Jess."

"I know, I love you, too."

"No, I mean, I really love you." I grabbed her in a hug. "And I'm sorry for dragging you into all this. I'm sorry for everything."

"I know. It's okay." She patted my back.

"No, I mean it. I'm really sorry."

"I know," she whispered, and I knew she understood. I also knew she forgave me for everything and with this knowledge I came undone.

"Hey, hey, hey." Jess held my shoulders at arm's length to look into my face. "What's all this. Stella, it's really okay."

"I just feel so bad about everything." I slumped to the floor. "I ruined your career. You shouldn't even be talking to me. And here you are, buying me Funyuns."

"I think you've had too much box wine."

"Maybe a little, but it doesn't mean I'm not serious."

"I'm serious, too, but right now I feel like singing." Jess flipped the TV to VH1 and jumped on the bed.

As I watched her sing into a hairbrush, making up words to a song she didn't know, I thought, *this is my friend for life.*

Chapter 26: Jessica

That's my friend for life, I thought as I watched Stella do an awful Elvis impersonation. I looked at the clock: 1 a.m. I turned off the TV; the room was spinning.

"You don't like my singing?" Stella asked, her words a bit slurred.

"Your singing is beautiful, but..."

"But what?"

"Where the hell is everyone?" I opened the door and peered down the hall as if they'd be standing there.

"Good point. They probably figured they weren't going to get any sleep, so might as well stay out all night. I bet they found some all night diner. Oh, say, that sounds good. I could go for some bacon and-" Stel tried to step off the bed, but she fell, which we found hilarious.

Next the phone rang, causing us to scream, then laugh harder at being scared by the phone.

"Hello?" I said, still laughing. "Marion? Is that you? Well, where the hell are you? Why don't you come on back and join the party? Course it's just Stel and me, but we're having the time of our lives."

I thought she said the police station, but that couldn't be right. "What? Where are you?" She did say the police station. I caught it the second time because she screamed in my ear. "Now, Marion, you didn't go and get yourself arrested, did you?" I joked, but stopped abruptly, "You did. No kidding?"

I told Marion not to worry, we'd be right there. However, we didn't know where *there* was. We finally located the police station purely by chance thirty minutes later. We stumbled to the front desk and said, "We're looking for that silly little tour guide lady you arrested awhile back, about yea high, intense, dresses like Jackie O, but looks like Donna Reed, but isn't either one. She's our guide. Her name's Marion. Are we speaking English?"

Maybe it was our outfits. Maybe it was our reeking breath. Or maybe it was the fact that nothing we said made any sense—but the police officer decided not to release Marion into our custody, but instead threw us in the clink with her, and charged us with public intoxication.

"What are you doing?" asked Marion. "I thought you came to get me out."

"So did we," I answered. "But that hairy guy in the uniform said we were to 'sober up and stop acting like a couple of yahoos.'"

Stel and I laughed. Marion did not.

"Are you drunk or something?" Marion asked.

"Oh, there's no 'or something' about it," Stella said. "We are drunk, a little. Okay. Maybe more so or a lot. I'm not sure. Did you say something?"

Marion sat on the bed and began to cry. I sat down next to her and started to pet her head. Stella slumped to the floor. "Oh, come on, ol' girl," I said. "Tell us your troubles."

"Yeah, we'll help," Stel backed me up. "We've been solving people's problems all night. It's like a game show– *Name That Misfortune*. Or a soap opera—*As the Sun Tours Roam* or *These are the Days of the Elvis Lovers* or . . ."

"Stel, shut up."

Marion began to cry harder. Stel asked, "Am I not helping?"

"No. Now, Marion, what's wrong?"

"Isn't it obvious," Marion answered. "Everything."

"That's not true." I told her.

"No? Take a look around. We're in prison. The leader of the Sun Tours has managed to get herself arrested."

"I meant to ask you about that." I looked around our little cell.

"It's all very simple really," Marion said as she stood up and began to pace. This wasn't easy as Stella was lying in the middle of the floor. "I was thrilled when I left the hotel," Marion began, stepping over Stella. "I thought I'd finally come up with a foolproof plan to get into Memphis in time to tour Graceland and set up for the candlelight vigil." Marion held her arms like a sprinter, ready to begin a race.

"However," she unfroze and continued pacing, "after printing only one copy of my masterpiece, my printer ran out of ink. I asked the desk clerk where an Office Max or Staples was located. He told me there wasn't one in town or within a fifty-mile radius. I asked where someone such as myself could make a few copies. And he said there was a lawyer in town who sometimes let people use his copier, but he would be gone for the day. I asked if there was anywhere else. He said I could try the grocery store.

"So I walked to the grocery store, but the copier was out of order." Marion held up her fingers to illustrate an "out of order" sign in case I was having trouble imagining the scene.

Marion continued, "I asked the cashier if she knew of a place in town to make copies. She said I could try the library. I walked to the library—closed! I started to crisscross Levesque in a panic. It's not like we could commence toward Memphis without an itinerary, without a plan. I had games to print out, and of course the itinerary itself, for all of you." She paused for confirmation.

"You're right," I added on cue. "Got to have a plan."

"I walked for hours when what do I find?" Marion paused again.

"A Starbucks," I guessed.

"No, a Kinko's. Silly me asked the hotel clerk for an Office Max. And he told me no, and he was right because they don't have an Office Max; they have a Kinko's. I thought I made it clear when I asked for a place to make copies, but apparently that's beyond his meager comprehension. Imbecile!" Marion took a few deep breaths.

"So I rush in and ask to make copies. But, wouldn't you know, the town is preparing for a watermelon festival. A watermelon festival!" Her screaming hurt my head. "What kind of town holds a watermelon festival a day before the anniversary of Elvis's disappearance? I ask you."

I shrugged. I couldn't imagine.

Marion continued her tirade. "All of their copiers were busy printing green posters except an old model they kept in the back, waiting to be shipped to wherever it is copiers go to die. After assuring the manager that this was an emergency and begging on my knees, he let me use it.

"The copier printed eight flawless pages when all of a sudden it sucked the paper back into the machine including my original copy! The itinerary, our reservations, phone numbers, medical waivers, hotel and tour confirmations for Graceland.... About to be shredded. I swear to you. I've never seen a copier do this. It was possessed. What was I to do? I mean, really, what was I to do? I ask you."

I shrugged again, trying not to laugh.

"I did the only thing possible, the only reasonable thing left to do." Marion paused not sure if she wanted to confess her crime. Then with conviction, she said, "I jumped on the monster's back and started tearing at his tentacles. I had no other choice. My itinerary was in its belly. I had to get it. Would you have done any different?"

I shook my head no.

"That's when the manager heard me screaming, although I don't remember screaming. He unplugged the machine and ordered me to stop. I yelled at him, explaining my dilemma. I told him it was all his fault, that he had forced me into this position. I wanted him to understand. He didn't. He called the police. The police showed up. They arrested me and brought me here."

"What are the charges?" asked Stella from the floor. I wasn't even aware she'd been listening. I thought she was sleeping.

Marion sighed. "Let's see." She counted the crimes off on her fingers. "Disturbing the peace, destruction of property and aggravated assault."

"Aggravated assault? Who did you assault?" I asked.

"The copier."

"But it's a machine."

"Exactly!" Marion held up her fist in triumph. Then she sank onto the bed and put her head in her hands. "I just wanted my itinerary. I just wanted something to go right. Is that too much to ask?"

Stel pushed herself into a sitting position and used the wall for support. "Marion, things might seem bad now—"

"They're worse than bad. They're shit. Char is right. The whole damn tour is shit!" Marion lifted her eyes to the ceiling and asked, "Why? Why have you forsaken me, when all I'm trying to do is please you?"

"God has not forsaken you," I reassured.

"What does God have to do with it? I'm talking to Elvis."

"Oh, yes, of course. Well, he hasn't forsaken you either. So some things haven't gone according to plan."

"Are you kidding me? Nothing has gone according to plan! Hell, we're on our fifth bus driver for Christ's sake, after being abandoned by the first, second, and fourth, and killing the third!"

"You need to calm down, Marion. You are starting to use foul language, and that's not like you," soothed Stel.

"Calm down!" Marion jumped up and crossed to the cell bars. "How can I, when tomorrow everyone is going to look to me for answers, and I'm not going to have an itinerary?" She said while staring down the hallway.

"Why do you need one?" I asked.

"Because without a plan, everything turns to chaos."

"Everything is chaos anyway," Stel pointed out.

Marion had no reply. She stood with her back to us.

"What are you so afraid of?" I asked slowly.

After a long pause, Marion whispered, "Failure. Looking like a dope. Losing my job. Losing the one thing I have going for me."

Marion turned to face us. "I know you think my life is pathetic, driven by my itinerary and chasing a former rock star, but it's all I have. You two have each other, your career, family, friends and Elvis. I have nothing except Elvis. He's everything to me. This tour is not my summer vacation. It's my life. And it's a complete disaster." A tear ran down her cheek unchecked.

I crossed the room to stand beside her. "That's where you're wrong. I've learned more about Elvis just by being on this tour and going through all this crazy shit. And that's the point. That's what Elvis would have wanted. My appreciation for Elvis has grown tremendously. This tour is so much more than I expected, and that's saying a lot coming from me."

For the first time that night, Marion smiled, a small one.

"There you go. That's better. You shouldn't be so hard on yourself. This tour isn't a disaster. Well, not completely anyway."

"Well, it'll probably be my last one."

"What do you mean? Why's that?" Stel asked getting off the floor.

"Once I turn in my report to the owner, Mr. Nelson, he'll probably fire me on the spot."

"No, he won't," came a baritone voice.

We looked up to see cowboy boots, an enormous belt buckle and his signature Stetson.

"Billy, what are you doing here?" Marion asked.

"The police have been calling the hotel for the last two hours hoping to find someone to claim 'three crazy women' as they put it."

Billy stood with the officer who threw us in here. He didn't look too happy to be releasing us. The officer opened the cell door. "You're free to go."

"What about the charges?" asked Marion as we stepped into the hallway.

"As the owner of Sun Tours, I've taken care of everything. You needn't worry."

"What?" Marion gasped, but Stella and I just smiled.

"I own Sun Tours. It's me, Percy, but don't tell anyone else. They'd string me up for sure."

"Oh, Percy! I'm so sorry," wailed Marion. "I didn't even know it was you! If you want to fire me, I'll understand," Marion said.

"I don't. In fact, I want to promote you." Billy put his big hand on her tiny shoulder. "Everything that has gone wrong with this tour is due to poor upper management. I've given you little to work with—a dilapidated bus and insane drivers. I'm hoping I can convince you to come work in my office and restructure the whole business. You are my only hope of salvaging my livelihood."

"Really?"

"Yes. Your organizational skills are just what I need. Maybe we can save each other."

"You don't know what this means to me. Oh, sir, you are the greatest." Marion wrapped her arms around her boss in a big hug.

It began to rain on our walk back to the hotel, but we didn't mind. Nobody felt the need to talk. When we reached the hotel, Marion said she needed more time to think. She continued walking when we stopped at the entrance.

"Night, Billy," I said. We turned to leave, but Billy stopped us.

"Say, I tried to call my wife earlier, I guess I can't stand being apart, but she wasn't in your room. In fact, no one answered. Do you know where she is?"

"She's with Char," Stel answered.

"With Char! What's going on? Where?"

"Don't worry, they made up. They're on a secret mission. I'm sure we'll find out tomorrow." This didn't seem to ease his worries.

"It's really okay," Stella assured. "Char won't do anything to her."

"Oh, I know," said Billy. "My Anastasia is stronger than she looks. Nobody pushes her around." We sat on a bus bench outside the hotel, and Bossman proceeded to tell us a story about his wife, which became my Journal Entry #23.

#

Anastasia's life began in a rundown trailer court. Her parents were alcoholics and the town's white trash. So Anastasia learned to fend for herself. She worked at a diner washing dishes after school and did yard work on the weekends to buy food and pay the heating bill. At school she ate hot meals and received kind words from most of the teachers. She was a good student and a voracious reader. She spent her free time in the library to avoid being teased for her ratty clothing.

When Anastasia was thirteen, her parents vanished for a weekend. For three days she heard nothing. When they came home, it was five weeks before they vanished again. This began a pattern that would last for the next three years. Then one time her mother came home alone. She was pregnant.

Without her husband around, Anastasia's mom mellowed and began talking about the future. She and Anastasia would move to California. For the last two months of her pregnancy, Anastasia's mother was confined to her bed. When her mother went into labor, she gave birth to a boy and a girl. Anastasia named them Christopher and Chloe.

Three months after the twins were born, Anastasia's father showed up drunk and with another woman. Anastasia grabbed her siblings and took them into her room while her parents fought. She pushed a dresser against the door and spent the night trying to calm the twins. The house quieted down around dawn, and Anastasia crept out of her room. Her mother was sleeping. Her father and his girlfriend had passed out on the couch. Anastasia went through her father's pockets and took a couple of hundreds from his wallet. Knowing she would need more, she went through the woman's pockets. There was nothing but keys to the Suburban parked outside.

She decided to search the car. When she looked in the toolbox, she found about two pounds of what looked like cocaine. Anastasia was shocked. She figured her parents dabbled in the stuff. But she'd always assumed they were users. This amount could only mean they were dealers as well. This meant there was more money around than she guessed.

Anastasia doubled her efforts. She found a paper bag underneath the driver seat, tucked into the wires and the stuffing of the seat itself. She carefully opened the bag. Inside was a wad of hundred dollar bills. She found a similar bag under the passenger seat. Anastasia guessed she was holding about ten grand in her hands.

She thought quickly. She could guarantee her mom was going to take off again, especially after this stunt by her dad. Her dad wasn't going to stay either. She and the twins needed this money desperately, but the minute it was discovered missing, her parents would only have a handful of suspects.

Anastasia came up with a plan. She hid the toolbox along with the money behind a loose board in the porch. She left the car doors wide open and slipped back inside. Leaning out the window of her room, she aimed the keychain at the car and activated the alarm. The reaction was instantaneous. A horrible high-pitched squeal came from the car, jolting the household awake. In unison, the twins added their screams of protest to the din. Through the thin trailer walls, she heard her father and girlfriend dashing to the car.

Turns out her father was not a dealer, but a drug runner, taking shipments from the supplier to the dealer. Without the drugs and money, he was in major trouble with both ends. Her father split with his girlfriend. When Anastasia got back from school she found a note with the babies. Her mom was gone as well. Anastasia didn't know if she was angry or relieved. She cursed her parents for leaving her with two newborns. She was barely sixteen and just a sophomore in high school.

She could go to the authorities and explain everything. Her sister and brother would be put into the system and would most likely be adopted, with any luck, by the same people. She was underage and would be placed in foster care. There wouldn't be a chance in hell she'd ever see her brother and sister again.

Anastasia retrieved the money. Altogether there was nearly twelve thousand dollars. She did some fast calculations. If she kept working, and used the money only when she needed to make ends meet, Anastasia had enough money to last a little over two years. If she wanted a good job, she would need to get her high school diploma. She would make it, with her babies at her side. At that moment, they became hers.

So began the greatest undertaking of her life. She found a nice mother in the trailer park who agreed to watch the twins while she was at school. She switched jobs from the diner to a small florist shop where the owner was nice enough to let Anastasia bring the children. Their blue-green gazes would follow their new mom around as she swept the shop or tucked flowers into vases.

Two years passed. Anastasia opted halfway through her final year to take her GED. Her marks were among the highest in the state. She also took the SATs and the ACTs, and her scores could have gotten her a scholarship to any college or university. She would apply—in three years, once the twins were in kindergarten.

By this time almost all of the twelve grand was gone. She worked as much as she could, but with most of her wages paying the babysitter, she struggled to make ends meet. She began working full time for a local factory. Then the twins came down with the chicken pox, and she had to stay home to care for them. She returned to work a week later to find out she no longer had a job.

Rent was due. Her landlord gave her a week extension, but wanted the money by next Sunday or else. She knew what the 'or else' meant. Friday rolled around and she still didn't have a job. She looked herself in the mirror and made a deal with herself. She hired a babysitter for the night and dressed up in some skimpy clothes.

That night Percy was driving through Anastasia's little city on his way to Dallas. He saw Anastasia hanging out on a corner, looking fearfully at every car that slowed down. She looked so young and scared. He pulled over and asked her if she'd like a cup of coffee.

She hesitated getting into the car. Later she told him it was the way Percy held the door for her that made her go with him.

After four cups of coffee and a piece of apple pie, Percy coaxed Anastasia into talking about herself. She told him about Christopher and Chloe and a bit about her parents. When he asked her what she was doing on the streets, something broke inside her. She started crying and the whole story came out. He listened patiently while inside was rigid with anger. Part of him wanted to hire a hit man to hunt down her mom and dad and send them both to hell. Another part ached for the lost childhood of this beautiful woman. But mostly he just admired her for her intelligence, her resilience and her courage. There aren't many people who are willing to tackle what she did.

And that's how Percy became Anastasia's benefactor. He moved her and the twins into the loft apartment above his garage. He put her through college. Anastasia majored in business management and joined his company. Two months after graduation, Percy asked Anastasia to marry him. And to his complete disbelief, she accepted.

#

"So you see," concluded Billy. "Tansy has been a fighter all her life. She's really amazing. I fell in love with her that night over pie and coffee. And I still can't believe she's mine."

We said goodnight for the second time and started to walk to the lobby via the adjacent restaurant and casino. Inside the entrance we could see Matt, Marcus, Luc and Elliot playing pool. Lester was sitting at the bar, moaning to Bus Driver Elvis about nobody understanding his gift. "I know I'm Vietnamese and all, but many people have told me I look and sound just like Elvis. In fact, I'm going to let you in on a little secret. I'm really Elvis's long lost twin."

"Bullshit!" Stella screamed at the top of her lungs before I dragged her back outside, both of us giggling. After that episode we couldn't very well go into the lobby. So we doubled back and planned to sneak through the bathroom window into our room. This was more difficult than we imagined.

First, we spotted Maggie and Eric talking on the deck of the guy's honeymoon suite. Not wanting to disturb them, we decided to sneak through the "Lover's Garden," but Vince and Ella were arguing in the gazebo. No other alternative presented itself to our alcohol-clouded brains, so we crawled on our bellies through the shrubbery. Once at our room, we slid open the window and climbed into our bathroom with relative ease, which was disturbing when we thought about it the next morning.

From inside the bathroom we could hear Char and Tansy laughing on the other side of the door.

"Trapped," Stella announced.

"Yep."

"What do you want to do now?" she asked.

"Take a bath."

We looked in the mirror and our reflection was shocking. Streaks of mud, blue eye shadow and mascara ran down our face. Our hair was a nappy, snarled mess, and the clothes we had borrowed were torn, dirty or otherwise ruined.

"They're going to kill us," Stel said.

"Yep." For some reason, we both found this funny and started giggling.

"How are we going to explain why we're wearing their clothes?" I picked at a torn hem.

"The same way we'll explain why we ransacked the room digging through their suitcases," Stel said, "Too much box wine."

"Oh well, I'm not going to think about it now. I want a bath." I stumbled to the tub.

"But Char and Tansy will hear."

"They have the music too loud." Soon I was soaking fully clothed in a tub of bubbles.

Stel sat on the floor beside me. "This has been one hell of a trip."

"Yeah."

"I've actually started to care for these people."

"Yeah, the bunch of weirdoes have grown on me, too. It's going to make one hell of a story, even if we never get a second assignment." This made me think of The Incident and the reality of our situation. "Stella, do you ever think about just giving up writing?"

"Jess, if we give up, Ursula and all those betting against us win. All we'd be remembered for is The Incident."

"Yeah. But I never thought, not in a million years, we'd end up here."

Chapter 27: Stella

How did I end up here?

I'm covered in mud and lying on the bathroom floor. The few memories of last night which I remember don't clarify the situation. Definitely don't explain why Jessica's in the tub, fully dressed and lying chin-deep in muddy water.

Those were my first thoughts on waking. Standing made my whole body hurt and my head throb. When I looked in the mirror, I discovered not only was I covered in mud, but apparently I ate some as well. I found a toothbrush and toothpaste in a drawer. I pondered the wisdom of using my discovery. Who knows where it came from, what it was doing there or what it had been used for prior to my dental needs?

Jess stirred in her sludge-filled bathtub. Char's shirt floated around her in tatters. Noticing my best friend in danger of drowning, I roused her with a friendly smack on the back of her head.

"Ow. Don't. My head. Hurts." Jessica stared at the dirty water. "Stel?"

"Yes?"

"I'm in the bathtub."

"Yes."

"What am I doing in the bathtub?"

"I don't know."

"Did we sleep here all night?"

"I think so."

Jess tried to stand, but didn't make it. "Oh, God help me." She slowly tried a second time. Rivulets of filthy water coursed down her legs. She joined me at the mirror. "What the hell happened to you?" she laughed.

My reflection answered, "By appearances, I would say the same thing that happened to you." Now I laughed. Mud hid Jessica's two front teeth.

"Well, hell," she said. She cupped her hand under the faucet and started rinsing her mouth.

"We can't let anyone on the tour see us like this," I told her reflection. "I think I remember passing a Kohl's on our trek back from jail. Think we could find it again to buy some clothes?" I grabbed a wad of toilet paper to remove my make-up.

"We also have to buy outfits for Ella, Char and Tansy because the ones we stole are ruined." Jessica followed my lead with the toilet paper. "Or at least find a dry cleaners."

"Crap, you're right. Jess, we have to hurry." We crawled back out the window as we still wanted to avoid being seen.

"Do you think they'll let us in the store looking like this?" Jess asked and gestured to our clothing.

"It's either this or go naked. Personally, I think our chances are better if we have clothes on."

#

We arrived at Ellen's Eatery two hours later dressed to the nines. Even though it was past ten, Stella and I were among the first to arrive. It was a long night for everyone.

Marion arrived, looking relaxed. I had never seen Marion relaxed before. She looked at us sheepishly. I didn't blame her; I wouldn't want to face the people who shared a jail cell with me, either. She nodded a greeting, but went to sit with Vince. She spoke quietly to him, and patted his hand.

By the looks of things—Ella sitting alone with the newspaper held between her and us like a wall—she and

Vince hadn't reached an agreement. If I had to bet my last ten dollars, I would say he's leaving for Vegas after this, and Ella is going to spend some time at home, rethinking her decision to get married. I felt bad for the two of them. Married for ten days and already on the rocks.

Sister Mary and Thomas were engrossed in a conversation in the next booth, and whatever they were talking about was making both of them glow. They noticed my stare and started laughing.

Through the window I saw Don and immediately felt nervous and excited. We were quite intimate at dinner last night when it was just the two of us, but I don't know how he'll act in front of the group. He was talking to bus driver Elvis a.k.a Aaron. When they entered the diner, Don caught my eye and walked over to our table.

"Are these seats taken?" Don asked.

"No please join us," I said too quickly. I felt my face flush, and I know I was smiling like a dope, but whatever. Aaron sat in the open chair across from Jess. He gave her that wicked grin of his.

"Good morning," he said.

Since Jess didn't answer and just stared at him, I said, "Good morning," and elbowed my friend.

"How did you two sleep?" asked Aaron.

"Uh," we both said. How to explain sleeping in the bathtub? Luckily we didn't have to as the waitress arrived to take our order. All of a sudden I was starving. I ordered the Lumberjack Breakfast, which came with eggs, bacon, sausage, hash browns and three pancakes. By the way the waitress' eyes widened, I realized I was being a pig, but Don saved me.

"Me too," he said. "I'll have the Lumberjack Breakfast as well."

Elliot and Lester came in, followed by Eric and Maggie. She smiled and flashed a thumbs-up. Our three college boys dragged into the diner next, followed by a worried Billy. He took a good look at the tour members present.

"Has anyone seen my wife?" he asked over the top of the conversations.

Everyone looked around. "Isn't she with you?" asked Maggie.

"No. I haven't seen her all morning. Has anyone seen Tansy?" One by one, we shook our heads. Billy started pacing, his movements almost jerky.

The bell on the door jingled.

"Honey, it's okay." Tansy stepped through the doorway, Char at her side. "Char and I just took a little time getting ready." Tansy was a knockout in simple, faded blue jeans and a plain cotton shirt. She left off most of her makeup, making judicial use of eyeliner, mascara, and a pale pink lip-gloss. Her skin shone pure without foundation or powder. Instead of some complicated over-sprayed hairstyle, she had tamed her locks with a brush and left them to curl loosely down her back, achieving a sexy, windblown look.

Char was no less stunning. Gone were her baggy, stained sweats and polyester suits. Wearing a simple cotton dress, Char flaunted her figure, which was simply voluptuous. Although not the grand beauty Tansy was, Char had a fantastic set of eyes, enhanced by a touch of makeup. Foundation smoothed her complexion. Her unruly, frizzy hair had been chopped into a bob. Her sides were brushed forward toward her high cheekbones; a devastating combination.

Like my fellow passengers, I was stunned. Lester was especially enthusiastic over the new Char. She shrugged him off, though—"I just decided I was due for a new look. Tansy helped me out with the hair and makeup. I swear, that girl could make millions as a Mary Kay Consultant."

Tansy, on the other hand, bit her lip and looked nervously at Billy, gauging his reaction to her less glamorized look. Unlike the others who immediately heaped praises on the duo, Billy stood silent and looked at his wife. Without all the makeup and fancy clothes, Tansy looked years younger, which only served to emphasize the gap in ages between them. When Billy still didn't say anything, Tansy looked ashamed. Not wanting to spark a fight, she lowered her head, sat in a vacant chair, and picked up the menu.

Char watched the exchange between the pair, eyes darkening. "You nasty old man," she snarled at Billy. "The least you could do is say she looks pretty. Anybody with eyes in their head can see that she does!"

Billy appraised his wife's defender. "Char," he said, "sit down and shut up." His look gave no room for argument, and Char obeyed. The rest of us waited in startled silence for what Billy would say next.

"Char, you demand I tell my wife she's pretty. My Anastasia, my little Tansy, could grow a mustache and wear a clown's red nose and still be beautiful to me. I have never loved her because of what she looks like on the outside. That can change. It will always be the depth of her soul that captures me. She hypnotized me one night in a diner where I shelled out a hundred dollars for coffee and apple pie, and I've never been free since. When I look at her, I see so much more than a pretty woman."

Billy pulled a chair next to his wife and took her hands. "Tansy, you are breathtaking. But it doesn't matter to me what you wear or how you fix your hair. I love you for everything you are: your intelligence, your wit, your courage. Your spirit strengthens me." Billy took her face in his hands. "Without you, I'm lost."

"I love you, Percy," Tansy cried. Words failed as the lovers embraced.

As one, we rose from our seats. We cried. We hugged. We smiled. We laughed. The nine days of our journey felt like nine decades given all we had been through. Our bus ride from Minneapolis to Memphis was more like a trek across Antarctica, fraught with ice caps and polar bears rather than psychotic drivers and malfunctioning toilets. However, we were down to five days and Memphis, looming only forty-five minutes away, was calling. Arm-in-arm, we turned to our fearless leader for direction.

The earth should have rumbled, and fire from heaven rained, when Marion uttered the words, "There is no itinerary." But it didn't. In place of a natural disaster of epic proportions, a slow smile spread across Marion's face. If peace could exist in a face, it resided at present in Marion's. The rest of the tour held their breath, afraid of a meltdown. But Jess and I knew one had already taken place and now things were going just as they should, just as fate—or Elvis—planned.

"So today we are going to wing it and see what happens. Okay?" Marion said.

Everyone cheered. We loaded the bus in record time. Memphis was so close we could smell it. A feeling of euphoria overtook the group. Little did we know, it wouldn't last. As we drove down the road, a slow grumble spread from member to member like an ugly infestation.

Jess and I were the only ones oblivious to the ensuing storm. We watched the buildings give way to the open road without knowing how we managed to provoke the entire tour. However, we were about to find out.

"Jessica!" Char bellowed, bringing us out of our peaceful reverie. "Since Estelle-"

Yes, she called me Estelle, my full name, but I don't remember telling her this. That was my first clue something was wrong. My second was her angry tone of voice and the crazed look in her eyes.

"Since Estelle shared with us why you two are on this assignment together, why don't you tell us why you hate Elvis."

The blood drained from my face and all of the oxygen left my lungs. Jess had more composure. She stood slowly to face her attacker. "Char, what are you talking about?" Jess measured her words. "I don't hate Elvis."

Glancing around, I realized everyone was glaring at us except Don, who sat across from me, and Aaron, who was keeping an eye on the unfolding drama from his rearview mirror.

"Yes, you do," snarled Char. "Your own hand betrays you!" With that thunderclap, Char raised a thick, leather-bound journal, containing our assignment, first impressions and, most damning, our opinions of Elvis and his fans.

"No," I gasped and stood up. Jess didn't deserve to face them alone. I was getting ready to go into bitch mode. To my surprise, Jess was giving me the subtlest of looks: *Sit down.*

Standoff. Jess asked Char to wait, to let us explain first, we were about to reveal everything, honest. But it was too late. Char opened our journal and read its secrets as loud as a blow horn as she paced up and down Cybill.

"'Day one: I find myself in the midst of Elvis freaks.' Shall I continue?" asked Char.

"No. Please. Let us explain," I pleaded. Jess gave me another *shut up* look.

"No need to explain. This explains everything quite clearly. You've written about everyone in here. Let's see, Stella," Char held up my journal. "You call Lester a screeching baboon, Don a dog-breathed lothario and Thomas a delusional zealot. What kind of journalism is this? Reads like my third grade diary." Everyone laughed.

My fear gave way to anger. How dare she compare my writing to a third grade diary. Granted my first entries were a bit snarly and childish, but they were never meant to be published or read aloud, especially the part about Don. I glanced at Don in terror; but to my surprise, it looked like he was stifling laughter.

Char continued to rattle off our iniquities. She must have prepared, because she read all the really incriminating material, without having to flip around to find it. An alarm began blaring in my ears. I believe the sound was the physical manifestation of their collective anger shot at Jess and me through their glaring eyes.

"Well, what do you have to say for yourselves?" Char demanded.

Jess stuttered, unable to produce one coherent sentence in our defense. Gone was her calm demeanor. It was replaced with nervous hands and red spots on her neck. I couldn't help but feel responsible for getting Jess into another mess. And damn it, I'm not going to let my best friend be treated like this. I stood and took my place by Jessica's side.

"How did you get our journals?" I asked coolly, evenly.

"You dropped them while loading the bus this morning. We figured since you went through our suitcases last night, you wouldn't mind us reading them. Little did we know how you two felt about the rest of us."

"But we didn't know you, and we don't feel that way now. We were wrong," said Jess.

"You knew very well what you were doing," said Maggie who was visibly upset. "You had no intention of writing a professional travel article. You set out to hurt us and expose your warped view of Elvis. We were wrong to think you were our friends."

That hurt coming from Maggie. "But we are your friends!" Jess protested.

"No, you're not," Char accused. "The only woman you love is Stella.'"

"What do you mean?" asked Jess.

"Oh, come on," Char jeered. "Don't try to fake it any longer. You know and the whole tour knows. Hell, you've made it pretty damn obvious."

"What?" I cried.

Char thrust a chubby finger in my face and screamed, "Lesbian!" Then she pointed her other hand at Jess and screamed, "Lesbian!"

Jess and I looked at our chests expecting to see scarlet L's stitched in our clothing. Jess looked at a hysterical Char and slapped her hand away. "You're an idiot."

Char began crisscrossing her hands, pointing at us and shouting, "Lesbians, lesbians, lesbians!"

"Have you lost your mind?" I asked. "We're not lesbians." Again I looked at Don for his reaction. He was laughing out loud at this. But I didn't think it was funny. In fact, I was downright pissed.

"We heard you the day Helix disappeared," continued Char. "Whispering about vaginas in the cornfield, wrestling on the hotel room floor, sharing a bathroom—oh we know about that, thanks to Marion, thanks to Ella."

I threw up my hands in disgust. "Oh get real. I don't know what you've heard or think you've heard, but you've got it all wrong. I don't see what the purpose of this witch trial is."

"Stop making up lies and excuses," shouted Char, "and tell us the truth."

"The truth about what?" I shouted. I heard a little voice inside my head saying, "Don't raise your voice. Don't get caught up in emotions. Try to resolve your conflict amicably." I told the voice to shut the hell up.

"Let's start with the truth of your assignment," said Char. She had the look of a cat playing with a mouse. "The truth is, you're not some big time travel writers. This is the only assignment you could get after…" she paused for effect, "The Incident."

In that moment, I knew the meaning of the words, blind rage. I felt the heat rush through my veins and reason leave my mind as my body went rigid with pure, unparalleled fury.

I snatched my journal out of Char's hands. My face inches from hers. "That's enough," I hissed. I reached for the other journal, but missed as Char moved it behind her back. I raised my fist and narrowed my eyes. Char's eyes widened in fear. She knew she crossed a line and pushed me to crazy angry, and she was afraid.

I felt Jessica's hand on my arm. "Stella, don't. Let it go. It doesn't matter."

But it did matter to me. Char has insulted my writing, attacked my best friend and called me a lesbian. Now she wants to expose one of the worst days of my life for her sick enjoyment.

And not one person has come to our defense. While we were changing our minds about these people and growing to love them, they were judging us and betraying us all along—spreading lies, and remaining silent while Char began hurling her halfwit accusations at us.

"So you want the truth, Char?" I asked, and I meant it to be a threat.

"What do you mean?" asked Char.

"You capitalize on everyone's mistakes and flaws to cover your own. You drive people away so you don't risk rejection, which is too bad for the nice person hiding behind your wall of defenses. You will die alone."

Char was silent. One down. I turned on the others for their silence, for believing Char and not letting us explain. "Tansy, if you didn't want to be labeled a trophy wife, then why did you dress the part? Billy, stop the fake southern accent all ready. You're from Fargo.

"Ella, stop mourning a marriage that ended before it started! You deserve better. Vince, I'm not even going to waste my time. You are too busy thinking of your penis and how many women you believe want it.

"Matt, Marcus and Luc, you're fine. I don't have a problem with you.

"Maggie, so you have a past. Everyone has a past. Eric, if you can't forgive her, then you're dumber than your CEO status and Ivy League education indicates. Elliot, your mother died, and I'm sorry. But your father loves Maggie. He has for a long time. It doesn't diminish what he felt and still feels for your mom.

"Mary, you're fine. I don't have a problem with you either.

"Thomas, if you try to convert me into one of your born-again Elvis worshipers one more time, I will kick your teeth in.

"Lester, you kill me. You really kill me. You think you are some long lost Elvis twin. I see just a few problems with this theory. Let's forget for a moment that you can't sing. You open your mouth and dogs start wailing, glass shatters and birds fall dead from the skies. But let's stick with logistics. If you were Elvis's twin, then you should be over sixty years old. You are thirty-two. Do I have to do the math? But what really gets me are your fake sideburns.

"Marion. Never mind the fact you dragged us to the most pointless, God-forsaken tourist traps and hotels that exist, you destroyed a small forest for your precious itineraries in your need for control. If you were really in control, you would have noticed we hauled Ted's rotting carcass across two states.

"What really blows my mind is none of you even know what Elvis looks like, because if you did, you would see he is driving this bus! What the hell is up with you anyway, Aaron or Sam or Tom or whoever you are? Are you some practical joke to drive Jess and me from sanity, because if you are, you are wasting your time. We lost sanity the moment we signed up with this traveling circus-freak sideshow of a tour.

"I don't know. Maybe I'm being a bit melodramatic. Maybe I'm a little tired after eight nights of zero sleep! After being stuck on a bus that reeks like some cesspool of human excrement. After witnessing the loss of not one or two or three but four bus drivers, one who pulls a gun on us and one who has the gall to die! After stowing that dead bus driver in the luggage compartment and singing 'Oh Danny Boy' at his funeral. After playing therapist from this Venus flytrap of a bus seat and trying to fix all of your screwed up lives. After all of this, don't I deserve a little breakdown of my own?

"I hated Elvis when this tour began. I will admit it. But now, I kind of like him. I appreciate his life and music. Isn't that enough for you? I have forgiven each of you as you, in turn confessed your sins and other pathetic tales of woe. Where is the love in return? Why did you all just sit there while Char went berserk?

"Furthermore, can someone explain why we're going to Memphis to honor the passing of someone none of you will admit ever died? Let me tell you, whether you want to believe it or not, the man is dead. That's right, folks, you heard it here first. Elvis has kicked the can, moved on to the sweet by and by, entered the happy hunting ground, met the spirit in the sky, Elvis has left the building. He is dead.

Capitol D-E-A-D, dead. As dead as dead can be, the never-coming-back kind of dead. Uh, huh. Dead."

I finished my tirade exhausted and just daring someone to argue with me. But nobody said anything. Heaviness spread across my heart and a sickness filled my belly. At that moment I realized my only success was to wound very deeply those I had come to care about, maybe even love. I could see the hurt in their faces, an irreconcilable hurt. I had crushed their most treasured belief, and I hated myself for it. Shame filled my whole being.

"You bitch," growled Char. She hurled Jessica's journal at me, nailing me square in the eye. Everyone rose to their feet as Char took a few steps forward.

"Cat fight!" yelled Matt. The entire bus surged forward to get a front row seat.

"Stop!" Don leapt between Char and me. All I saw was a lean figure between us, my knight. In the process of rescuing me, however, he clipped the corner of my mouth with his elbow. I tasted blood and stumbled back.

Aaron slammed on the brakes. Bodies rocketed into the windshield. They crashed into me and I tasted the dashboard—plastic, dust, blood. I lost my balance and toppled down the stairs. The doors flew open, and I tasted the road—rubber and asphalt and dirt; then weeds, dust and the thick smell of grass in summer.

I was lying in the ditch on the side of a lonely road.

Cybill was idling ten feet away. In her doorway was Don, staring wide-eyed at me from the top step. His muscular body held back the pulsing mob. Faces bubbled and jumped behind him; or maybe they were just trying to find their balance again. But Char's bloodshot eyes were glowing in the chaos. The only thought in my pulsating head was, *did I just fall off the bus?*

Don shouted at me, "Run! Run! For the love of God, run!" He shouted at Aaron, "Drive, man, Drive!"

I didn't run. I barely managed to roll out of Cybill's way before she sped off in a squeal of rubber. Left in the wake of Cybill's exhaust, I lay in the ditch for an eternity. I watched the clouds roll by and listened to the sudden stillness. Felt the heat coming from the ground and wondered if that lump in my back was a rock or discarded dirty diaper. I made no effort to find out.

Gradually I realized Jess and our day bags were in the ditch with me. "Cawcaw cawcaw," I croaked the secret call.

"Cawcaw," Jess returned.

"Jessica," I moaned. But with my swollen upper lip, it sounded more like, "Pleshica."

"Are you alive?" Jess asked.

"Thespnnoo."

"Is that a yes?"

"Thespnoo."

"How did you get out?"

"I think I fell or maybe I was pushed," I told her in garbled tongue. "I'm not sure. You?"

She flopped onto her back. "When I saw you were going berserk, I grabbed our stuff and army-crawled to the back of the bus. I tried to go out the bathroom window, but I got stuck. When I wiggled free, I landed on my head and rolled to safety just before Cybill took off." Jess crawled to where I lay. "We have to get up."

"Thespnoo."

"Yes."

"What's the point?" I garbled. "We're never going to see Graceland." I began laughing. Laughing hurt, so I tried to stop, but Jess was laughing, so I couldn't help it.

We rolled to a sitting position, side by side. Leaning against each other, we stared down the road to where it disappeared over the horizon. We sighed and sat in silence, listening to the intermittent sound of a car whizzing by.

"We have to get up," Jess repeated.

"Why? Eventually someone will stop," I reasoned.

"Probably, but just to rape our corpses and keep driving."

"Fine."

We managed to stand and gather our stuff. We sat on our suitcases on the side of the road. "Where are we?" I asked.

"As near as I can figure, this is Highway 64. We just passed Ebony, and I remember seeing a sign for West Memphis, so we have to be close."

"So, what do we do now?"

Without saying a word, we picked up our bags and began limping toward Memphis. "I'm going to walk behind you a ways and try to hitch a ride," said Jess. "The way you look, nobody is going to pull over. If I get someone to stop, we'll pull ahead and get you."

"Sure," I said. I stumbled forward. With each step, I discovered a new injury. I'd twisted my ankle falling off the bus. My left eye began to swell shut. Cars passed every few minutes, but the drivers barreled onward without so much as a glance in the rearview mirror.

We walked for miles. I thought I saw my journal in the ditch, but it turned out to be a Harlequin Romance novel. I stared at the scandalous cover for a long while before trudging on.

"I keep looking ahead expecting to see Memphis," moaned Jessica. "I know it has to be only miles down the road." She had given up on hitching a ride, so there we were: Two beat-up, worn-out friends-for-life trudging toward Memphis in the ditch.

Sweat ran down my back as the sun marched across the sky. By late afternoon, long shadows stretched across the landscape.

Propelled my inertia, we kept moving. In the glare of the setting sun, I thought I saw a figure of a human in the distance. I dismissed the figure as a mirage until it grew bigger and bigger.

Before I knew it, Don was coming to a stop in front of me. I stumbled forward and his hands caught my shoulders. I looked up at him with my good eye and tried to say something. I wanted to know why he came back for me, but all that came out was "Plesihekfoienskl."

Don smiled. "Hey pretty thing, going my way?" He brushed a blood-crusted strand of hair from my face. "Char might have overreacted. She read the rest of the journal, and ran out of ammunition on Day 3. Mary and I wrestled her for it, and got the truth, and I think there was enough in there to make us all look like fools." Don's hair was messed up, but eyes were smiling. "Marion said there's a room for you and Jessica at the Heartbreak Hotel."

Then he bent forward and kissed my forehead tenderly as the sun set in the west and the lights of Memphis glowed in the east.

Epilogue

Lester and Vince missed participating in the Ultimate Elvis Tribute Artist Contest. Stella and Jessica missed running in the 27th Annual Elvis Presley Run, Walk, Rock & Roll charity race. Marion missed making connections at the Fan Club Presidents' Event. And Mary missed the Elvis Film Fest. However, the Sun Tours Elvis Extravaganza members made it to Memphis in time to stand outside Graceland with a candle in hand, shoulder to shoulder with people of all ages from around the world, and honor the life and legend of the King of Rock and Roll.

Afterwards, Jess and Stel returned to their tiny apartment in Denver exhausted, but confident they had a moving, if somewhat unbelievable, story for Ursula. But will she like it? Will they land a second assignment? Or will their careers as travel journalists come to an end?

Find out in the second novel of the J&S Survival Series, *Surviving Black Friday*. Coming soon!

You can follow Jess and Stel and share your Elvis story at www.SurvivingElvisWeek.com.

About the Authors

Vanessa Grace and Amy Bea met at Augustana College in Sioux Falls, SD. To their shock and horror, they realized each possessed half of the same brain. These Non-twins shared many adventures, both on campus and off, in this county and others. For the sake of National security, they now reside on opposite sides of the county, Amy in Georgia and Vanessa in Montana. Although separated by distance, they remain close enough to continue co-authoring books and having misadventures.